OTHERWISE FABLES

GOBBLE-UP STORIES

CHI-PO AND THE SORCERER

THE HISTORY OF SIGISMUND, PRINCE OF POLAND

T0163887

OSCAR MANDEL

PROSPECT
·PARK·
BOOKS

Published by Prospect Park Books
969 S. Raymond Avenue
Pasadena, California 91105
prospectparkbooks.com

Distributed by Consortium Book Sales & Distribution
cbsd.com

Library of Congress Cataloging-in-Publication Data
Mandel, Oscar.
 [Short stories. Selections]
 Otherwise fables / Oscar Mandel.
    pages cm
  ISBN 978-1-938849-21-3 (pbk.)
 I. Mandel, Oscar. Gobble-up stories. II. Title.
PS3563.A44O85 2014
813'.54--dc23

                                       2013037767

Cover design by Brad Norr. Book layout by Amy Inouye.
Printed in the United States of America.

CONTENTS

Gobble-Up
STORIES

GOBBLE-UP STORIES

(in alphabetical order)

FOREWORD

Once upon a time I found a letter in my mailbox from a friend upbraiding me for offering him advice which he thought unethical. I had suggested that he mail the manuscript of a hopeless novel to two publishers at the same time. In his letter he invoked the moral majesties of Moses, Socrates, Spinoza, and Kant. He and they were right, my advice had been naughty (if wise), but the heaviness of the artillery deployed against my insignificant target amazed me. Out of this amazement, and the blameworthy amusement that followed, grew, I don't know why—yet with the rapidity of a mushroom after the rain—the fable "How God Learned What Measure Is." I could, I suppose, explain that having been brought up in Belgium speaking French, I inevitably knew and loved my La Fontaine. But La Fontaine in particular, and fables in general, were far from my conscious mind on the day, indeed in the year, my friend's letter arrived. Hence I must fall back on that convenient darkness, the subconscious mind, a mental tunnel where I see nothing, though a well-lit fable emerges at the exit.

Even more mysteriously, once I had composed my little apologue, a troop of others came running as if at a signal— as if they had been lying in wait for years in that darkness. I remember this, decades later, as one of the stranger circumstances of my life. For a few months the stories lined up, so to speak, urging my pencil to materialize them. A dozen stragglers came later; in afteryears a few others; a pair fairly recently. Thus the collection grew from thirty-three (the original *Gobble-Up Stories*) to forty-six fables.

This augmented edition, published here for the first time in English, also brings to light the sometimes deep revisions I made on many if not most of the original thirty-three. Indeed, revision has been the one task my diminished imagination has always been up to. I continued and have never ceased to revisit most of these texts, and, like a fond parent who cannot let his children go, I have kept trying to comb out their imperfections and to brush up their attractions.

Why "Gobble-Up"? The word can be taken as alluding to the pleasure (the presumed pleasure) of "consuming" these fables, but I meant it more, at the time I thought it up, as an eat-or-be-eaten reference to the cruel world with which, alas, so many fables must cope.

Three of these gladly admit to a clear pedigree. One is my variant of the famous tale of the Crow and the Fox— *Le Corbeau et le Renard*—the one every child and adult in the French-speaking world knows by heart. "The Cock Who Made the Sun Rise" goes back to Edmond Rostand's *Chantecler* (his extravagant comedy of roosters), though Rostand had it from Aesop or Phaedrus, I don't know which. And the source of "In the Belly of the Whale" is an obscure political pamphlet by August von Kotzebue, which I read while writing a book on that singular contemporary of Goethe. If there are predecessors for some of the other fables, I have forgotten what they are. Be that as it may, even the three stories I have named are original in the ordinary sense of that word. They are not "creative imitations" of their models, but new fables inspired by and rooted in old ones.

Plato tells us that Socrates was about to versify Aesop before his fate overtook him. This is proof enough, I think, that fables are serious literature. The well-turned traditional apologue, as practiced by ever so many writers since antiquity, is a means of conveying grave and often cruel truths without torturing its readers. It does not lose substance because of its brevity; it does not forgo significance by inviting cows and baboons to take the podium. I do, however, admit to a touch of vexation toward the world for not quite believing in our severity. It is, of course, a forgiving vexation, for who is more temperately aggrieved than a fabulist?

A BONE OF CONTENTION

A fox terrier and a spaniel were fighting over a steak bone. Merciful heavens, they went for each other with teeth, claws, shoves, barks, and kicks. "Get away from my bone!" "This bone belongs to me!" "Mongrel!" "Flotsam!" "I'll throttle you with your own tail!" "I'll throw you to the cats!" "Oaf!" "Fleaface!" "Lickspittle!" "Perpetrator!" It was a fearful spectacle, for both dogs were bleeding out of a dozen wounds.

Considering this opportunity, a young hawk, inexperienced in the sad ways of the world, came down from a tree in order to pick up the bone for himself.

The dogs stopped fighting at once. "Who's this?" rasped the spaniel. "A foreigner!" the fox terrier howled. "Brother dogs, unite!" And both dogs flung themselves on the bird.

The hawk was lucky he escaped alive that day with a small loss of feathers. No doubt, had I reached out a hand for the bone, the three would have leagued together as Animals against Man. And if a Martian had landed at that moment, I would have roused them personally to battle as Earth dwellers against Mars. For there isn't anybody with whom we couldn't make a faction.

Meantime, the spaniel chewed one end of the bone and the fox terrier nibbled the other. They were still bleeding, but they were bleeding in peace.

⸺⧫⸺

THE CATERPILLAR AND THE LEAF

Why are you nibbling me up?" said the leaf to the caterpillar. "It hurts; I am bleeding; I will die."

"Believe me," answered the caterpillar, "I have nothing against you personally."

"Then why don't you go elsewhere?" wept the leaf.

"I have nothing *for* you personally either," answered the caterpillar, munching on.

⟞⟝

THE COCK
WHO MADE THE SUN RISE

Every day before dawn, the rooster Kukkurrik uttered a mighty volley of crows, watched the sun come up, and said to himself, "I've done it again." For he believed that his crowing made the sun rise. Once, however, it happened that his chum, the chiffchaff, risen from his twigs before his usual time, overheard Kukkurrik and urged him to explain what he meant by "I've done it again." At first Kukkurrik was reluctant, for he felt that getting the sun to rise was his own private affair. But as he was proud of his mission in life, his friend finally wormed the truth out of him. However, instead of being impressed, the chiffchaff went into gales of laughter.

"You superstitious henpecker, you arrogant eggnog—*you* bring out the sun? Ha, ha, ha, go on and prove it to me."

"I don't know why I should bother," said Kukkurrik coldly, "but even a fool like you must have heard of logic."

"Logic?"

"Yes, logic. Every morning I crow, and every morning as soon as I have finished crowing, the sun rises. Cause and effect. Logic. *Ergum probatus est.*"

"It so happens," answered the chiffchaff, "that the sun comes out in the morning because a god, whose name if you please is Fibbus, takes it out for a ride. Did you say logic? I drank FACTS with my mother's milk." And there the quarrel ended, because the sweet voice of his favorite hen was calling Kukkurrik to business.

One winter night, however, Kukkurrik and that same hen (her name was Mistress Pertelote) had a falling out, and Kukkurrik left her roost in a huff. It was long past midnight and very frosty, and poor Kukkurrik caught a ferocious cold. He could feel the fever gripping his lungs, his head was in a whirl, he coughed grit and gravel, he cursed Mistress Pertelote, and, as the time to crow came on, he found that he couldn't bring out so much as a semiquaver. "I don't care, it'll be dark for once," he thought, and staggered up his loft, where he fell into a deep sleep.

Hours later, the chiffchaff woke him up. It was a bright day. "Friend Kukkurrik," he sang, "wake up, it's me, your best friend, you've been furiously sick, your wives tell me you couldn't crow, and yet here's the blissful sun blushing all over the world, and to add insult to infamy, there's not a cloud to be seen from poop to stern."

"What's that?" mumbled Kukkurrik.

"You didn't crow, and the sun is up," the chiffchaff shouted into his ear. "Pray explicate." He thought the hour of victory had struck and the Fibbus hypothesis was confirmed forever. But not at all!

"I guess," Kukkurrik brought out in a hoarse whisper, "I crowed so long yesterday that it carried for two days."

"I'll be damned," said the chiffchaff.

"In fact," wheezed the rooster, "I wouldn't be surprised if I lasted the sun a week." And he left the chiffchaff agape at the compelling power of logic.

THE CONCEITED MINNOW

A fisherman had already caught three handsome trout—they were lying in a basket next to him—when he hooked a minnow. He was about to throw it back into the stream when the minnow, catching sight of his grimace, cried out, "And what's the matter with me, if I may ask? Let me inform you that I'm as good as any trout that swims in these waters. I'm small, but I am good-looking, smart, and appetizing. In short, I resent your gesture of contempt and demand to be treated with the respect I deserve."

"Oh well, if you insist," said the fisherman, and he tossed the minnow into his basket.

I don't know about people, but with minnows, once the ego breaks loose, there's no telling where it will stop.

A CONFERENCE OF KINGS

Two kings met to adjust a border dispute. One was clothed in gold and silver, the other was dressed in rags and his face was full of cuts. The king in gold and silver was so shocked when he saw his neighbor that he forgot all about borders. For even though kings like to make war against each other, they hate to see one of their own in *real* trouble. Even when one king kills another, he wants to be sure that behind the one he killed, there's another ready to take his place. Anyway, the king in gold and silver grasped the other by the shoulders and cried, "What has happened to you, brother?"

"Don't ask," the king in rags replied, "I've been all but hacked to death. I'm a good king. I raised everybody's wages and salaries and profits and interest and dividends and pensions and royalties, and the people got used to fingering money, so they asked for more; but the treasury was empty, I sold the queen's jewels, the rich denounced me, the rabble besieged me, everybody threw stones at me, and if it hadn't been for our blessed border dispute, they would have murdered me to pieces. While look at you, oh look at you. Gorgeous and merry, and looking twenty years younger than you are. Brother, brother, how do you do it?"

"Unlike you," said the rich king, "I imposed on my people a tax so heavy it would have ruined five generations to come. At the last moment, when the only noise in the realm was that of sobs and groans, I made an unforgettable gesture from my balcony and reduced the tax by one entire tenth. And now, brother, I am rich enough to buy Mammon, and the people, though hungry, bless me everywhere I go."

A CONVERSATION BETWEEN A BULLDOZER AND A MOUSE

A large bulldozer was tearing up a field in which a family of mice had made their nest. As the bulldozer carved its way nearer and nearer to their home, the mice could hear the groans of wounded bitterweeds and the gasps of slain beetles rising from all sides of the field. "What shall we do?" the miceling were crying, but their parents only stared and trembled as the terrible jaws gnashed the earth. At last the father mouse leaped forward and ran up to the machine, which he addressed as follows: "Lord Bulldozer, spare my little family; we are poor but honest mice who have lived in this useless lot for many years without disturbing the peace."

"And what makes you think that I have come to disturb the peace?" replied the bulldozer.

"Well—" said the mouse.

"Nonsense," the bulldozer retorted, "you are thoroughly mistaken. I am leveling the ground for an eighty-five-story apartment house as a special favor to you mice." "As a special favor to us mice?"

"Yes, sir. You have been disgracefully happy in a sordid nest with an occasional dandelion in your gullet; but after I have finished my work, you will take your pick of five dozen rooms, each one overflowing with bread and cheese, potatoes, and lamb chops. The nation of mice will thrive; you will publish odes to me."

"I am very glad that the nation of mice will thrive," said the mouse, "but what about us?"

"Who is *us*?" "Us, me, my woman, and my two miceling!"

"I don't know us, my and me," said the bulldozer. "I deal in principles."

The mouse ran back to his family, and said as cheerfully as he could, "The bulldozer brought me good news: he is growing an apartment house here especially for the nation of mice, and we are going to live in whipped cream to the end of time." But before the mother could make a comment (and that was a pity, because she was a sensible beast), a ton of earth fell on top of them and the bulldozer churned on.

Let you and me be more careful than these mice, and when we see progress coming our way, jump aside in time.

———⋙◆⋘———

THE CROW AND THE BEGGAR

A beggar was standing with his cap in his hand far from the road, all alone in a field of boulders and stubble. A cold wind crept from gray horizon to gray horizon. Puzzled by the sight, a crow landed among the weeds a few paces from the man. "Beggar," said the crow, "no one will give you anything in this desert."

"Crow," replied the beggar, "no one will deny me anything in this desert."

———⋙◆⋘———

THE DRAGON OF HELGOLAND

We harm those we hate; we also hate those we harm; otherwise our conscience would sting us, and who likes to be stung?

The dragon of Helgoland had vowed to exterminate all the unicorns of the realm. History does not record why, but we must hope that he had his reasons. One day, as he was prowling through the woods, he thought he saw a unicorn concealed in the undergrowth. He quickly belched out a jet of flames which burned out an acre of land in front of him. The wave gone, he heard a feeble lament almost under his enormous paw, and, looking down, he saw a litter of tiny badgers, all burnt to death except one, who was still alive enough to despond. "Why did you kill us?" wailed the last of the badgers. "What harm did we do you in our short small lives; why did you strike us down who are innocent?"

"Innocent devils!" bellowed the dragon, "I hate you weasels; all the world knows you've been plotting against me with the unicorns!"

"But we are not weasels; we are badgers," said the little victim.

"Well, I hate badgers too," grumbled the dragon. "They're always standing in the way of my fire." And from that time, he never thought of badgers without spitting a flame in disgust.

⋙◦◦⋘

THE EAGLE ON THE MOUNTAIN

Five sportsmen were climbing a huge mountain which no human being had ever scaled. The gales blew and whistled between the crags, on all sides chasms opened, the air was thin, the men gasped and tottered in the hurls of snow, three were buried in an avalanche which tore the face of the mountain, a fourth lost hold of a ledge and fell headlong to his death, and at last the fifth stumbled to the top, where, under a cold sun, he planted the flag of his favorite nation. The top of the flagpole happened to be adorned with a large brass knob. An eagle, attracted by this shiny new object, descended and perched on the knob, even as the last sportsman was beginning his journey down. The brass ball made an elegant seat, he thought, and after taking a few nibbles from the flag he decided he liked it too; it had a colorful taste. Another eagle flew by. "What have you got there?" he called.

"Oh, nothing. Just a new perch and things," replied the first eagle.

"How did you ever find them?" asked his friend, who was strongly impressed.

"I hate to boast," said the eagle, "but do you see that biped lumbering downhill? He brought them up for me." The other eagle could hardly deny the evidence. Word soon spread, and the lucky bird on the flagpole became the most considered eagle of the range.

⇒◦⇐

THE FAITHFUL GARDENER

An old gardener was shearing and trimming a privet hedge around one of the gardens of a famous duke, when, looking up from his work, he saw a dark figure standing beside him. "Who are you?" the gardener asked.

"I am your death," replied the figure, "your time has come, gardener, and I must take you away."

The gardener's arms fell as he looked at Death. For a few moments he could not speak, but then he said: "My hedge is not yet done. Look, it is evened here as smooth as a baby's cheek, but yonder it is as wrinkled and rough as my own. Let me finish my work, it will not take me long; I wish to leave the garden in order."

Death answered him: "Why care about leaving the garden in order? Presently, when I extend my fingers into your old heart, the garden will not matter to you."

"I have been the duke's gardener for sixty years," said the old man, "what will he think of me if I leave him with a rough privet hedge?"

"What will he think of you! Fool, I repeat that in another minute, you will have ceased to care about privets and trimmings and masters."

"But I care now," cried the gardener with his last tears in his eyes, "I care, I do, let me complete my work!"

"Death waits for nothing and no one."

"Yes it does! We are debating, so you've delayed!"

"You are mistaken," Death said, "the moment hadn't come; but now it has." And he extended his long fingers into the old man's heart.

———◆———

THE FARMER, HIS SON, AND HIS MULE

A farmer had loaded two sacks of potatoes on his mule and gone to the market-town, accompanied by his little son. After selling the potatoes, feeding the mule, and stopping at a tavern with his boy for a loaf of bread and cheese and a mug of ale, he spoke as follows: "Son, the road home is a long one. As I'm feelin' my age and a heaviness in my head, I'll ride our Meg till we reach the little stone bridge. By that time I'll be my chipper self again, we'll change places, and it'll be your turn to ride old Meg as far as the roadside chapel to Our Lady. That's where we'll reward her for carrying our potatoes and you and me, and give her leave to trot home easy on her own."

The lad happily agreed, and so, I think, did the mule, who had her own way, after so many years spent together, of understanding her master. Off they went, with the farmer astride the mule and singing a ditty, and the boy walking at his side, now hopping on one foot, now on the other. Presently they came across a philosopher and his disciples who were going toward the town for a convention of sages. The farmer raised his hat to them, gave them a cheerful word, and rode on. The philosopher didn't reply, but he turned around to watch the threesome ambling on their way. After they were out of earshot, he said to his disciples, who had, of course, turned around with him: "The older, the more selfish. Proof? The gross father, smelling of cheap beer, takes his ease; the delicate child is left to fend for himself. Let the poor boy stumble! Let his feet bleed! The old codger is comfortable, so he no longer cares if the rest of the world, including wife, children, and mules, goes to the devil."

Upon reaching the little stone bridge, the farmer said to his son: "Your turn, my boy!" He lifted his son onto the back of the mule, and off they went again, the farmer singing another ditty and the lad and the mule beginning to dream of supper.

After an hour or so, they met another philosopher on his way to the sages' convention. This one was alone, muttering aphorisms to himself. The farmer raised his hat, gave his how-d'you-do again and walked on without noticing that the philosopher had turned around to watch the little group. The sage took out a notepad and scribbled: "The world, I repeat, is topsy-turvy. The child rides the mule, the old man trudges on foot. Mark my words: soon the man will be carrying the mule on his shoulders."

After reaching the chapel, where the humans crossed themselves and the mule saluted with a pious nod, the farmer said, "All right now, Meg has been a good girl; let's set her free. We'll walk on our four feet each side o' her and try to reach home before sunset."

Off they went again, with the mule braying contentedly, the farmer singing, and the boy hopping now on one foot and now on the other.

They were nearing home when they crossed the path of two more philosophers on their way to the convention. The farmer raised his hat again, and again the philosophers turned around to watch the little family down the road and away. "Folly," said the older philosopher to the younger one, "folly wins out; it is congenital in mankind and education cannot root it out. Two supposedly rational creatures walk alongside a mule, and to neither, it seems, does the idea occur that one of them, or both, could ride the beast."

"One does despair at last, does one not," his colleague sighed.

At suppertime on the farm that evening, the boy asked his father, "Dad, who was all them fine folk you raised your hat to so polite-like?"

"They are philosophers, my son," replied the farmer.

"What are philosophers?" asked the boy.

"They are folk who understand things which the likes of us won't never fathom, and that's why, when I pass them on the road, I raise my hat, and so must you, my boy, when you grow old enough to wear one."

❖◆❖

THE FLATTERED HIPPOPOTAMUS

The hippopotamus was delighted. "What are you delight-ed about?" asked his best friend, the crocodile, who could not bear to see him so happy.

"Why," said the hippopotamus, "when the lion spoke to us last night on behalf of the pension for retired lions, he smiled at me and said in the hearing of all present: 'Without Handsome Hippo's assistance, I am powerless here.' "

"Ha!" sneered the crocodile. "I hate to disillusion you,

my dear friend, but you make me laugh. Handsome Hippo! Are you truly taken in by this obvious piece of flattery?"

"No, I am not," answered the hippopotamus. "I am not flattered by what the lion said; but I am flattered to be the one he chose to flatter."

A FLEA PROTESTS

I despise you." So said the dog to the flea as he lifted his indignant rear leg to scratch his flank. "You parasite," he added.

The flea happened to be a reasoner. "You call me a parasite," he squeaked from behind a tuft of bristles which the dog could not reach, "but don't you live off rabbits, don't cats live off mice, don't people live off chickens, don't lions live off zebras? Why does everybody hate us so?"

Unfortunately, the dog was a reasoner too. "We despise you," he said, "because you live off those who are bigger and stronger than yourself; that makes you a parasite. We live off those who are smaller and weaker than us; that makes us normal."

What could the flea reply? Rules are made by rulers, and those who bother the rulers must not expect to be called by pretty names.

THE FOX AND THE CROW

One hand, they say, washes the other.

A crow was sitting on a branch with a piece of cheese in his bill when a hungry fox, drawn by the smell, stopped under the tree and spoke as follows: "Master Crow, I find you at last! How often your voice has brought down my tears when I heard it in the distance through the foliage! I beg you, sing a ditty for me now, so that I may taste, savor, and relish!"

This was an irresistible speech. The crow opened his beak, dropped the cheese, and cawed his creaky uttermost, high, middle, and low. "Enchanting!" cried the fox, who didn't like to make enemies, "but, oh dear, what is this?"

"It's a cheese I was about—" the crow began to answer, but the fox broke in passionately with, "A cheese? So it is. A vile Golgondola! It must not, it shall not beslobber your windpipe!" And picking it up with all his teeth, he gulped it down in a wink. "There," he said, "I have removed the temptation. Your voice is saved."

The crow thanked the fox, the fox thanked the crow, and they parted company in high spirits both. And why not? The fox had won a luscious cheese, the crow a glowing compliment, and neither is easy to come by in this world.

———◆———

HANK THE SALESMAN

Above all the salesmen working for him, the President of the company loved and prized a man whose name was Hank. Hank had eyes that made the ladies dream of naughty adventures in ancient Persia. Beneath his comely nose, a long black moustache pointed to the right and the left like a pair of wings. His hair was curly and neatly trimmed around his attentive ears, his cheekbones looked like small ruddy apples, and his arms seemed to have been forged to carry the helpless out of fire-swept buildings. He was, furthermore, a man of merry monologue who believed in the quality of the product his company sold (I have, alas, forgotten what this was) as devoutly as the Pope believes in the Trinity. As a result, he scoured his territory like a conqueror, selling more units of the product than anyone the company had ever employed. No wonder he was the President's favorite, and the darling of all the Directors too.

And no wonder, either, that, one morning, as the meeting of the Board of Directors was getting under way, the Chairman confronted the President with rage rampaging in his face, gestures, and words. "The news has come to me," he thundered, "that our President has fired Hank. Why, Mr. Weamish, did you fire Hank?"

The Board was dumbfounded. The President said nothing.

"Why, why, why?" the Chairman shouted. "What made you do it?"

And still the President was silent. But now the Board was finding its voice. "Confess," said a cunning Director. "Wasn't it envy? Was Hank too successful? Did he steal the sunlight from you?"

"Oh no!" cried the President. "I? I envy Hank, I who admired him so, I who gave him raise after raise?"

"What then?" asked another Director. "Did he debauch the typists?"

"He did," replied the President, "but that was stipulated in his contract." Several tears were beginning to sprout from his eyes.

"Did he peculate and malversate?" suggested another Director.

"Hank malversate or peculate? Hank? Oh Hank," blubbered the President, "you who lunched on yogurt when you traveled in order to save the company's pennies! I never knew a boy as honest as you, except my grandmother in Heaven."

"Enough!" bawled the Chairman. "Mr. Weamish, you fired our most brilliant salesman, though you were aware that the competition was luring him with bonuses, stock options, and limousines. One last time, tell us the cause, or else *you* in turn—the rest is blank, but as you all know, my silences are even more terrible than my words."

And indeed the President was trembling. "Mr.

Oglethorpe," he whispered, "forgive me, but you named the cause yourself."

"Fiddlesticks! Where? When?"

"The offers from our competitors...every day a new one... oh, I was so afraid that he was going to leave us...so nervous, so terrified..."

"That you fired him?"

"That I fired him."

And there my story ends. Hank, as you might guess, went on to sell innumerable units of the next product, while the President was condemned to wrap parcels with twine and tape in the stockroom. There, for years to come, he would impart to newcomers and old-timers alike his settled conviction that doing mischief in order to prevent it is a very sad mistake.

HOW GOD BESTED THE DEVIL

Some people believe that the devil is busy day and night tormenting mankind. But that's a pretty medieval way of thinking. Actually, the devil turned the whole machinery on, so to speak, right from the start; I mean, he made people as ornery as he could and then he left them to their own devices. Now and then he lands here to make sure that everything is going wrong, but then he goes about his interests elsewhere, or else between trips, he relaxes on the homestead in Gehenna.

On one of his tours on Earth, the devil happened into the troposphere just when a few physicists and generals were trying out a hydrogen bomb. The devil's a tough piece of steak, as you can imagine, but he got burned and jolted all the same, like that time long ago when AX-469 exploded in Galaxy Azazel and the universal pottlewibblets were exterminated. Anyway, after he recovered from the shock, the devil went to talk to the generals and physicists. "Something new is cooking, I see," he said.

"Yes," replied the chief physicist, "and we're pretty proud of it; believe me, it took brains."

"Tell me more," said Lucifer. So the physicist gave him the lecture—hydrogen isotopes, tritium, and deuterium, critical mass, self-sustaining reactions, annihilation of matter.... "Excellent, excellent," said the devil, rubbing his hands together, "but what do you propose to do with it? It seems a pity just to let it drift."

"Who said anything about drifting?" retorted one of the generals. "This gizmo of ours ain't no drifter; it's a proliferator!"

The chief physicist explained: "My colleague is suggesting that scientific discoveries can't be kept secret forever, as indeed they shouldn't be when they're as luminous and far-reaching as this one."

"I couldn't agree more," said Lucifer, "congratulations to one and all. I look forward to a heartwarming bash. But after the concussion I had today, I think I'll go watch it from neutral ground."

"I'm afraid, sir—" the physicist began, but the general got ahead of him with a big laugh. "Neutral ground? Never heard of it! Tell me what it is and where I can find it, haw, haw, haw!" Now, everybody knows the devil has a sense of humor, but he didn't laugh this time; in fact, he began to feel a little worried.

"Neutral ground—you know what I mean, the kind of place where people just sit around; you know, just sit around and live. With geranium pots." At this, the general turned serious. "You read too many Happy Birthday cards, Mr. Fangs. After the last of these gewgaws has blown its lid, there won't be no geraniums left to tell the tale, the watering cans'll be scrap and so will the people that were gonna use them on the geraniums that ain't there anymore."

"Technically, sir, we call it the nuclear winter," said the physicist. "Allow me to explain: as the radioactive cloud—"

but Lucifer was gone, gone like a shot, gone in a panic that was a pity to see. The truth is, the devil needs people for his mischief, because there's no such thing as disembodied mischief. Mischief is absolutely void until it gets into living creatures. So the devil flew like a bullet to the mansion of the lord, where he didn't even announce himself; he merely plunged in and demanded an immediate audience.

When God took him into his private cabinet, he couldn't hold himself back. "Murder," he bawled, "it's murder, it's massacre, it's a plot against me, don't tell me it isn't, I ought to know a plot when I see one, and what in hell am I going to do without people?"

The lord chuckled. He'd never seen Lucifer in such a broil. "At last," he said, and then he repeated, "at last and at long last I have found the way of besting you. The forces of evil are smashed. Hang up your pitchfork, Satanas, I've outsmarted you. I'm almighty after all."

"You mean—" said the devil, gasping. "I do. From now on, it's cosmic dust for you; enjoy it if you can."

And that is the story of how evil had to quit the Earth forever.

—————◈◆◈—————

HOW GOD LEARNED
WHAT MEASURE IS

There is a Spanish proverb that goes, "Don't saddle a horse to go next door." And in Estonia people say of a fool, "He hoists a sail to cross a puddle." I know a man of such rectitude that he will bring Moses, Plato, Spinoza, and Kant down on your head for crossing the street against a red light or fibbing on a questionnaire. The world operates by degrees, however, and it took God himself a few experiments to discover this, as I will prove by what happened to him in the beginning of things.

When Jehovah began his career, he really enjoyed tossing his thunderbolt around. He had his standards, you see, and moreover he was the only object in the whole universe with standards; in fact (to get to the bottom of it all), it was at the pinpoint moment when the idea of standards erupted into the universe that Jehovah had made his appearance. Be that as it may, now that he was chief, he meant to see that the wildlife all over the galaxies toed the line. Not that I know what he found in the galaxies, but on Earth there was plenty of trouble. One day an electron refused to whirl, it just stood and dawdled; and that was against the standards, so Jehovah slammed the electron with his hottest flash of lightning, and it has never stopped spinning since. Another day a pebble fell up instead of down a cliff, and that was against the standards too. Jehovah lit into that pebble with his faithful thunderbolt. It stopped midair and started down so fast, Jehovah himself had to laugh. Another time a geranium leaf ate a caterpillar instead of the caterpillar eating the geranium leaf, and that wasn't in the rules either, so Jehovah bashed the geranium with a hefty thunderstroke.

In short, God was doing a thorough job, and he praised himself no end. Besides, there wasn't anybody around to contradict him, which is always nice too. But then one day, Cain killed Abel, and that made Jehovah far and away the maddest he had been yet. Talk about standards! He thought he'd crush Cain with a whopper like nothing let loose on the universe yet. And nobody can deny that the case called for harsh measures. Only it turned out that Jehovah had already used the ultimate weapon on those geraniums and pebbles. He was red-faced with shame and grief, but as he couldn't make a bigger bomb than the biggest, he had to once again fetch down his old thunderbolt—it was badly worn at the edges by now—and he picked Cain off with it. Only he didn't enjoy it at all. "I have learned my lesson," said God to himself. "Next time I will use my tweezers on those electrons."

IN THE BELLY OF THE WHALE

 whale had opened his jaws and swallowed a row of herring. The unfortunate fish were flopping about helplessly in the vast stomach, each looking with anguish at another for signs of help or hope. Instead, one of them began to cry, "Oh my God, oh Jesus in Heaven, we are all undone! Don't you see the hole gaping at the end of this cavern? There begins the gut, thither we are bound, and yonder we shall be digested into herring paste!"

The other herring made an uproar at this. On every side, in the dark, came shouts of "Alarmist!" "Rumor-monger!" and "Pessimist!" Then, after the hubbub had subsided a little, one of the herring, looking about in the faint phosphorescent glow, announced, "The indisputable fact, gentlemen, is that we have slipped, somehow, into a quiet, restful place." "Almost a resort," chimed in another. "Say rather a haven," remarked a third, "a vault under which neither sharks nor fishing nets are to be feared." Thereupon they all went, "Hear, hear!"

At that moment, they heard a familiar voice from afar. It was that of a fellow herring the whale had missed in his gulp. "Do you hear me down there, all you herring?" the voice was crying.

"Yes, we hear you, Ferdinand!" "Good! The monster has fallen asleep. You can all swim out again, but do it quietly!"

Well! The herring forgot their fine words, and with a terrified "Hush, hush!" they darted and scrambled all over each other to the exit. Safe again, they happily swam home to their families, each one crying to his kith and kin, "Listen to what happened to me! Let me tell you how, not one hour ago, I who am hugging you now was looking the Grim Reaper straight in the eye!"

THE INNOVATION

Two farmers were looking at a strange new apple tree.

"My landlord invented it," said the first farmer to the other. "He's a famous experimentalizer with ten framed diplomas on his wall."

"Sure is the oddest apple tree I ever run up against," answered the second farmer. "Who ever seen an apple tree with a purple trunk?"

"Who indeed!" said the first farmer proudly. "And instead of leaves, it grows feathers."

"Yeller feathers! And dang me if the apples ain't square instead of round!"

"Yep, they're uncommon all right. Try one. Nice and ripe."

"Thanks," said the second farmer, and, plucking one of the apples, he bit into it. "Ouch!" he yelled. "I'm bleedin'!"

"Yep," said his friend, "cuts your lip like a razor blade, don't it? Here's my hanky."

The lip was soon healed, but its owner's frown hung on as he thought and thought. At last he concluded, "Not much of a tree, I reckon," and he gave the trunk a kick.

The first farmer grew red with indignation.

"Not much of a tree? What do you mean, not much of a tree? Don't tell me *you* could have growed it!"

"No, I couldn't," replied the other. "I'm stoopid, and some jackass notions it takes a genius to dream up."

THE JOURNEY OF A COW

In a charming meadow of lower Carinthia, the cows were feasting on the sappy grass with joy in their souls. There was no better meadow to be found in the world, no jollier

cowherd, no friskier dog, and no happier fate. Most of the
day the cows ate dinner, but from time to time they also
took a walk (two steps or three) and then they lay down for
a sunbath or a sleepy friendly confabulation. One of these
cows, however, was a different sort. She had acquired a
little philosophy, I don't know where, and this had got her
to grumbling a good deal about life, and also (to speak the
whole truth) about death. "Oh sisters, sisters," she would say
to the other cows, "I admire your serenity, I envy your bliss.
Do you think that this cowherd, whose face you lick, and for
whose hand pats you compete, bestows his goodwill on you
because he loves you? I am sorry indeed to disabuse you, I
wish I could leave you ruminating with a grateful heart, but
you must be told that this cowherd and his rich employer
are merely fattening you for the kill. The kill, my sisters!
For your death! You listen complacently to the bells around
your necks, but these bells do not peal for you; they peal to
cheer the cowherd. For you there is only the eternal nothing,
and yet you graze, you smile, you grow fat in order to be
condemned the sooner, and you dare to be happy!"

The other cows listened as carefully as they could, but
it is not easy to pay close attention to metaphysics on a full
stomach, and these cows had a full stomach most of the
time. They admired the philosophical cow enormously—how
she could talk!—they knew too that she was giving them
distressing information, and they were grateful that she was
trying so hard to conceal it from them; but in the end, could
she deny that the grass was luscious and the cowherd a sweet
gentleman? These facts were too obvious to be refuted, and
so it was hard to see how one could prove that they ought to
be unhappy. "These animals are hopeless," the philosophical
cow concluded. "I must look out for myself; each cow
is alone in her universe; we can only make a pretense of
communicating; we moo in the void."

It had come to her attention that in India cows are
goddesses, they cannot be slaughtered, and they are wor-
shipped instead of broiled. For a long time she revolved this

wonder in her mind, and she even inquired of some migrant geese in what direction India lay. One day, when her companions looked more paunchy than the philosophic mind could bear, she set out without farewells on the long and dangerous walk to India. She was a courageous beast. She took the side roads, ate the wild grass along their borders, slept among strange herds in alien fields, her heart ever high though weary, her whole mind pointed to India, where cows are goddesses and men do not slaughter them. How many weeks, how many months she traveled, in the dust, in the cold, in the windstorms, in the rain, she did not reckon and I do not know; but one day she stood in a village in which cows roamed at will in the streets, without a dog to bark at them or a herdsman to march them back and forth.

"Am I in India?" she asked joyously of the first cow who crossed her path. The cow, who was pale and thin and whose head was bent low, looked up in surprise and said, "Poor wretch, you are."

The Indian cow could not take her eyes off the traveler. "Where do you come from?" she asked. "Because one look at your girth is enough to tell me you are not one of us."

"I come from Carinthia," said the other. "Carinthia? I don't know where that is, but oh it must be heaven. You are the chubbiest, cheeriest cow I have seen in my whole fly-bitten life." And here the Indian cow broke down and wept.

"What's the matter with you?" cried the philosophical cow. "Why are you crying? I came here to live among you. In Carinthia men fatten us for the slaughterhouse, we die assassinated in the flower of our youth; I came here to be a goddess and to live out in peace the years which nature counted out to me." Before her new friend could answer, two men with sticks approached. "Run, run," whispered the Indian cow. But she was so weak, she could only crawl. The Carinthian cow did not understand what the danger was, since they were goddesses, but then the men fell upon them cursing, shouting, "Out of the way, you loafers!" and hitting them with their sticks. Our cow had never been beaten, so now she dodged this way and that, her head in a whirl, mooing bitterly at each blow, until she found herself in another street, where the men left off beating her at last.

After she had recovered herself a little, she looked around, and saw that all the cows were as thin as her new companion, who had painfully trotted after her; they shuffled along with their heads down, looking as though they would perish any moment. "Was it all a mistake?" cried our cow. "Are you not goddesses here at all? Was I misled?"

The Indian cow had not spoken because the blows had nearly killed her; but now she found breath enough to reply. "No," she said, "you were not misled, my dear; but when goddesses swarm by the thousands, even goddesses starve. If we chance on a rich man's field, his servants fall upon us with sticks, as you just saw. So we return brokenhearted to our daily stubble, rice husks, and refuse which the very beetles disdain. Once in a long while our worshippers squeeze three drops of milk from our wrinkled udders. They love our dung better than our souls. They groan when we are too weak to give them a baby ox. At long last we drop with our jowls to the earth, and expire knowing that our hides will be turned into common purses. Let them! But shall I die of old age without once curling my tongue around a plentiful meal like the thousands, forgive me for weeping, the thousands you have chewed in your time?"

The philosophical cow was dumbfounded. For many a day she said nothing, only snatching at a tuft of grass now and then and, because she was stronger than the others, shoving them away from the better morsels. Shoving them? Ye gods, in Carinthia the cows invited one another to partake! She could not make up her mind what to do next. Remain where she was, live out her natural life as a goddess but live it out in misery? Or return to the joys of Carinthia, so sure but ever so brief?

I have heard that she is in India to this day debating with herself, because she cannot decide. And neither can I.

LA FONTAINE'S APOLOGY

My master Jean de La Fontaine was being teased one day by his vivacious patroness, Madame de la Sablière. "My dear La Fontaine," she was saying, tapping his knee with her fan, "are you not a shocking idler? Your best friends are doing wonders this year in homage to the Muse. It is said that they scorn Parnassus itself as a mean hillock, far beneath their own mountaintops. Racine, for example—"

"Ah yes, Racine," sighed La Fontaine.

"Racine," the lady continued, "has made our king himself shed tears over the unhappy Bérénice, abandoned by her royal lover. Not even Sophocles has imagined a more tragic, a more agreeable heroine. While Molière—"

"Ah, Molière, Molière," interposed La Fontaine with yet another sigh, at the same time raising his eyes as if to the heavens (and indeed, three cupids and a Venus were frolicking upon Madame de la Sablière's ceiling)—"don't I know all about Molière?"

"Molière, my lazy friend, has conquered court and town alike with his Monsieur Jourdain, who will be remembered so long as there are fools fooling in this world, and other fools to laugh at them. As for Boileau—"

"As for Boileau—" echoed La Fontaine, sighing even more deeply.

"Here in my own salon," said his pretty tormentor, "Boileau read us two hundred lines of his *Art of Poetry*, so telling, so graceful too, that we cried out as with a single voice, 'Horace has met his master!' While you, in all that time—"

"Have mercy on me, my dear lady," cried La Fontaine.

"You! You mope and dream and take snuff and play with my poodle and write fables in which foxes and monkeys chatter. What do you say in your defense, you wasted man?"

"In my defense, madam?" queried La Fontaine, scratching his ear. "I hardly know. Shall I venture another parable?"

"The man is incorrigible! But let me hear it all the same."

"Thank you, madam. You and I know that great nations must be governed by extremely wise men. And the wise men who govern them with care deserve our admiration. But the world has its small countries too. Shall they be governed by nitwits, madam, merely because they are small? Or shall small countries be abolished altogether?"

"By no means, you rogue," said Madame de la Sablière.

"Well then, my acres are few; you, dear lady, wish me to enlarge them, I only wish to rule them well. Yet this is where I tremble. Have I, have I ruled them well?"

"Were I to deny it, I would be lying instead of teasing. Yes, Monsieur de La Fontaine, you have been a wise governor of your few acres."

"If this is your true opinion," said La Fontaine, taking Madame de la Sablière's hand into his own and kissing it, "good luck and farewell potentates; the monarch who governs my little realm is happy."

——◆◆◆——

LANDSCAPE
WITH CLOUD AND DUNES

benevolent cloud which had spent its life wandering above tender meadows and fruitful valleys turned one day to the wind with the following surprising words: "I am sick at heart, oh my friend. The world is not all tender meadow and fruitful valley. I have had glimpses, in the farthest distance, of a wretched desert deprived of all life except a few bristles of heartless vegetation. Send me, I beg you, to that pitiful sand; I have in me rain, milk, blood, call it what you will, to bring the desert to life." The wind protested that not in a hundred years had he driven a cloud over the barren region she spoke of. Indeed, no cloud had ever made this singular request. Why choose to hover over a desert instead of billowing gracefully above green grass and buttercups?

"I am different," said the idealistic cloud, "the grass and the buttercups do not need me. The poor desert does. Lead me to the desert, my friendly wind."

The wind, who was an intelligent spirit, said nothing more, and blew soft and steady until the cloud had her wish and stood high over a burning tract of dunes that seemed never to end.

The dunes looked up in horror. "What is this thing?" cried the highest of them, as if choking in its sand.

"It's a cloud," whispered the wind.

A shiver of hatred spread through the desert. "A cloud, a cloud, a cloud," ran the grainy voices from crest to crest.

The chief of the dunes looked up again and snarled, "What are you looking for, you cloud? You're sitting on our sun. Don't bully us. Go home!"

"Gently," replied the cloud. "I am your sister. I have come to quench your terrible thirst. I am here to die for you. And afterward, you will turn to grass and trees, to fruit, to fountains and brooks, to barley, wheat, and corn."

"Nobody is thirsty here. Die for somebody else!" growled a heap of sand.

"Take your barley to the North Pole!" shouted a sarcastic cactus.

"Ugly bundle of fumes," bawled a half-buried rock, "We'll burn up your rain if you dare to touch us."

"Wind, wind," hissed a cunning little dune, "blow up a nasty storm, whisk us aloft, we'll scratch her face and blot out her rain."

Such, and rougher, were their words. The kindly wind scattered the worst of them before they could reach the cloud. He allowed only as many to pass as he thought she needed. And to be sure, after hanging undecided for some hours, she turned to him and said, "Guide me back to the land of meadows, my friend. Ah bitterness: the desert is the desert it wants to be."

THE LUCKY PEBBLE

Two peasant lads named Robin and Colin were sitting at the edge of a footpath, chewing grass and tossing pebbles into the meadow which lay before them. One of Robin's pebbles happened to strike a hunter who was asleep behind a thicket. The hunter gave a cry, leaped up, and strode toward the boys.

"Who threw that pebble?" he shouted. "I demand to know who threw that pebble!"

The two boys were terrified.

"I threw it, sir," said Robin as piteously as possible.

"Wonderful boy! You saved my life!" cried the hunter. "Look at me: I am none other than your Prince. I was pursuing a fox with my retinue, but I galloped so nobly that I lost my way. Exhausted, I lay down and fell asleep. Your blessed pebble woke me. I saw a deadly snake on my breast ready to strike. I killed it, and thanks to you, my dearest and patriotic boy, our country will continue to rejoice in my rule."

"I was glad to do it, sir," said Robin.

At this point the Prince's retainers arrived. They dismounted in alarm, but the Prince reassured them and told the miraculous story of how his life had been spared. "See to it, Lord Chancellor, that this charming and loyal youth is taken to my palace to be reared among my pages; ennoble his parents at once and give them 20,000 ducats for vestments and furnishings. When the boy grows up I shall make him Captain of my Dragoons."

The Lord Chancellor folded Robin in his arms. "Come with me, charming and loyal youth," he said, "from now on your eyes must light on nothing baser than gold, ermine, and pearls."

As everybody was once again mounting his horse—the Prince's steed, I am happy to report, was grazing nearby— and Robin sat proudly on a margrave's pillion, Colin tugged at the Chancellor's robe, whose hem he could just reach.

"What about me?" he piped. "I was throwing pebbles too."

The Chancellor nipped his robe out of Colin's hand. "How dare you compare your vulgar pebble-throwing with his?" he thundered.

"Upstart," said Robin from his horse.

"He has shifty eyes," added the margrave.

Whereupon the cavalcade departed, covering Colin with a great cloud of dust. What remains to be said? Colin went home to spend the rest of his living days planting turnips and beans, and Robin grew up to become a rich, pampered, and dreaded Captain of Dragoons.

THE LUNATIC PIGEON

Three tubby pigeons were sitting on the gravel in a park.
"What happiness it is," said one of them, "to possess a magnificent tail like mine."

"Magnificent tail?" answered one of the other pigeons, "what magnificent tail?"

"Look behind my head," the first pigeon retorted. "Behold the luminous expanse of green and blue." And now he began to strut about the gravel, wagging his little rump. "Admire if you please, the shimmering discs, praised by the better poets."

"You are out of your small mind," said the third pigeon, "the tail you are talking about belongs to the peacocks who live in the park with us; I wish you could turn your head and look at your own rear."

"So do I," replied the deluded bird, "but my consolation is that I can watch the children who surround me hoping to catch one of my feathers. I take delight in their innocent pleasure."

The other two pigeons stared at each other, excused themselves and walked away.

"Strange lunacy," said one of the normal pigeons.

"All the stranger," the second normal pigeon added, "when you consider that just as God made us—and never mind these tawdry peacocks—we pigeons are the most bewitching birds in the world."

"As is plain to see," his friend agreed.

THE MOTH WHO DISGUISED HIMSELF AS A DRAGON

There was a moth who became tired of always being afraid. "Why did the gods make us so frail?" he cried. "We are at the mercy of a thousand large and ferocious animals (like titmice and chickadees) that fly faster than we do, animals with teeth, or claws, or simple unadorned brutality." And so it occurred to the moth to paint his wings up with huge eyes like a dragon's and scarlet stripes more flaming than the tiger's. "It's worth a try, anyway," said the moth to himself. The first time, he crept up from behind a leaf to test his effect on a snail. He rushed at the snail like a wild bull, spat, and displayed his wings. The snail sucked his head back into his shell so fast, he fell off the leaf. The sight of that awful dragon took five years from his life. "Not bad for a beginning," chuckled the moth, resting his wings on his back. Next, he tried a large grasshopper, who took one look at the horrible wings and leaped seven feet over a fence, never to be heard from again. To a horsefly that happened on the scene, the moth gave a heart attack without even trying. For his last test, the moth flaunted himself about, waiting for a bird to pounce. Soon enough a hungry blue jay descended to make an antipasto of him. But the moth was ready. At twelve inches, out went the wings, the ghastly eyes stared at the blue jay like those of a fiend in hell, the jay screeched in horror and vanished over the horizon. The other birds fared no better. It was a triumph on every front.

Presently the moth became the terror of his neighborhood. He grew fat (as befits the terror of a neighborhood) and became reconciled to the justice of the gods. "It isn't size that counts," he would crow to less fortunate moths, "it's brains." After a while, he took to frightening birds, and even cats and dogs, for the sheer sassy sport of it. He would creep up on an oriole or a pigeon, erect his monstrous wings, and go boo as loud as he could. It never failed, and the moth grew ever fatter and sassier.

One day, however, he ran up against an owl, which is a bird that doesn't see much of anything, at least in daytime. Only the moth didn't know it, so he thought he'd have another laugh. He got near the owl, struck out his wings, and said boo. The owl was half asleep, but the sound interested him, and he opened his eyes a little. All he saw, though, was a blur.

"Boo," went the moth.

"I beg your pardon?" murmured the owl.

"I said boo."

Owls, it so happens, work mostly by ear. That last boo did it. The owl made a dart at the noise and gobbled up the moth. "Ye gods, I must have slipped," was the last thought which the disappointed moth had on this earth.

And to be sure, one always does in the end.

<hr />

THE NAMELESS TREE

In a remote corner of the world which no human being has ever seen, there flourished some trees which, as no one has ever seen them, I can't describe to you, though I like to imagine them as looking like grand cabbages sitting on their trunks, why not? One day a seedling was wafted into their midst from eastern New Jersey. The seedling took root next to one of these trees, and it too flourished. First a sapling came up, and then, many years later, a pine tree mature enough at last to know the rules of civility and to greet its neighbor with a "Good morning to you, neighbor!"

The tree it thus addressed responded with a cordial, "And a sunny day to you, young growth. I've watched you pushing up season after season. I can see that you've reached ripeness and wisdom, and I wish you hundreds more years of the same."

"How very kind of you," exclaimed the pine tree. "Allow me therefore to introduce myself: I am a pine tree. And you?"

"I am me, and I'm not quite sure, dear friend, that I understand your question."

"Forgive me!" said the pine tree from New Jersey, "I was simply asking for your name, not wishing, however, to go beyond the bounds of decent curiosity."

"Your curiosity is welcome," replied the other tree, "but I know nothing about names; what is a name?" The pine tree was surprised.

"A name is, well, a name. As I told you, I am not only a tree, like you, I am a pine tree, as they say in New Jersey, or a *Tannenbaum* in German or, better still, a *Pinus ponderosa* in Latin."

At this point it was the native's turn to be surprised. "What can I say? I am nothing but what you see, and so are my relatives up yonder slope; we have no names that I know of. Tell me, what good are names?"

"I'm not sure, but I can inform you that without a name, one doesn't know who or what one is; in fact, one doesn't altogether exist—if you'll forgive my saying so."

"How very awful," sighed the nameless tree. "And I suppose that without a name you stop growing, you lose your leaves, your roots wither, and the creatures give up on you and fly elsewhere."

"Oh no! Please don't be frightened! No such thing! Just look at yourself! Any mother-tree would be proud to call you her own!"

"Then may I be your friend without a name?"

"You may be and you are," said the pine tree, shaking all his needles. "Besides," he added, "I hereby allow you to forget *my* name; for the more I gaze at your head of leaves, the more I feel that I too shall manage to exist without one."

THE PARLIAMENT OF ANIMALS

The white rabbit was showing his country off to his uncle from across the river. He took him to the Parliament of Animals, where they crouched in the gallery with the other small creatures while the leaders of the animals spoke and debated. "What a glorious thing you have there," said the uncle, "all these wonderful animals speaking their minds! On our side, it's hold your snout or else. Who is the majestic figure in the center?"

"That is the lion, our king," said the white rabbit proudly, "but all king that he is, we tell him off any hour of the day." But now the session had begun and the two rabbits were quiet.

First an elephant took the floor. "I am sick of your stupid policy of cutting down banana trees," he told the lion, "and I demand drastic reforms."

"Oh my God," the foreign rabbit whispered to his nephew, "now surely a pride of lions is going to tear the poor elephant to shreds."

"Not in the least," said the nephew, "the elephant can say whatever he pleases."

"Can he, can he?" the visitor marveled. And indeed, they heard the king reply, "Banana trees deserve our attentive solicitude."

Next they saw a cobra wind himself up to the rostrum. He spat, hissed, and said, "Banana trees or no banana trees, it's time we took our kings from another species."

"You are certainly entitled to your opinion," said the lion courteously, "it is very helpful to get a number of constructive views."

The visiting rabbit could hardly keep from dancing with pleasure and clapping his paws. "The beauty of it," he cried, "oh the beauty of it! 'A number of constructive views!' What a king, what a country!"

And now a bear stood up and said, "I do not necessarily support our good cobra; but I want to make it perfectly clear that unless you lions subsidize the culture of honeybees, I might subject his proposal to an objective examination."

"I do trust that we can satisfy you," murmured the lion, "meantime, I want to thank you for your important contribution to this debate."

"He thanks him, he thanks him!" cried the rabbit in ecstasy. "But nephew, surely this is all a game! It can't be serious. They're all in the plot together, so to speak, and they're pulling our legs."

This slur made the white rabbit mad. "I'll show you, and when I've shown you, you can cross the river again and give your spineless friends a report about us." And leaving his uncle speechless, he leaped into the midst of the assembly.

The uncle thought he was dreaming when he saw his own kinsman jump onto the platform and heard him state with great dignity, "And I the rabbit am dissatisfied with the way you lions and elephants and bears trample all over our vegetables without any regard for our interests. I demand that you guarantee the integrity of our cabbage and lettuce."

"I believe your speech is out of order," said the lion politely.

"He certainly failed to follow Parliamentary procedure," the bear remarked.

A panther added, "The rules are clear: a *cuique suum* petition must be filed *ad usum* with the clerk before the opening of the session under subsection 16b."

"I am indeed sorry," said the lion, and he gobbled up the

white rabbit.

"Wait!" cried the visiting rabbit; and he was about to shout, "You're eating my nephew," when he looked at the little animals who were in the gallery with him. Nobody seemed to have noticed a thing. Then he looked at the Parliament: the lion, the bear, the cobra, the panther, the orangutan, the elephant, the rhinoceros—my heavens, didn't they look big and dangerous! So the uncle thought it over and went back to his side of the river. He was used to keeping quiet.

As for me, rather than give you my opinion of the case, I'll sing you a few couplets as follows:

> *Rule the happy realm who will,*
> *Master Jack or Mistress Jill,*
> *Haughty captain, sober prelate,*
> *Jeweled king or bearded senate—*
> *Brother, mind this homely truth:*
> *VAIN IS THE BITE WITHOUT A TOOTH.*

THE PERFIDIOUS SPIDER

Evil is what others do. What you and I do is always good, and what is more, we are ready to prove it. So it was with the spider who caught a fly in his web. As he was running toward his prey on all eight legs, the fly went on his knees (as far as the web allowed him) and begged for mercy. "Why should I let you go?" said the spider. "The law of nature demands that I eat you; and on top of nature, I'm hungry."

"But I don't want to die," cried the fly.

"Neither do I," answered the spider. "I am eating you, my dear, in order to keep alive."

"Of course," said the fly, "you have the right to live too. But if you'll let me go, I promise to send another fly your way. Your web hangs in a dark corner (God knows how I fell into it) but I'll send somebody on an errand straight into your clutches, word of honor, my own sister if necessary."

The spider thought it over for a moment, and then he said, "I'd be a bit of a fool to free you on the basis of a promise. But I'm not heartless either. Call over one of your friends, tell him you've found a piece of meat in this corner, and the moment he is caught, I'll release you."

It was not the best bargain in the world—the fly would have preferred his own offer—but what could he do? So he whistled "dinnertime" as bravely as he could, and presently a cousin of his was caught in the net.

"You son of a cockroach," cried the new victim, "why did you lure me into the web with you?" "In order to save my life," said the fly, "there never was a better reason." And then he called on the spider to unbind him at once, now that he had lived up to his part of the agreement.

"Unbind you?" the spider exclaimed, "a cowardly traitor who coldly sacrifices his neighbor to save his own skin? I couldn't live with myself if I did!"

And in the name of decency, he gobbled up both flies.

⊰•◆•⊱

THE PONY
WHO CAME TO A STREAM

A young pony who was traveling to enrich his life found himself at the edge of a rapid stream. Since he had never crossed a stream before in his few years, he cautiously dipped one hoof in, then another, then his third, and then his fourth. He was standing up to his nostrils in water, wondering what to do next, when two good-natured trout came swimming down the current.

"Is anything the matter, my friend?" asked one of the trout.

"Nothing much, thank you for asking," replied the pony. "I am obliged to cross to the other bank in order to improve my knowledge of the world, but I am afraid of drowning."

"Come now," said the affable trout, "it's a well-known fact that all mammals, with the exception of man, swim by instinct."

"Swim by what?"

"By instinct, or inborn disposition, or congenital ability. I thought everybody knew it."

"Oh, of course," said the pony, ashamed of his ignorance; and so encouraged, he lurched into the middle of the rapid. The current toppled him at once.

"Help!" cried the pony as the stream carried him off. "Help! I'm drowning!"

"I really thought," remarked the first trout, "that all mammals can swim."

"All mammals can swim in quiet waters," said the trout who had been silent so far. "One should always speak in complete sentences, my dear."

THE QUEEN AND THE POODLE

A poodle had strayed into the boudoir of the Queen of Patagonia. She was beautiful, her eyes shone like two pearls, and her skin was the color of early morning. The poodle was greatly impressed, for this was the first queen he had ever met. But the queen too was delighted. "Come here, pretty, pretty poodle," she warbled, and she made the poodle sit on her lap, she gave him a piece of sugar out of her own silver dish, she tied a blue ribbon around his neck, and she kissed his cold nose a dozen times. The poodle licked her hand in return as daintily as he could, first scraping his tongue against his teeth in order to make it perfectly clean.

That same afternoon the queen was presiding over a

meeting of the Patagonian cabinet. It was a dreadful affair. Never in her life had so much urgent business fallen on her shoulders all at once. The Minister of Transportation was bitterly complaining about the shortage of camels. The Minister of Information needed more telephones. The Minister of Culture moaned that the peasants used bad grammar in the fields. And the Minister of Foreign Relations announced that no one was speaking to Patagonia. Seven bundles of documents lay before the queen. She had to read them all, sign them, and understand them too.

Just then the poodle ran into the Council Room—one of the guards had left the door ajar in order to listen—and blissfully wagging his tail, he jumped onto the queen's lap and raised his muzzle to her face. He was still wearing his blue ribbon.

"Who left the door open?" the queen shouted. "Who let that mongrel in? Is this a cabinet meeting or a zoo?"

The terrified guard came running. He picked the poodle up by the scruff of the neck, ran out again, and threw the dog out of the palace.

"What happened? What did I do wrong?" wailed the unhappy poodle. And he told his fearful story to a philosophical mutt who lived in a ditch nearby.

"Don't you know the saying of the wise men," said the mutt, "that there is a time and a place for everything?"

"But not for love!" groaned the poodle.

"Even for love," replied the mutt.

A few days went by. The poodle could hardly eat. Now and then he chewed listlessly on a worn-out bone, because he was really famished, but he paid attention only to his disappointed heart. Finally he could bear it no longer. He ran back to the palace, and without hesitation, without a single wrong turn, he found his way once more to the queen's apartment.

The queen was reading a romance when she saw the poodle at the foot of her couch. "My pretty poodle is back!" she exclaimed. "Come here, my poor darling, forgive me for being mean to you, it was such a dreadful day! And look!

My ribbon is still tied around your neck, but all wilted, all bedraggled, and I'm sure you haven't swallowed a morsel in days!"

The poodle was beside himself with joy and frisked in his queen's arms as happily as a lamb in clover. But when a footman arrived carrying a dish of delicacies for him, he remembered his hunger and fell to eating with loud and generous gulps. It was the finest meat in the palace. Even the footman ogled it with envy. As for the queen, she was delighted to see her pet enjoying the dinner she had given him.

"That's enough," she said mirthfully after a while, "now I want to play with you." And she bent down to take the poodle's dish away. Imprudent queen! A gobbet of meat was left in the dish. The poodle bit her hand and snatched up the meat. It was gone in a second.

"My hand is bleeding!" cried the queen.

The footman was concerned. "Shall I destroy the hound, your Majesty?" he inquired.

The poodle looked at the queen, and the queen looked at the poodle. "No," she said. "Please bandage my hand." After the footman had left, the queen took the poodle into her arms. He licked her hand remorsefully. "Never mind," she said, stroking his head, "I should have remembered there's a time and a place for everything."

"Even for love," thought the poodle.

❦

THE RICH IBIS
AND THE PAUPER THRUSH

The ibis and the thrush had been good friends in their student days. They had shared many a spittlebug and even a bit of frog, and warbled all night long in praise of ladies they were too poor to entertain. Today they were still friends—friends, of course, as one is friends when one is quite grown up, has married, brought children into the world, and learned to look at life maturely. The ibis had become extremely rich by working hard, and the thrush had remained poor, also by working hard. The thrush lived with his family in a rough nest of decayed wood and cow dung. It perched in a dusty bush close to a factory that manufactured gloomy carburetors. The ibis, on the other hand, had just acquired a magnificent hideaway made of the finest Amazonian twigs. One of its two nests sheltered the young ones; it faced the mountains and oversaw a lovely ground of roses, azaleas, and camellias. The other, quite close to the first yet snuggled in a delicious rash of leaves, which gave it privacy, housed the ibis couple and faced a lake, receiving over it the orange rays of the setting sun.

The thrush and his wife never visited the ibis, it would have been too awkward, but the ibis liked his old friend and sometimes flew over for an informal visit. Lately, though, he could see that the thrush was making but a dreary show of good humor in his company. Every other topic of conversation seemed to depress him, until little was left to talk about except the old school days when ibis and thrush had been equals in full hopes and empty craws. But the ibis would not give up his old chum. Instead he thought about him so hard that finally an ingenious idea occurred to him. On his next visit, after the greetings and a sip of apple juice, the ibis produced a deep sigh that could not be ignored.

"What's the matter?" asked the thrush's wife distrustfully. She always hated these visits.

"The matter is," replied the ibis, "that I sit here and envy you two."

"Envy us?"

"Indeed I do. Oh you don't feed on imported snails, I know, but you love each other, your children respect you, you lead your quiet unruffled lives, singing much better than any ibis ever will, and ever would, do you hear, even if he owned all the gold mines of Araby. No, my old friends, believe me, it is not possessions that make a bird happy, happiness is not for sale."

"Is something specific the matter?" asked his friend, looking more hopeful than he had in months.

"I shouldn't worry you with my troubles," said the ibis.

"Of course you should," retorted the thrush's wife, leaving her sodden kitchen and coming close. "We've been your friends long enough, I hope."

"What shall I say?" groaned the ibis. "Living with my wife has become intolerable."

"We had no idea—" said the thrush as tactfully as possible. Both he and his wife were becoming hugely interested. "We spend entire evenings not exchanging a single word. She wants fur-lined nests, flights over the Pacific, lotions for her feathers, God knows what, while all I want from life is a dish of worms every day and a good chat with friends like you. We haven't a thing in common. And the children—I haven't told this to anyone—but our girl has taken up with a stork who cackles in free verse and drinks. She intends to live with him on top of a chimney. As for the boy, he says he wishes he'd been born something with four legs and a set of teeth. I don't know how much longer I can bear it."

This was all news to the thrushes. They were amazed. But they consoled their friend as best they could and dolefully shook their heads. "You see," the thrush said to his wife after the ibis had left them, "haven't I always told you? It takes the rich to be really wretched in this world. Come here and give us a peck."

"Poor ibis," the thrush's wife sighed cheerfully. She kissed her husband and they spent a happy evening together.

Meantime, the ibis had flown back in haste to his nest, where he embraced his wife, folded his children under his wings, and sat down with them for a late supper under the moon, in full view of the agreeable lake. When his wife asked him what he had done that day, he only said, "I have done a good deed." But later that evening, over a rare nectar of chrysanthemum, he spoke again: "The fable has it, my dears, that the rich are unhappy. It is a fable we the rich should cultivate. We must pay priests, philosophers, and poets to spread it. For it cheers up the world a little, and buys us (I hope) the forgiveness we crave."

———≈◆≈———

THE ROCK AND THE SEA

I stand with hard torso, high forehead, and headstrong pride," said the rock to the sea.

"And I am flexible and insinuating," said the sea in reply.

"When you come leaping at me," said the rock, "I hold out my fist and split you dozens of times and split you again."

"When I lap at you," answered the sea, "I deviously divide myself and erode you with a dozen fingers at once."

"I shake you off, poor fool, every time you advance."

"I leave off, proud imbecile, only to attack again."

"You attack me with the chips of myself, as you are too weak to do your own damage."

"I use you against yourself instead of wasting my own substance."

"I have proved that I am better than you," concluded the rock.

"My superiority over you is established," settled the sea.

At that moment, a seagull landed on the rock.

"You heard us," cried the rock.

"Yes, you heard us," cried the sea. "Which one of us is right?"

"Everybody is always right," sang the seagull. "That's what words are for."

And away he flew.

THE SOCIABLE SWALLOW

flock of migrant swallows had landed at break of day on a small island in the ocean. One of the swallows, more sociable than the others, decided to strike up a conversation with a seal nearby.

"Ah what a flight we had last night!" said the swallow for a beginning.

The seal was half asleep, so he lifted only one of his two eyelids and said as vaguely as possible, "Oh?"

"Oh yes," the swallow went on, "a thick fog came in maybe a hundred miles from here, we lost sight of the stars, and if we hadn't put a fairly clever leader in charge, we might never have landed here for our rest."

"Oh?" said the sleepy seal.

"Oh yes. Not that I, for example, couldn't have found the way as well as he. But I'm one of the younger ones, I have to keep my place. However, once we land in the north, I'll find a healthy wife, make a few babies, and become top-swallow in my turn."

"Oh?" said the sleepy seal.

"Oh yes. Of course it's a long way from here. Thousands of miles. More fog, storms, nasty wind currents, gulls and boobies that cross your flight line. But we know what we're doing and we know where we're going. It's been in our blood for millions of years; swallows are smarties."

"Oh?" said the sleepy seal.

"Oh yes. Look at me for instance. Notice this metal strip around my ankle?"

"Umph," replied the seal. He thought he was having a noisy dream.

"Some fool of a fellow took me in his hands when I was an infant and slipped this ring on me. Thanks, I said. Somebody makes me a present, I don't ask why. It looks distinguished, don't you agree? Maybe I can pass it on to my children. Heredity, you know. This is known as a decorative mutation."

"Oh?" said the sleepy seal.

"Oh yes. Of course everybody is used to seeing it by now and it doesn't flutter feathers anymore. But on the return trip at the end of the season, when it's always more crowded, I'll attract a lot of attention with this bauble flashing in the sun. It will help my career. To be sure, we travel mostly by night, but even then there's the occasional lighthouse. Did you know that lighthouses are dangerous?"

"Oh?" said the sleepy seal.

"Oh yes. Fools rush into them, and then it's a short plop to kingdom come. The trouble is we fly low, most of the time we skim the waves. And we're crazy about light, we're sun worshippers, though we do fly at night, I'm not sure I know why, maybe because the stars are useful, who knows?"

Just then the swallows' leader called his flock together, and they all flew away to make up for the time they had lost in the fog.

"Why were you wasting your breath talking to that lump of a seal?" the leader asked the sociable swallow while they were aloft.

"Because I for one have an alert mind and like to keep in touch."

"Keep in touch with a blubbery seal?"

"What do you mean, blubbery? Let me tell you that this seal happened to be one of the most interesting personalities I have ever met."

So spoke the sociable swallow, not without a touch of indignation. And now that I think of it, I too am utterly fascinated by anyone willing to listen to me.

THE SPARROW
AND THE EXECUTIVE

n a certain day in spring, an executive was checking into notes receivable relating principally to current wholesale financing of the Corporation's products, when a sparrow sat down on the sill of the open window. "Poor executive," said the sparrow, "what are you doing?"

"I am checking into notes receivable relating principally to current wholesale financing of the Corporation's products," said the executive. "That's really too bad," said the sparrow. "I like your face, so I'm going to tip you off to a good thing."

"Namely?"

"Namely that the sun is shining, the park is full of pretty girls, the fountains are squirting in the wind like clowns, and you should be out playing hopscotch instead of tallying notes receivable." Another lecture on the Crass Commercial Spirit of the Age, thought the executive.

"Look, little sparrow," he said aloud, "I could buy you by the shipload."

"Just try," the sparrow replied, "you'll soon find out that poets can't be bought."

"Oh yeah?" said the executive. And he rang for the office boy, whispered something into his ear, and gave him a ten-dollar bill. "Relax," he told the sparrow, and went back to his accounts. Soon after, the office boy returned, carrying the most beautiful white cake the sparrow had ever seen. It had whipped cream all over itself in hills and dales, fudge, half peaches, walnuts and almonds, and a large message traced in pink cream: "Sparrows Welcome." Alas, that was more than our guttersnipe could bear. Such a cake! He had never eaten anything better than an abandoned danish. So he flew into the office, gobbled up a chunk of cake, and found himself in the executive's hand.

"Where am I?" cried the sparrow, his bill full of cake.

"In a cage," chuckled the executive. For in the meantime the office boy had quietly brought an empty birdcage, into which the executive clapped the sparrow like a shot. "I've bought you," he stated, "and what's more, you'll like it." And he threw the cake into the cage after the sparrow.

The prisoner drooped. "You were right," he said, "I see now that the likes of me are free spirits only because nobody will buy us. I'll eat your cakes, and I'll sing for you while you collude price structures with your competitors."

"Shake here," said the executive. And every day he made the office boy put a new feast in the cage: once it was a puff framboise, another time a mother's homemade factory-fresh apple pie, then a meringue chantilly, and on another occasion a nesselrode supreme. But strange to report, as day followed day, the cakes began to taste less good, the sparrow took to dreaming of dirty bread crumbs in gutters, and he longed so hard for the park full of pretty girls that at last he lost his voice. If only he could have had his cakes in the park, or the park in his cage! But that was asking for too much luck. And finally he died, for even those who can be bought can die. "I'm sorry for my poetic sparrow," said the executive, holding the cold little body in his hand. "How frail life is! And how solid, instead, are my notes receivable."

<hr />

THE SPINSTER, THE CANARY, AND THE CAT

A spinster was living quietly with her cat and her canary. One day she left the birdcage unlatched by mistake, and while she was busy in her kitchen boiling a chicken for dinner, the cat put his paw into the cage. But the canary was no fool, and the moment he saw a claw where a claw had never been before, he began to chirp like a madman and shake the cage by flying against its bars. The spinster came running in. "You horrible thing!" she cried, pulling the cat away. "You mean, horrible, cruel thing; you were going to murder an innocent little bird!" And, though she was a lady, she gave her cat a memorable whack on his rump.

That evening, as she was putting fork and knife into her meal, the cat sat himself down on a chair by the table and said: "What are you eating there, my mistress?"

"Chicken," answered the spinster.

"Isn't chicken a bird?"

"I suppose it is."

"Why do I get beaten up for wanting to eat a bird, and why don't you beat yourself up for eating another?"

"That is not a nice question," said the spinster. "You were going to murder the little bird practically in front of me. Dear Jesus, I would have seen the feathers in your jaw and the blood on the linoleum. Whereas the chicken was scientifically processed a hundred miles from here, so that I have nothing to do with it."

"Why didn't you tell me before?" the cat exclaimed. "Leave the cage open again, and I promise I'll eat the canary clean and quiet while you're away."

"You wicked animal," said the spinster, biting into the chicken's thigh, "you don't want to understand. The canary is a pet, the chicken is food."

"Not for me," said the cat. "For me the chicken is food and the canary is food."

"Very well," answered the spinster, "but as I nourish you loyally and plentifully, and at no small expense to myself, there's no reason why you need a canary."

"Yes, there is," said the cat, "canary is caviar for cats, and that's more than I get loyally and plentifully."

"Enough!" cried the spinster, and this time she stood up and shook her fork. "The canary is mine, mine, mine, and you won't touch him!"

Mine, mine, mine! Cats and you and I know when we come to the unanswerable argument. The cat slunk off the chair and went to lap up his liver chunks, and he never ogled the canary again.

———◆———

THE SQUIRREL
WHO WAS CAUGHT IN A WAR

Though much is better than little, little is better than nothing.

The gibbons were making war on each other and raising a tumult in the forest. One day, as they were pelting each other with coconuts from adjoining trees, a missile struck a squirrel who was bringing the afternoon's harvest home to his family, and inflicted a mortal wound on him. A mortal wound! What is that? It is the one wound, alas, from which no one recovers; and so (to hold nothing back), the unfortunate squirrel soon lay dead at the feet of his spouse, while all around them the bombardment continued. The mother squirrel was in despair; she wept, she cursed the gibbons, and then she thought of her young. She herded them back into a hollow of her tree and ran up to gibbon headquarters a dozen branches higher, jumping out of the way of the coconuts and pineapples that flew all about her. When she reached the gibbon general, she raised a pitiful clamor about her dead husband and her unprovided-for children. "That coconut," she cried (and she had brought it along for proof), "was meant for one of you. We squirrels, thank heaven, have nothing to do with your war, we don't even know what it's about."

Here the general interrupted her. "It's about ideals, madam, and it might not be amiss if you learned something about the important issues of our world."

"I don't care about ideals," cried the squirrel. "My husband is dead of a mortal wound, my children are going to starve, I demand compensation, namely a winter's supply of cashew nuts and an escort out of this infernal tree."

"You're out of your mind," said an aide-de-camp. "Don't bother our general. I'd like to know how we could carry on a decent war if every time a bystander was hit we were obliged to dip into the treasury to compensate him. Get out of here, and next time tell your husband to duck. Besides, he was hit by the enemy and not by us, so take your complaint to the next tree." With this, the squirrel was booted off the branch, and the gibbons went back to their affairs.

The squirrel stopped by the hollow to see that her children were safe, and then, taking advantage of a lull in the bombardment, she ran across to the tree where the enemy was lodged. She quickly made her way to the general of the hostile gibbons, and reported her complaint. "Look at the weapon," she said, exhibiting the coconut once more. "You can't deny that it's yours. It killed my innocent husband and left my children without provision. I demand that you make some restitution to us, namely half a winter's supply of cashew nuts."

"Are you on our side in the fight?" asked the general of the gibbons. "What do you mean on your side? I'm a squirrel, a different species and a mother of three, I'm a neutral, I have no ideals, I don't belong to any side."

"God strike you," shouted the general. "We don't like neutrals around here. Get out of my tree before I have you shot as a spy."

Terrified, the mother squirrel ran away as fast as she could. On the way down, a kindly old buzzard who had watched the scene took her aside and whispered into her ear, "Go back to your children, madam, take them away while you can, and don't make trouble merely because you are right. You must always smile; smile at everybody, and keep saying thank you."

With this, the widowed squirrel went back to the hollow, and began to move out her children and three or four berries she still had in a hutch. As she was clambering down the bole with her brood, an armed gibbon stopped her. "Where do you think you're going with all these supplies?" he snapped.

"To the authorities," said the widow, smiling and curtseying, "in order to help the brave soldiers."

"That's enough," said the gibbon, "just hand them over to me, I'll take 'em to headquarters. Let's see you out of here by the time I've swung my tail around this branch."

"Thank you," said the widow, and she left the tree with the little squirrels, bereaved, battered, and robbed, but alive.

THE STORK
WHO PRAISED LONG NECKS

In their Academy of Science, on the shore of a pretty lagoon, the animals were debating the question of long necks. The stork pointed out that with a long neck you could keep your body in place and send your face ahead to look for worms and frogs practically anywhere you liked. You could gaze in every direction there is, you could peck your own tail clean (if he might say so without offense), you could rest your weary cheek on your own bosom, and best of all, he concluded, you could enjoy your meals longer, because it took a morsel all that marvelous time to travel down the esophagus into the stomach.

In my opinion it was a good and scholarly speech. But suddenly a noise was heard in the reeds. A silly goose who had eavesdropped on the proceedings was madly clapping his wings. The stork's speech had carried him away. "Me too," he honked for all to hear, "me too honk honk I like long necks!"

It was most embarrassing for the stork. And now the owl spoke up. He hadn't liked the speech about long necks for reasons of his own. "I, for one," he said sarcastically, "do not see eye to eye with a goose, but I am glad that our esteemed colleague has found someone, unfit to be sure for the Academy, to honk in support of his theories." The stork blushed to the tip of his beak, and the animals decided unanimously in favor of short necks.

For a goose can be as right as Aristotle, but no one cares to be right in his company.

THE STUBBORN COBBLER

What is the worst human failing?" asked the scholar Apollodorus one morning as he, Socrates, and several other gentlemen were coming from the baths.

"Strange as it may sound, I feel that irritability is the worst," said the physician Eryximachus after all had considered the question a while. "I do not need to tell you that man is not among the gentle and frightened animals. He belongs with the creatures that counterattack more often than they fly. But of course he stands above these creatures in the possession of a resourceful and supple intelligence. We might say that his claw terminates in a brain, or his brain in a claw. It is this peculiar and deadly combination—irritability and intelligence—which makes him man, and vicious."

"You are painting a frightful picture of us," said the warrior Alcibiades with a laugh.

"And yet I think that envy is worse," the poet Agathon cried out. "For consider this, my friends. All our failings are in some degree pleasurable to ourselves. If I am avaricious, I hide my money from you but enjoy it on the sly myself; if I am irritable, I punish my offender and satisfy my anger; if I am gluttonous, I may cram myself to death, but I will have rejoiced in a quantity of excellent meals on the way. Envy, on the other hand, is grievous above all to the envious man himself. It hurts the striker more than the struck. Furthermore, envy is a wound out of which the pus never stops flowing, for the objects of envy are never exhausted: the emperor of the world still envies Zeus."

"Or a common cobbler," Aristophanes chimed in.

"Well spoken, Agathon," said Alcibiades, "but spoken like a true poet. You artists know the stench of envy better than most other men. But perhaps because I am a soldier, I say that the worst human failing is cowardice, not irritability, nor envy. Do you not agree, my friends, that man differs from all animals in the peculiarity of his daring?"

"I do not quite understand you," said Socrates. "Are not many animals courageous?"

"No. For each animal is circumscribed by instinct in his own province of behavior, beyond which he never goes, indeed cannot go, for if he did, he would no longer be the same animal, but another."

"I am lost!" Apollodorus exclaimed.

"You see," said Socrates, "you are leading us beyond our lights."

"I am sure you are both mocking me, for what I am saying is by no means hard to follow. A goose, for example, may be called daring when she clamors at the fox who approaches her goslings, but she acts by mere instinct, thus far and no farther, like a mechanical toy. If she countered the intruder with a scheme of the sort Eryximachus was suggesting when he spoke of our brains, as for example to organize an invasion of foxholes or to set a trap for the fox and all his relations—then she would be authentically daring. But such actions are not possible in goose-land; she would cease to be a goose."

"I agree with you," said Eryximachus. "The very notions of daring and cowardice exist only when a mind is able to consider the difference between flight and attack."

"Then I proceed. True daring is the glory of man. It made him lord of nature, and then begot all the arts and sciences. Only man aspires, whether in the body or the spirit;

therefore, only man dares; and only man truly conquers. Now since daring is the highest virtue in man, since, indeed, it is that which makes him most peculiarly man, it follows that cowardice, or timidity, is his most ignoble failing."

"I suppose," said Agathon, "that Socrates will now invent for us a failing still worse than those we have named."

Socrates replied, "Why not? If you promise not to accuse me of being irritated by your arguments, or filled with envy, or anxious to be more daring than any of you, I shall propose that the greatest of our failings is obstinacy."

"Why should obstinacy be such a monstrous vice?" Alcibiades exclaimed.

"I do not say that it is monstrous. But it stands in a category apart, above the others, I might even say in a commanding position over the other vices. For it does not concern itself so much with the world as with these other vices."

"I think I understand you," said Apollodorus. "It is a vice about vice."

"Yes, you might say so. Take a man who has a resentful disposition. That is a serious failing, yet by means of good arguments, we may hope to make him relent. But if the man is stubborn about his resentment, all hope is lost. And so with the other vices. Obstinacy is the vice of freezing our vices within ourselves."

"I have no theories of my own," said Aristophanes, "and if I had, who would listen to the theories of a comedian? But I mentioned a cobbler before, and your words, Socrates, remind me of a fable that Aesop is supposed to have told, though few men have heard it. It concerns a certain cobbler who was living in a village deep in the mountains, and who was angry with his wife because she had brought him a bowl of cold soup. It happened to be raining very hard, and the mountain streams were swelling by the hour. As the waters began to flood the village, the wife urged her husband to fly with her to higher ground. But the cobbler's anger over the cold soup would not abate, and instead of attending to his wife, he kept furiously putting more nails into a neighbor's shoe which he was mending. When the water began to pour into the house, the wife fell on her knees and cried, 'Dearest husband, relent, for God's sake, and forgive me for the cold soup. You cannot see that I am kneeling because the water has come up to my bosom, but I beg you to postpone your anger long enough to run away with me. Take the shoe along; it belongs to Cleonymus, who has already made his escape; in another hour it will be too late for us.' 'Get away from me, you bitch of a wife,' shouted the cobbler. 'I work the nails off my fingers to support you and all I get for my reward is cold soup.' When she heard these words, the cobbler's wife decided to save her own life. She fled from the house, and in a refuge far above the flood, she found her one-shoed neighbor Cleonymus, who readily forgave her for coming without the other shoe, and who went even further: he took very proper care of her as long as the rain continued to fall. When the water subsided at last, the cobbler was found stubbornly drowned near his workbench. Thereupon the wife and the neighbor agreed to marry, and as far as is known, they lived happily together for the rest of their lives."

"After the fearful story Aristophanes has told us," said Socrates, smiling, "I hope you all agree that obstinacy is really the worst of our failings."

"Of course we do," Agathon replied. "Were we not placed in this world expressly to agree with Socrates?"

———◆———

THE TERMITE AND THE ANT

What are you doing in that hole?" asked a pretty ant of a burly termite as she was strolling on an old log.

"I live here, my dear," replied the termite. "How odd! Do you enjoy it down there? And what's it like?"

"I enjoy it very much, and it's safe and peaceful and comfortable; my pantry is always full of delicacies; and I am not mauled as you are by nasty winds, ugly frosts, flaming suns, marauding enemies, and beastly men."

"It does sound jolly," said the ant. "Did you say a full pantry?"

"I did indeed say a full pantry. Would you like to come and see?"

"Why not?" said the pretty ant, and down she went into the hole. It was awfully black at first, and when she got used to it, it was still awfully black, but she could feel that she was in a gallery. "Where are you, friend termite?" she called.

"Right here, my dear," said the termite, touching her nose with one of his fingers. "Follow me and make yourself at home. I don't get many visitors, you know." And they walked down the gallery. It was not too difficult, because the gallery was so narrow that you couldn't get lost in it, it led you onward all by itself. But the blackness was giving the ant terrible flashes, and she became anxious to arrive in a respectable room. After a dreadfully long time, she heard the termite say, "Well, here we are. This is my dining room. Feel the antique paneling and the sturdy furniture. Relax, my dear, and let me give you a timber sandwich."

"Where am I? Where am I?" cried the ant. She thought she had gone blind. "It's as black here as in your hallway. I can't see a thing!"

"Why would you want to see anything?" said the termite, a little surprised. "What good would it do you down here? Seeing is all right where there's danger, but down here we don't need all these glares and shadows and visions. Enjoy yourself, sit down, here's a comfortable splinter." But the ant was terrified. She almost wept, and the flashes were getting worse.

"I don't want to sit down! I want the light! Oh where's the way out?" And she ran around groping for the opening to the gallery, bumping here and bumping there, so that the termite was quite bewildered.

"I'll help you, my dear," he called out, "but why don't you like it here? Didn't God make the darkness for his creatures to enjoy?"

"It's not true!" wailed the ant, still dashing to and fro. "God made the darkness to punish horrible animals like you. Where's the light, oh, where's the light?" The termite was so dumbfounded by what the ant had said that for a while he forgot to move. But the ant was still crying with terror, so he finally caught her and turned her into the gallery.

"Shall I see you out?" he asked sadly.

"Let me go!" she gasped, and she ran toward the blessed hole—ah, there, after an elbow in the gallery, there it was at last—and she jumped out into the world, upon which a quiet moon was shining. "Heavenly moon!" she exclaimed full of joy, sitting on her hind legs as though she wanted to embrace it. "Sweet shapes of the world, take me back!"

As for the termite, he remained behind to puzzle over the miserable novelty he had heard. "Did God make us his good termites to enjoy his darkness, or was she right, did he make the darkness to hate us with?" He was still thinking about it as he ate his dinner, and the question ran after him even on his snug little plank as he was falling asleep. But next morning, when the blackness seemed to be laid fresh and thick in every cranny, he rose from his sleep invigorated again. "To work!" he cried, and biting with relish into the log, he dug a deeper room for yet a darker night.

THE THREE REVOLTING ANIMALS

A rat, a skunk, and a porcupine were bemoaning their evil destiny.

"I have lost my appetite for life," said the skunk. "I am hated and shunned. My name is used for petty ridicule. Fame, honor, and affection are forever denied me. Why, last week, when I waved a friendly tail at a little impertinent monkey, he stuck out his tongue at me and flung me an obscene grimace."

"And I?" said the porcupine. "Though I lack your beauty, master skunk, I am an honest family man, a decent provider, in my rib cage beats a simple heart. And yet for every quill on my body, the world has stung me with a barb of derision. Yesterday I gave a kindly greeting to a gazelle, who tittered in reply, 'A genteel porcupine! I've seen everything now!' and ran laughing into the woods."

"Gentlemen," said the rat in his turn, "they may laugh at you or avoid you, but they do not loathe you as they loathe me, the rat, whom they call plague, vicious killer, lover of sewage. My intellect and my agility only excite their horror. Last month I nodded at a rabbit—"

"Everybody loves a bunny," interrupted the skunk in a sarcastic voice.

"I nodded at a rabbit, and he screamed, 'A rat! A disgusting rat!' as only a rabbit can scream when he sets his mind to it."

The three unhappy creatures decided to complain to the lion, who was king of the animals. They arrived at court as the monarch was dining, but a jackal, who was the king's majordomo, invited them to watch their king at his meal and to present their petition after dessert. "You are not," said the jackal, "among his favorites"—and he shuddered a little—"but his majesty gives a hearing to even the lowest."

The lion was sitting at table with an enormous bib under his beard.

"What's after soup, stupid?" he roared.

"Your Majesty," replied the majordomo, lifting several silver covers, "here is a homely but excellent rabbit stew, a superb *emincé* of gazelle, and *singe en brochette*, the chef's specialty."

"*Singe en brochette?*" asked the lion.

"Monkey on a spit," replied the jackal. After the lion had finished eating, and as he was wiping the grease off his whiskers, the jackal told him, "Your Majesty, here are three of your citizens, the skunk, the porcupine, and the rat, who say they wish to file a claim."

"A claim? What kind of a claim? Step forward, don't dawdle, speak up and have done."

The three animals had watched the lion's dinner with wide-open eyes and mouths. The rat, who was indeed no fool, cried out, "A misunderstanding, your highness! Not a claim, your highness, but acclaim, my lord, enthusiastic acclaim." And he led his friends in a round of applause for the king. This done, they bowed to the ground and left the supreme presence as hastily as their legs would move.

"Revolting beggars," the lion remarked. "I was glad to see them go before the cognac."

The three citizens found themselves in the open field again.

"Ah God," said the porcupine, "I feel faint when I think of that sweet gazelle, that droll monkey, and that cuddlesome bunny."

"Turned into main courses," whispered the skunk.

"Turned into main courses, gentlemen, because they were not repulsive enough," said the rat.

And from that time on, not one of them ever complained of his fate again.

———◦◦◦———

THE TIGER WHO BECAME HUMANE

If only the world would see me as I see myself!

Once there was a tiger who decided to become humane against the advice of all his friends. "I want to show the world," he said, "that in spite of our sharp teeth, our ferocious growl, and the beastly traditions of our race, some few of us are not beyond redemption." "But what about our nature?" his friends objected. "We must overcome it," he replied. And so this tiger gave up killing people and animals. Instead he ate bunches of forget-me-nots, he picked up bananas and mangos, and occasionally he even grazed like a cow. It was not much fun—the vegetation tasted vile as far as he was concerned—but he made up for his discomfort by his moral satisfaction. One day, however, a crowd of hunters spotted him as he was nibbling at some mushrooms.

"There's the killer!" whispered a boy, and one of the hunters raised his rifle. But the tiger looked up at that moment and cried out: "Stop! I am the kindly tiger, the famous tiger who has become peaceful!"

"I'll show you what a peaceful tiger is," said the hunter, and he shot the good beast dead between the eyes.

THE TROJAN HORSE

Agamemnon and his generals were considering for the three thousandth time how to set about capturing Troy. Achilles was dead, the city was standing as stiff as it had stood ten years before, and it seemed that everything had been tried—catapults, battering rams, showers of fire, volleys of treachery, and even negotiations. What to do next? The warriors thought and thought as hard as warriors can, but Diomedes had no special idea, except to build a bigger ram; Ajax scratched his head and said, "Why not send another thousand foot soldiers out to have a bash at the gate?"; Odysseus just looked wily; and Nestor stroked his beard and said, "We must be wise." Finally they decided to shoot a few more arrows into the town, and then the meeting broke up.

Now Agamemnon was alone with his servants, and he sat in his tent a weary man. The only way out, he thought, was to send for Sinon, the Thracian military expert. It was a humiliating step to take, and expensive besides, but what else was left, except a ludicrous retreat? His mind still far away, Agamemnon noticed that his sixteen-year-old cupbearer, Alycus, was standing timidly before him, waiting for a pause in the hero's thoughts to speak to him.

"What is it, Alycus?" Agamemnon asked.

"My lord," Alycus replied, "you should build a great wooden animal on wheels, hollow inside, and fill it with our best soldiers, and then pretend to break up camp and sail home; the Trojans will be sure to tow the animal into the city, and then at night our soldiers can climb out of it and open the gate for the whole Greek army."

"Lovely," said Agamemnon, smiling, "but now go tell Phrynacus that he might as well serve; I am dining alone tonight. And bring me pen and paper before you go." That was when Agamemnon wrote to Sinon and summoned him to the Greek camp. Sinon demanded ten talents, which was half of what the entire booty taken at Thebe had amounted to; ten talents, that is, for his services, with another two talents if his measures were successful, and three if they failed—"to compensate him," he wrote, "for his grief and the injury to his reputation." But there was no bargaining; Agamemnon was even afraid that Sinon might take service with the Trojans (but thank God they could not afford him). So Sinon arrived with his staff, and got busy right away. He was really a brain. He poked at the Trojan battlements, looked for secret drains, measured the walls, counted Greek heads, examined supplies and equipment, reassessed the lines of communication, and even infiltrated Troy itself by disguising two assistants as old Cappadocian crones peddling sausages. After four months, he submitted his full report, over a thousand pages long and entitled "The Siege of Troy. Background and Prospects. Tables of Casualties, Equipment Losses, Forces Committed, Temporary and Permanent Allies, and Losses Due to Desertion. Analysis of Strategy Shifts. Recommendations for Action in the Light of Existing Conditions." In the report, which was read to the assembled chiefs, Sinon suggested that a hollow horse be built of wood, stuffed with soldiers and planted in front of Troy while the main body of the Greeks feigned a withdrawal. It was supposed that the Trojans would lead the horse triumphantly into the city, and that the Greeks could issue forth at night, open the gate, and make possible the massive invasion of the city and its final destruction.

"An idea worthy of the gods!" exclaimed Agamemnon.

"I adopt it, I make it mine!" cried the crafty Odysseus.

"Smashing!" said Ajax.

"The contrivance of a sage," added Nestor. The poor cupbearer, who happened to be present, did not dare remind even himself that he had thought up the selfsame stratagem half a year before, and gratis at that. "I must have said something different with a silly twist to it," he reflected.

"Gentlemen," said Sinon with a frosty smile, "I am glad you are satisfied. The task of implementation is yours. Tomorrow I return to Thrace." The Greeks paid him, and on the next day he and his staff departed. Presently the Greeks built the horse (there was no one like Odysseus for the handling of hammer and nails) and soon thereafter Troy was captured and sacked to the last footstool.

The story of Agamemnon's cupbearer is perhaps not known to you. I have it from Arctinus of Miletus, who adds his own curious comment to it: "What father will listen to the advice of his son, what professor will heed a pupil's hypothesis, what millionaire will adopt the faith of his mechanic? We Greeks, alas, weigh the man instead of the idea: we had rather keep our heads empty than stoop to be instructed."

<hr />

TWO BLIND MEN

A blind man who was taking a walk passed by a blind man who was squatting quietly against a wall with a hat in his hand. The first blind man dropped a silver coin into the hat.

"Blind man," said the blind beggar, "how did you know

that I was here, and how did you know that my hat was out?"

"Blind man," replied the other, "how did you know that I was blind?"

Each believed the other lied; each longed to see the other; yet both were blind and truly blind. Explain it? I can't. Meantime one gave, the other thanked and took. What else on earth matters?

———◆———

THE TWO MICE

The country mouse was spending a holiday with his cousin, the city mouse. Though he didn't come exactly from the country, but from a decent small town in Ohio where life burns slow, if steady. Now he was in Greenwich Village, where his cousin had taken up painting. Most of the day the cousin mashed cream cheese on pieces of cardboard, and the other village mice thought he was doing pretty powerful work. The country mouse, however, was more interested in finding a nice mousie to settle down with, so he didn't say much about the cream cheese on the cardboard. But he did tell his cousin that he was a little shocked by the pace of life around him. Dear me, his cousin used words, and tossed notions about, and read magazines, and had friends that made his own fur stand up on his back. And the mice-ladies were much the same. They and the cousin talked about subjects—situations—private goings-on—I hardly know how to put it—in fact, sometimes not even normal ones—and not only sometimes, but, to be blunt, almost all the time. In short, the country mouse was acquiring quite an education, and when he confessed that he didn't enjoy it as much as he felt he ought to be enjoying it, his cousin laughed at him and told him to stop being a limp lollipop.

One evening they were disarraying themselves for an avant-garde party for which they had been promised electronic guitars, communal sniffing of Tibetan floor wax, and the agreeably revolting poems of a rat on parole. "Now listen," said the city mouse to his cousin, "I'm taking you to this party because our mothers know each other. But for God's sake don't make me look like a fool by staring and fidgeting if a couple of mice go off into the bednook, or if a mouse is using the needle to get more *with* the music, you know, into the gut, where it's alive, or if some dame takes off things, you know what I mean, we live the free life, if a mouse wants to feel unconstrained, who the hell are we to butt in with middle-class prejudices, so for God's sake don't act like a forlorn cheesehole."

"You mean," squeaked the country mouse, "some girl mouse might undress?"

"That's the true innocence, *mon cher.*"

"Yes, but wouldn't it be nicer to have a quiet sort of party? A little talk, a little singing, a glass of lemonade, cookies, musical chairs maybe, because all this freedom, you see—"

"Freedom ain't the kind of thing you turn off and on," remarked the city mouse. "When you're free, you've *got* to be free, or else the other mice put the hex on you."

"You mean if I'm not free tonight—"

"If you're not free tonight like the rest of us, whether you like it or not, we'll be hooted and cackled at till I'll never dare show my whiskers out of this hole again."

"Oh cousin," said the country mouse, "is this what freedom is? I see that you are as much a slave as I, and if slave I am and slave must be, I'd rather be a slave where I feel at home." Thereupon, instead of going to the party, he ran all the way back to Ohio, where soon afterward he married the daughter of a churchmouse, and begot, in the most conventional manner possible, a happy litter of miceling, both boys and girls. And was he not right in his way? Freedom, he had found, is but the slavery we happen to enjoy.

THE TWO MOSQUITOES

e usually see what we think we are going to see.

This maxim was not known to two mosquitoes of my acquaintance, good friends who shared an interest in scientific research. One night, one of these mosquitoes noticed a small hole in a window screen in our dear president's bedchamber, a hole that had gone undetected by the President's three hundred strong security guards. He wormed his way through the hole, and waiting till the President was asleep (for being slapped to death is a mosquito's chief worry), he took a deep drink of blood that could have satisfied half a dozen of his kin.

At about the same time, his friend was sipping the blood of a vagabond whose domicile was a cardboard box leaning against a masonry wall bright with hate-graffiti not far from the President's mansion.

The two friends met on a large tree leaf in order to compare the blood of a president with that of a homeless beggar. Each regurgitated a drop. The two drops were identical.

The mosquitoes examined the drops of blood with the greatest care. At last the mosquito who had bitten our President said: "Well, the difference is unmistakable."

"Though subtle!" cried the one who had drunk the vagabond's blood, putting in for his bit of credit.

"Yet clear in the end."

"Clear, my friend, to the trained eye."

THE TYCOON AND THE ARCHITECT

A tycoon whose name was Enceladus Grably was determined to live in the most magnificent of mansions and on the most impressive of estates and to enjoy himself like no tycoon recorded by historians. To make this dream turn into brick and marble, tree and flower as fast as possible, he spent all his days (and a good part of his nights) making deals. Let no one ask me for a list of his deals. Even for those of a single business year I'd be sitting a week at my table itemizing. So many and important were his deals, he had his private satellite running high around the globe, his discreet microsensors taped under the executive chairs of his major competitors, and a high-resolution videoconferencing system sitting in the small place to which even popes and presidents must go. He also ran banks of computers that told him every moment how the stocks and bonds were behaving in New York and Singapore, and all day long people pressed inside information on him to make him earn even more money. He was a man who bribed only the best people. He was a man whom only the best people bribed. On his desk, next to the framed first million-dollar bill he had ever earned, he kept a golden tablet with the word SUCCESS engraved on it. I must report, too, that he smoked cigars (smuggled in from Cuba), for he was the true and perfect tycoon. And every time he made a deal—whether it was to sell out his tin interests in Bolivia, or to acquire a controlling position in United Automotives, or to raise new capital for his Pan-Asian Progressive Chips—huge but huge amounts of money fell into his hands, and these he would make over to his architect in order to have built for him the most beautiful of mansions and most extensive of estates.

He had found an architect who suited him and whom he trusted. It helped, too, that he had met the man in a queer sort of way, "as if destiny had done it just for me," he sometimes said, speaking poetically to the right or the left of his Havana cigar. One day, in his youth, when he was still a mere plutocrat, he had leaned back on his great leather chair and, wondering mistily "Where is all this going to take me?"—for he had that same afternoon rid himself of a hundred thousand shares of Duraflex on private advice of an imminent takeover, and this at a profit of thirteen and a quarter per share (besides, he split the broker's fee fifty-fifty)—wondering, at that moment, "Where is all this going to take me?" the thought of the mansion had struck him for the first time. From that moment he knew that his life would be ruled at last by a glorious purpose. And the very next moment his executive assistant called him to say that a certain architect, recommended by a fellow mogul, was asking for the privilege of a brief interview.

The coincidence was so impressive that Enceladus admitted the man at once: a tall, thin gentleman of no ascertainable age, pale, bony, dressed in black, unsmiling, distinguished, even a little stiff. Enceladus, who was short, ruddy, and chubby, was impressed. The architect showed him photographs, sketches and plans of the buildings he had already created—churches, banks, hospitals, jails, crematoriums, and orphanages—all of exemplary quality, but especially the blueprints of a huge palace, twice the size of Versailles, designed for the Arch-Emperor of Togo (formerly Sergeant Bobbs), left unbuilt due to the lynching of that interesting monarch by a famished mob.

Again Enceladus was impressed. He gave the architect a lecture on the sort of mansion he had in mind for himself but also for posterity. The man listened; it was clear that he understood; and when Enceladus was done, he asked, "When, sir, would you like the work to be completed?"

"Tomorrow," replied the tycoon with a laugh. "I'm in a hurry to enjoy it." At this, the architect seemed to smile, though it was hard to tell. Be that as it may, they made a deal, and presently a contract of 132 pages, drawn up by Grably's attorneys, was signed by both parties. Several shy little articles favorable to the tycoon slumbered under a tropical profusion of impenetrable clauses. The architect declared himself satisfied. "Here, have a Havana cigar," said the tycoon after penning his name to the document.

"Thank you, sir," replied the architect with a polite gesture of refusal.

"Hell, you don't know how to live!" cried Enceladus, giving his man a pat on the shoulder.

Soon the grounds were bought, generous miles of lovely, hilly, wooded, and also grassy land, and the foundations of the great mansion were laid. Slowly the edifice rose. Two hundred bedrooms were drawn in the blueprints. Each came with its bathroom, of course, and each bathroom with its luster, its heavy carpeting, its mink-covered walls, its sunken bath, its private patio with fountain, and its personalized liquor cabinet. Ballrooms were in the plan, reception rooms, drawing rooms, conference rooms, dining rooms, servants' rooms, bowling rooms, television and cinema rooms, rooms bristling with the latest amusing electronic gear, a dozen kitchens, two wine cellars (with sprayed authentic artificial cobwebs over the bottles and barrels), boudoirs, dens, one library, listening rooms, billiard rooms, two hundred fireplaces, and parking for a thousand automobiles. There were to be patios, cloisters, solariums, hanging gardens, illuminations, music piped out of imitation grass blades concealed in the meadows, greenhouses, golf courses, swimming pools, a heliport, and of course the park itself, some of it wild and stocked with game, some of it grassy, sprinkled with innocent sheep, some of it gardened, both in the English and the Italian manner, as well as an artificial lake infused with succulent, suicidal fish.

The truth was that Enceladus not only saw himself, supported by a bank of young sirens, enjoying his life to its final minute; he had larger thoughts and dreamed of an Enceladus Grably Entertainment Center for Tycoons, Magnates, and Moguls to perpetuate his memory for all the ages remaining to the universe itself.

Every three months the architect reported to the tycoon. As soon as the first story was built, Enceladus became anxious to move in. "Pal," he said, taking the cigar he was smoking out of his mouth, "you're building me a shack that's gonna make the Traj Majal look like a hot dog stand on Highway 40, and howsomever it ain't finished, I'm moving in next week."

The architect demurred. "The house, Mr. Grably," he took the liberty of saying, "is not quite fit to receive you. It is far from completed—the park, of course, is virtually untouched—and the palace does not appear to my eyes to be as habitable, as comfortable, as splendid, as it ought to be for a man in your position. And may I remind you that you are in the midst of your petroleum worries? Hence I wonder: truly, is this the time to move, with five thousand workers on strike in Saudi Arabia?" "I guess it ain't," Enceladus agreed; "keep up the good work and put air conditioning in the cook's linen closet."

Many times afterward, Enceladus expressed his urgent desire to move into the unfinished yet grandiose building. One year the architect reminded him that he must go to the Congo to look after his uranium interests. Another year, just when Enceladus was getting ready to move in at last (the furniture vans were ordered), an antitrust suit that fell into his lap distracted him. It was a hard year for him, because one wing of the government was suing him for overpricing while another was awarding him a lucrative contract, and the two herds of lawyers got all entangled. Another year the tycoon married an eighteen-year-old assistant to the architect, a bewitching girl who talked him into taking a slow cruise around the world. When the cruise ended, and a baby boy had been born, Enceladus instructed his wife to organize the servants for the great move. Instead, the young darling, who had been conscientiously visiting the estate, decided to run away with a brawny, well-bronzed gardener, a man by the name of Mellows, specialist in fertilizers. The shock of indignation soured the tycoon on mansions and estates for a year or two.

The year his good mood returned, the architect was gone on a faraway mission and the tycoon dared not move without his trusted builder's supervision or a wife's advice. The architect returned in time to warn his patron against undertaking the move while his brain was churning over his deal with Niguchi Motors of Kanagawa (the one that opened the immense Chinese market to his tractors and harvesting equipment), his move to establish dominion over the film industry of India, and the judicious spreading of confusing rumors on Wall Street.

"We must find the right time, sir," said the architect, "the moment of serenity worthy of your extraordinary mansion, the construction of which I intend to bring to a close in the near future." "Serenity, hell!" Enceladus replied. "A tycoon who ain't busy day and night won't be a tycoon for long!" "I stand corrected, sir. So then, perhaps next month—"

But a month after this conversation, a fearful series of terrorist attacks broke out in the civilized world. The architect looked worried. "Your mansion, sir, is an appealing target for a band of fanatics who hate your capitalist magnificence. I blame myself, how bitterly! for failing to surround the buildings with adequate protections. On the other hand, if you still wish to move at this time—"

"Are you crazy?" cried Enceladus. "You expect me to sit there like a clay pipe in a shooting gallery? Put up concrete barriers, hire armed guards, reinforce the windows, build shelters, and after that you can call me."

When he was seventy years old, Enceladus began to feel it was time to think of his last will and testament. Though he intended to live to a hundred and ten, he thought it wise to bequeath his possessions to his son in order to prevent litigation, with instructions to turn the grand estate, as planned from the start, into the Enceladus Grably Entertainment Center for Tycoons, Magnates, and Moguls. Some fifty pages of details for the amusements to be provided—some, perhaps, not intended for the eyes of the multimillionaires' wives—completed the document.

The larger the deals made by the tycoon—and they kept increasing in dimension; for wealth, as people say, attracts wealth—the more the architect grumbled, with due deference, about the difficulties of completing the mansion while his employer invested, divested, trafficked, lent, borrowed, structured, restructured, speculated, litigated, and counted his billions.

At the age of seventy-eight Enceladus had a cerebral seizure. He was now paralyzed in his lower extremities and confined to a wheelchair. One morning he summoned the architect to his office. "I'm getting on, pal," he said, "and I don't care what you'll say next; finished or not, I'll be moving into that fancy cabin of mine."

To his surprise, the architect replied: "Now is a most propitious time, my dear sir, for I have just completed the last pavilion in the park; it is to be called the Winter Rotunda."

"Great," said the tycoon, "ring the buzzer the minute it's ready, and I'll order the vans again."

At last the day came when the architect called the tycoon to report that the Winter Rotunda was ready. That Sunday—it was a hot day in July—Enceladus took the grand tour through the property, wheeled by the architect himself. He saw each one of the rooms (they used five different elevators to visit them, and each had its own Muskabad carpet, its Second Empire sofa covered with silk, and its candelabrum with electric candlelight) and inspected all the gardens, cloisters, solariums, swimming pools, verandas, gazebos, towers, and terraces. Afterward, the architect wheeled the tycoon across the park. They paused by the lake and Enceladus looked lovingly at it, saying, "God, I'm going to enjoy fishing here."

In the distance, across the lake, stood the mansion. It was truly outstanding, reminding one of France, Italy, the American South, Tudor England, Seville, and India. Suddenly the architect broke the silence. "Sir, I see your son (I forget his name) standing in front of your palace, as though he were examining it."

"Where, where?" asked the tycoon, whose eyesight was failing, "and what's he doing there anyway? Who invited him?"

"I don't know, sir, but I find it a little disturbing..."

"Disturbing? Why? Tell me why!"

"Why, I ask myself, is he studying the place, as though...?"

"Call him over!" cried Enceladus, in high alarm. "No need, sir. He has seen us, and he is coming of his own will."

"Yeah, I can see him now. Damn this heat! I hope he hurries."

Fortunately, a rowboat was tied to the lakeshore on the mansion's side, and the son rowed himself across the water to rejoin his father and the architect.

"What brings you here, son?" asked the father mistrustfully. "And you've grown a beard since I last saw you, was it three or four years ago?"

"Father," said the son, "I want your blessing, for I am about to become a novice in the Franciscan order of friars."

"Suits me fine," replied the tycoon. "So why were you staring at my *chattoh*?"

"Because, when the time comes, which, God willing, is yet far away, I have vowed to donate it to my beloved Capuchins so it can be turned into a hospital for orphans of every race and nation."

"Like hell you will!" shouted Enceladus. "First of all, I'm gonna live to a hundred and ten. My old man lived to be ninety-eight, 'spite the doctors being no good in his time. Second, I'm disinheriting you as of today. This mansion of mine is gonna be the Enceladus Grably Entertainment Center for Tycoons, Magnates, and Moguls, and anything else will have to happen over my dead body, so get out of my sight, vacate the premises, my blessing be damned, and go pray in church that I invite you for lunch on my next birthday."

"Go, young man," whispered the architect into the son's ear. "All will be well in the end." The son knelt for a moment before the wheelchair, then rose and walked away without another word. The tycoon was sweating in the sun. "I'm calling my lawyers as soon as I get back to the office. But first I need a drink of water and a bit of shade."

"May I suggest the Winter Rotunda, sir?" suggested the architect. "It stands right behind us, and it will provide us with all the shade we need."

"Fine," replied the tycoon. "Children!" he grumbled as

the architect wheeled him away. "They can't wait to rob you!"

When they came to the Winter Rotunda, the tycoon was pleased at first. "Good work," he said, "I hope there's a faucet inside." The rotunda stood ensconced in a grove of poplars and cypresses; it had been built of white marble, with fluted columns, and in the center one could see a kind of room protected by a heavy grill. Over the grill the tycoon noticed his own name chiseled in the stone and neatly gilded. His satisfaction vanished. "Winter Rotunda!" he exclaimed. "Hell, it looks more like a mausoleum to me!"

The architect said nothing, but he leaned over his employer, and for the first time ever, touched him by placing a hand on his shoulder. "What is it?" asked the tycoon, shivering a little.

"Old man," said the architect in a serious low voice, "here is your château, here! The other one, beyond the lake, will never be yours."

"You're fired!" yelled the tycoon from his wheelchair, trying in vain to rise from it and run away. The hand on his shoulder was too heavy for him. "Take your goddam hand off of me. I'm telling you again, you're fired!" he shouted, wriggling desperately. But the architect set the cold palm of his hand on the tycoon's forehead, and kept it there, until Enceladus became still, and died.

The architect himself was so good as to compose his employer's epitaph, in Latin, but with a translation underneath:

PERSPECTANTE DEO VIXIT

He lived under the watchful eye of God.

In afteryears visitors to the orphanage would say, as they passed by the mausoleum: "Under the watchful eye of God? Indeed? Lucky man!"

VENICE ENTERTAINS
THE KING OF PODOLIA

The young king of Podolia was traveling to broaden his views and make friends for Podolia. In Venice he was received with satisfying pomp and shown the wonders of the city, its art treasures, its dungeons, and its famous Arsenal. One late afternoon, after several hours of banqueting in the Ducal Palace, the king turned to the doge who was sitting to his right and said: "My friend and respected host, tomorrow I must pursue my journey. Allow me therefore to make a last request of you. Bring before me two citizens of Venice. Let one of them be the happiest, and the other the unhappiest man in the state. For to climax the memorable entertainment I have enjoyed in your city, I wish to ask your happiest Venetian for his secret, and to help your most wretched citizen out of his misery—if any misery be allowed in your fair republic." This request was thought by all the guests to be a notably witty one, quite worthy of the Podolian monarch. Much wine had been drunk; the doge had even permitted himself two gales of laughter. Now the whispers went eagerly back and forth among the senators and counselors, and a good-humored contention took place, until the doge's own advice prevailed and two messengers were dispatched into very different districts to summon the chosen men.

An hour later the two citizens appeared. The contrast between them was all that was to be expected, for one man was smiling, and he was arrayed in the richest furs, silks, and jewels imaginable, while the other, clad in malodorous rags, tottered along by leaning on a stick, and a nervous anxiety contorted his wrinkled face.

"Well met," said the king of Podolia to the two men; and, turning to his host, "How awesome is the distance from happiness to misery when they stand so nakedly illustrated before our eyes." And he spoke to the two citizens again.

"You, sir, shall tell me whether riches alone have made you happy; and you, my poor man, must ask me for the means to make a new and fairer beginning in life."

Before either of the men could answer, the guests all began to titter, and the doge spoke as follows: "Your highness, you are mistaken about our two worthy visitors. This beaming citizen, our Overseer of Public Charities, is the unhappiest man in Venice. And the happiest Venetian is yonder unwashed and fidgeting beggar."

"How can this be?" asked the king. "The rich man is all smiles, the poor man looks wretched. All is as it should be, unless a comedy is being played at my expense."

"No," the Overseer of Public Charities now broke in, "no, your highness, this is no comedy! I am smiling because, on the way to the palace, I was informed that your highness had promised to relieve the unhappiest man in Venice, and now, when I stood before you, I heard the confirmation from your own munificent lips." And the Overseer prostrated himself before the king.

"What ails you?" the latter asked, greatly surprised. "I owned ten galleons trading with the Orient. News came this morning that three are lost at sea. My credit is fatally hurt, I am compelled to dismiss half my cooks and lackeys, and I must either commit suicide, or else suffer the sneers of my odious rival, the Director of Urban Works." Hot tears spurted out of the Overseer's eyes, moistening the carpet under him. "And you," said the king, turning toward the poor cripple, "if you are the happiest man in Venice, why these rags, why this tormented expression?"

"He is mute, your majesty," the doge interjected, "but I shall reply for him. The man was born on the pavement and has slept all his life on cold flagstones. This morning he inherited a pallet filled with worms and rotten straw from a thief whom we hanged, and tonight he will sleep in a bed for the first time since he was born. My messenger hauled him away as the sun was going down; he longs for his cot; he had been the blissfullest man in Venice, perhaps in the whole world, and will be so again if your highness will detain him no longer."

The young king waved his hand in dismissal, and as the doge had foretold, a joyful smile drew itself out on the poor man's face, and he hobbled away on his crutch as speedily as he could.

"As for you," said the Podolian king to the Overseer of Public Charities, "I should like to relieve you, but three galleons are two galleons more than Podolia owns. Here, however, is a garnet ring. Wear it; you are now a Knight of the Pewter of Podolia."

This was no common distinction, and the Overseer departed a little less distraught than he had arrived.

"Your highness," said the doge with a smile, "you forgot to ask the happiest man for his secret."

"I think I know it already, your excellency," answered the king. "To be happy is to take a leap forward, though it be from nothing to little; and to be miserable is to be thrust backward, though it be from very much to much."

"There is great wisdom in Podolia," said the doge, lifting his glass to the king.

"It lay dormant until Venice brought it out," retorted the king, raising his to the doge.

APPENDIX
GOBBLE-UP STORIES 1966-2014

Gobble-Up Stories was published by the Bostonian house of Bruce Humphries in 1966, a couple of years before that estimable publisher vanished. The yellow-covered hardback, crudely printed yet containing some witty illustrations by the late Pasadena artist Jack Carr, to whose spirit mine remains grateful, has now undoubtedly become what the trade calls a collector's item, to be seized by way of the Internet.

Some new and some revised fables appeared in various journals after 1966: in the Winter 1967 issue of the *San Marino Quarterly* ("The Rich Ibis and the Pauper Thrush," "The Flattered Hippopotamus," "The Conceited Minnow"); the Spring 1972 issue of the *Prairie Schooner* ("The Lucky Pebble," "The Lunatic Pigeon," "The Pony Who Came to a Stream," "The Innovation," "The Talkative Swallow," which was later renamed "The Sociable Swallow"); the December 1976 issue of the *Literary Cavalcade* ("Two Blind Men," "The Termite and the Ant"); the Spring 1991 issue of *Columbia: the Magazine of Columbia University* ("The Lunatic Pigeon," "A Flea Protests," "The Parliament of Animals," "The Stork Who Praised Long Necks"), and the 2006 issue of the malodorously named *The Dirty Goat* ("A Bone of Contention," "The Caterpillar and the Leaf," "The Conceited Minnow," "The Sociable Swallow," "The Cock Who Made the Sun Rise," "The Crow and the Beggar," "A Conference of Kings," "A Conversation Between a Bulldozer and a Mouse," "The Dragon of Helgoland"). Of these magazines, I believe that only *Prairie Schooner* survives.

Well before the Bruce Humphries volume appeared, it had occurred to me that the fables lend themselves happily to readings aloud by myself or others, and to live performances by two or more actors. Readings and performances—of varying selections from the book—have in fact taken place in theaters, restaurants, college campuses, galleries, shops, private homes and circles, and over the radio. The actors have usually performed script in hand.

The actors Donald Elson and Elizabeth Gardner, accompanied by the flutist David Agresti (a graduate student in physics at the California Institute of Technology) gave two readings at the Elson-Robyns Gallery in Los Angeles on August 21 and 22, 1964. This presentation was broadcast by the Los Angeles radio station KPFK on December 23 and 24 of the same year.

A performance by Elson and Joan Tomkins, again accompanied by Agresti, was staged at the California Institute of Technology on January 16, 1965. This was repeated on the stage of the Pasadena Playhouse on February 12, 1965. And broadcast by KPFK on April 12 and April 19, 1966. The same cast was heard at the Jack Carr Gallery in Pasadena on November 30 and December 1 and 2, 1967. (Carr and his wife owned an elegant art-supplies and frame shop on Colorado Boulevard.)

In 1970, Elson and Olive Dunbar performed a selection of fables at the New Hope Inn in Santa Monica. This show was repeated at the California Institute of Technology on February 20.

A translation into French having been made by Professor Micheline Sakharoff of a number of my fables, I read them with her before the Alliance Française of Pasadena on January 20, 1971. I gave this group of tales the title *Fables crocasses*, a made-up word punning on *cocasse*, meaning droll, and *croquer*, meaning to gobble up. On December 14 of the same year, this program was presented to the Alliance Française of Los Angeles at Immaculate Heart College. And again to the Alliance Française of Santa Barbara, in the McGuire House, on January 15, 1972.

On November 30, December 1 and 2 of 1973, Elson, Philip Diskin and Joy Matthews, accompanied by two musicians, John Ferejohn and Keith Elliott, offered a group of fables at the Wedgwood Phillips Antiques store on 8644 Sunset Boulevard in Hollywood. The same musicians accompanied an unprecedented fully staged production May 24 and 25 at the Theatre Vanguard in Los Angeles. Ellen Bailey directed, Barry Frost designed the sets. The actors were Shirley Marneus, Allen Arkus, and Ralph Lucas.

On July 17, 1976, Beatrice Manley gave a solo performance, with musical accompaniment by Alan Solomon, for the Garden Theatre Festival, Barnsdall Park, Los Angeles. This program was repeated at the Theatre Vanguard on February 4 and 5, 1977.

On February 25, March 5, and March 11, 1977, I read my fables at Gallery 8 in Pasadena.

On June 15, 17, and 18, 1977, a program of fables was included in the Sixth Internationales Festival Kleiner Bühnen in Bern, at the Galerietheater "Die Rampe." The performers were Elson, Mary Tiffany, Douglas Lance and John Fahringer.

In June 1983, performances were given at the Théâtre de Dix Heures in Paris (Montmartre) by Tiffany, Eddie Creech, Stefan Haves, and Bruce Lanoil, with music by Stacy Stein and costumes and props by Maureen O'Heron. Marneus directed.

I directed a set of readings by Elson and Maylou Maier, with Toby Caplan-Mintz at the flute, in the Sculpture Garden Café Restaurant in Venice (California) on October 25 and November 22, and at the Athenaeum of Caltech on November 22, 1986. With Dunbar replacing Maier, these readings were repeated at the Sculpture Gardens on January 31, February 28, and September 18, 1987; and, again with Maier, in 1989.

I published a dramatized version of these tales under the title *The Kukkurrik Fables: 43 Mini-Dramas for all Media* in 1987, and reprinted the little book in 2006 (Los Angeles: Spectrum Productions). The firm of Samuel French became their amateur-theater representative. *The Kukkurrik Fables* was presented at the Ristorante Lido in the Pacific Palisades (Los Angeles) on November 16, 1989, and February 8, 1990, by Maier and Elson. On March 16, 1991, Ellen Jane and Douglas Coler performed under the direction of Dan W. Davis at the Ramo Auditorium of Caltech.

In the seventies, I had begun to translate the fables into French. This work was completed many years later in collaboration with madame Jacqueline Lahana, and a book was created which L'Harmattan, in Paris, brought out in 2002 under the title *Le Pigeon qui était fou*. This edition was bought out by another Paris house, Editions de l'Herne, and republished in 2007 under a new title: *La Reine de Patagonie et son caniche*. An annotated set of twenty-four of these fables was published by Flammarion in 2013 in a collection called "Etonnants Classiques" for use in *collèges* and *lycées*.

The Dutch composer John Sernee set several of these fables to music: "Une puce proteste," "Le goujon vaniteux," "La chenille et la feuille," and "Le rocher et la mer." They were sung by the soprano Yuri Komai at the Cathédrale Sainte-

Croix des Arméniens de Paris on October 25, 2008. They were sung again at a concert presented on June 19, 2010, at the Cité Internationale des Arts de Paris. In 2012, the fable "Paysage avec nuage et dunes" was sung by Léa Kamoun at the Eglise de Bon Secours in Paris to the music of the French composer Yves Rinaldi.

CHI PO
AND THE
SORCERER

Chi Po lived in a province full of mountains, grass, weather, and people. It lay deep in China, far from the sea, a little south of where it might have been, and all in all a trifle west of where it was. Chi Po was eleven years old, and he went to school because there was no remedy for it. But the schoolmaster always kept a branch or a flower on his desk—plum blossoms in the winter, a peony in the spring, a lotus in the summer, and a chrysanthemum in the fall—and this consoled Chi Po for having to memorize the classics. He would stare and stare at the peony, and count its petals, and wonder about having such a fine glob of color right under the blackboard.

"Subjunctives, children, are the preserve of the aristocracy and villagers must not meddle with them," said the teacher. He also told them that if anyone in the school could draw, or make, a cube, one side of which was wider and longer than the other five, that youngster was destined to become emperor, even if a girl. All the same, Chi Po kept staring at the flower until his eyes became round, and then he would ask himself: "Am I watching the peony, or is the peony watching me?"

The teacher noticed this, of course, and he sometimes thought that really he ought to take the flowers away, but he almost preferred his flowers to Chi Po, and besides, he had twenty-two other students who were gratifyingly spellbound by his discourses on Geometry and Decorum. So the flowers remained on the desk, and the soul of Chi Po buzzed about them like an ignorant bumblebee.

After classes, Chi Po went out with his friends Lo Fing, Fee Sh'ing, Joh King, and a lot of others to play wild games from cliff to cliff, over the meadows, and across a dozen brooks. Chi Po had the sharpest eyes and the quickest legs of anybody in the class. Nobody could catch him, and nobody could tire him out. But he really preferred to sit on a stone in the middle of a stream and watch how the water, without ever tiring, broke against it and how the spray tried to swat the water-flies. So he would lead his friends on a crooked chase, until they became fuddled and lost him; then he would sit on the stone I have just named, memorize the water, and when it was time for high green tea, go back to his playmates and laugh at them and hug them. Then he would go home and paint the water on a sheet of paper. Ah! I forgot to tell you that this story is about how Chi Po became the greatest painter of all China.

Chi Po's mother and father were proud of him. They never scolded him for coming home all mucky, provided he painted a bold pine tree or a swinging monkey to prove he had not wasted the afternoon. His father was the village carpenter. He hoped that the boy would grow up to adorn his tables, chairs, carts, and wheelbarrow, and rise at last to become the supreme artist of the district's signboards and panels.

Chi Po had his own low, long table in a corner of the room, where the light was good. On top of the table he kept his water jar, his inkstone, his inkstick, his colors, his plates, and his brushes, all in a neat row. Under the table, in a lacquered box, he kept rolls of paper, and even silk, to paint on. When he painted, he placed the paper flat on the floor, licked the brush, gulped three times, and then went zing, zing, zing with his brush like a madman, so that he scared the cat.

You must not believe that the lad had never seen anything. Far from it! The uncle of his mother's father was a peddler (the family called him a merchant) who traveled far and wide. One day he brought back from the city of Yan some fifteen paintings on paper, some in black and gray, others in colors. To speak the truth, they were only copies made from copies of masters like Wang Wei, Wu Daozi, and Liang Kai, but they filled Chi Po's soul with delight, and set ablaze within him the fires of knowledge, love, and ambition. So there was virtue in them after all, you see. As for the grandfather's uncle, he gave the lad a pretty *Springtime in Jiangnan* before selling the rest to the nearby peasantry.

Chi Po's father and mother were poor, because the rule is that you cannot have a son who will be a great painter unless you are poor. However, they didn't mind having no money. Nobody in the village had any money, so it didn't show. Once there had lived a rich mandarin in the village, and it made everybody mad to see how he pranced on his horses, followed by a horde of lackeys, and stuffed himself with delicacies brought from India. One day this mandarin went into the woods in the direction where the sorcerer Bu Fu lived, and he never returned. That evening Bu Fu came to the village square, and, as all the villagers agreed (even those who didn't see him), he glared. Since he didn't open his mouth, he said nothing about Kuang Su-mei (that was the wicked rich man), but the villagers were no fools, and they understood. Besides, they knew better than to question him. If you asked a question of Bu Fu which he refused to answer, there was no help for it but to keep on asking it (without changing a word) once every three hours for the rest of your wretched life. Anyway, when the mandarin was gone, the villagers went back to not noticing that they had nothing.

But all this happened long before Chi Po was born. None of the children had ever seen Bu Fu, because he had stopped coming to the village for his wine and for the rice and marmalade that were all he ever ate, besides what he picked from the foliage. Instead, the two village idiots, T'ing and Ling, carried the victuals to his cave once a week. T'ing carried the rice and marmalade, and Ling carried the wine. Once a year, at the time of the Holiday of the Lanterns, they brought him a full change of garments, because a sorcerer, for all his power, is pretty helpless when it comes to gowns and underwear.

Bu Fu would hear of no other food than the rice and

marmalade. One time the two boys had brought him mustard butter instead of marmalade, and he had spoken but one wrathful word—"*P'u!*"—and not very loud at that. That same night a storm fell on the village, swooping three houses off their stones and setting them in the middle of their own rice paddies.

There was just about nothing Bu Fu couldn't do, and only a little less that he *wouldn't* do. He was a particular friend of the Sky Dragon, who makes the rain, and he knew so much scandal about the genie and the Lady of the West that they all trembled before him and did him any favor he wanted. It was a good thing, Bu Fu let the villagers know, that he happened to want so little. He didn't allow anybody, not even T'ing and Ling, inside his cave, because that was where he kept his trigrams, his crucibles, the Eight Diagrams of Wen Wang, his Book of the Four Prearranged Mysteries, and the Amulets of Kuan Yin, the latter doing duty sometimes as toys for his bulbul.

The bulbul is a bird with a black head that sings tolerably on pitch when the nightingales are quiet. Bu Fu would send his bulbul about the village, and of course nobody could tell it from all the legal bulbuls, so that was how Bu Fu knew pretty well who was saying what, when, and where, because the bulbul reported back to him. This was such a bird that many villagers said he could even read thoughts. They could prove it by what had happened to Mi Fen.

Mi Fen's cow had given birth to a two-headed, one-legged calf that almost drove him crazy with fright when he first saw it. He was questioned as severely as possible by the six village Ancients, and he finally admitted that a few months back the thought had crossed his miserable head, "Why don't we get rid of Bu Fu so we can save the cost of all that wine and marmalade?" But he hadn't *said* it to anyone, not even to his wife, nor to his concubine. Hence, there was not much question about the bulbul's having caught a whiff of that thought as he was flying over Mi Fen's farm. On the other hand, some of the younger men declared that the six

Ancients were an old-fashioned superstitious lot. Bu Fu, they said, didn't need a bulbul to read people's thoughts, for a thought is a wind, the wind is a traveler, the language of this traveler is the language of the Spirit, and Bu Fu knew the language of the Spirit by heart. It was to be deduced that he had detected Mi Fen's thought without the supernatural aid of a bird.

Another uncanny thing Bu Fu could do was to send his portrait to people's dreams. People might be dreaming about the tax collector coming round to count their sacks of rice, or maybe about their pig running away into the woods, and then suddenly Bu Fu stood on the tax collector's right shoulder or hung from the pig's tail. Why did he keep doing it? The villagers had sent him an eloquent letter, handsomely written by the village scribe. The letter, rolled into the rice bowl by T'ing and Ling, asked the sorcerer whether he showed himself in dreams like everyone else, that is to say, for no reason, or whether he did so on purpose. "On purpose, can you doubt it?" was the reply on the blank side of the letter. "But do not worry. I wander among you on patrol, in case my bulbul has missed something." Of course, it was also his way of making sure they wouldn't be tempted to skip some of the rice and marmalade or put the Yangtze into his wine.

Mi Fen could have offered in his defense that he was not the only man in the village who had thought of sending Bu Fu to another province. One day, in the time when Bu Fu still occasionally visited the village, one of the truly old Ancients (note, if you please, that some Ancients are less old than they would like us to believe)—this Chao Chou, as he was called, threw a stone at the sorcerer to keep him from crossing his garden. Chao Chou was so very old that he didn't care, and was planning on becoming a Demon of the Breeze shortly, out of any sorcerer's reach. But Bu Fu tossed his curse on the whole village, and exactly thirty-four days later a band of robbers swooped in and stole eighteen cows, five horses, one hundred sixteen chickens, including two already dead, and a few wives that happened to be strolling nearby.

The next day a great assembly was called, presided by the mayor, and everybody talked about uprooting an old willow, but of course even T'ing and Ling wouldn't have been fooled about who the old willow was. But it all came to nothing, because another elder, Kai Yuan-lao, reminded them that because of Bu Fu, the name of their village had actually been uttered by the Emperor while reading a report on sorcerers of the realm. No other village within two-hundred *li* had ever been mentioned at court, let alone by the Emperor, and it was not certain that, without Bu Fu, the court would have known that their very province existed—it was that far away.

As a result of Kai Yuan-lao's honorable reminder, the assembly decided to keep the old sorcerer, and they made a treaty with him, granting him all the rice, marmalade, and wine he could digest in exchange for his promise to take no more walks in the village. Then they made sure that none of their children ever went to the mountain. And that is why neither Chi Po nor any of his friends had ever seen Bu Fu.

One day Chi Po and his friends were playing Tartars and Mandarins after school. Chi Po as usual had to be one of the Tartars, who must be caught, brought back to camp, and skewered. You couldn't let him be a mandarin because he could always catch the other boys, and that spoiled the fun. Well, this time he ran and ran up a mountain—you've guessed which one!—and still, every time he looked back between the trees or down from the top of a rock, he could see one or two mandarins grubbling through the underbrush after him. So he ran farther and farther up, he didn't know where, full of the finest merriment, and under the trees it was so cool that he breathed with his mouth wide open and it felt like drinking from a cold waterfall. Finally he was alone on the mountain. Here and there he could lean over from a clearing and see his dear village, a pretty speck in the plain far below him.

Chi Po stopped to watch a squirrel fooling merrily with a few pine cones he rolled on the ground. He made no noise, but sat down where he could enjoy the little spectacle. The squirrel could see him too, but he didn't mind because he understood from a look at Chi Po's face that the boy was too much of a gentleman to eat him. In fact, the squirrel was so glad to have somebody watch him for a change (his own family paid no attention to him) that he gave one of his best performances, inventing a hundred drolleries with his pine cones and running up and down a tree with them. Presently Chi Po began to move his arms and his body as nearly like the squirrel as he could; and, drawing in the air all the wonderful curves of the squirrel, he began to dance too, all the time trying to memorize the squirrel so he could paint him when he returned home.

He had just fetched the best caper of them all and touched ground again when he heard a horrible voice behind him thunder: "Upstart, what are you doing here?"

The squirrel just laughed from the top of a tree, especially on seeing Chi Po spin round like a toy top to face the voice. As for the boy, he didn't need much guessing to guess that what stared at him was none other than the sorcerer Bu Fu.

Now I have to tell you that Bu Fu was a large sorcerer every way you looked at him, up and down, sideways, or back to front. Maybe it was all that marmalade he ate. And his face was all beard. You couldn't tell where the beard ended and the head of hair began, nor whether it was hair or beard that covered his ears. Through this wilderness pierced the mouth, containing six whole teeth and one broken one. There was nothing noteworthy about his nose, but Bu Fu's eyes were strangely yellow, throwing out the most unreassuring light, and bubbling out, *I* think, like the marbles children play with.

Chi Po saw them in his own way. "You look like a thick wood with two yellow birds perched in it," he said with amazing bravery (I would have fainted in his place), meditating on that face and those eyes.

Now Bu Fu didn't mind not scaring squirrels, but it pained him that a sorcerer couldn't at least scare an eleven-

year-old boy enough to make him cry "Mother!" What was
the world coming to? "Demons of the abyss!" shouted Bu Fu.
"I am Bu Fu!"

"*My* name is Chi Po, son of Chi Huang-ju and grandson
of Chi Liao-ni. I lost my way on your mountain, sir, but I
meant no harm, the squirrel is my witness."

It so happened that Bu Fu had been busy all morning
fingering the Amulets of Kuan Yin, which, if you finger
them right, produce tall midgets, beauteous crones, tuneful
silences, and four-sided triangles. Alas, Bu Fu's triangles
had been resisting him like a pack of mules, not to mention
the silences that wouldn't budge, so now, like the squirrel, he
was rather glad to have company

"Don't you know that these orogenous formations are
interdicted to the deambulations of little boys?" shouted Bu
Fu, not to seem too friendly at once.

"Please forgive me," said Chi Po, who knew how to catch
a drift, and he bowed respectfully several times. However,
between bows and afterward he kept looking at Bu Fu's face
with the sharpness of the true artist who examines all that
he sees. Suddenly a bird came flying down to settle on Bu
Fu's shoulder. It was the bulbul himself, and Chi Po noticed
he had only one eye.

"Welcome our guest," Bu Fu told the bulbul, "and curtsy
as many times as he bowed to me."

To Chi Po's astonishment, the bulbul dipped his head,
winked with his good eye, and went *"Wek-kaw Wek-kaw"*
three times as hospitably as anyone could wish.

"You are a mighty sorcerer," said Chi Po. "Who else
could make a bulbul speak Chinese?"

"No one," answered Bu Fu. "But compared to the amazing
and monstrous magic I do all day long, this is a trifle. I have
had my bulbul sing in Latin and Greek, and I could turn him
into a tiger before your very eyes. A tiger with an appetite.
And this tiger turns into the squirrel you just saw. Say it for
me, honorable ancestors: I can make continents of trouble,
and my fulminations are fulgurous. However, tell me, child,

why you were dancing like a marionette when I caught you."

Chi Po said that he had been trying to imitate the squirrel's gestures in order to paint him the better when he got home. "I also paint tigers," he added.

"So you paint in order to while away your time?"

"Oh no!"

"Then why?"

"In order to become immortal."

"So, so, so," said Bu Fu, and tried to look indifferent, and then he hummed a tune and pulled at one of his earlobes deep inside his mane. "I tried my hand at painting when I was young, until I was called away to pursue nobler studies." However, his beard fluttered. For he knew from the Scroll of Utterness that he who has the Way of the Brush is a greater sorcerer than Hung Fo himself, the father of all skullduggers, because the sorcerer can only command Nature, but he who has the Way of the Brush creates it.

"I can make a waterfall rise up instead of falling down," said Bu Fu. "I can make a week have four Thursdays, and, in certain moods, I can make 10,349 times 636,871 come out 6,590,977,978."

"Everybody is terribly afraid of you."

"Not without reason, young one." Bu Fu leaned over so close that Chi Po's heart missed a beat. "Sometimes I really go too far," he said mysteriously. "Several of my curses have singed the countryside just flying to their destination, killing any wildlife that happened to lie in their path. Can awe-inspiring power go further?"

The bulbul quapped gravely.

Then a ray of the descending sun made its way between the trees. It touched Chi Po's nose and made him say, "I must be going home, sir." He bowed again and asked the sorcerer's permission to take his leave.

"Go home, go home," said Bu Fu, but he was sorry to see Chi Po leave, because those tiresome amulets were waiting for him in the cave, and there wasn't much conversation in them. So he called Chi Po back, and sternly said to him: "Come here. Whatever you paint next, you shall meekly bring to me for my yea or nay. Swear!" And now his yellow eyes began to roll furiously in their orbits. "Swear!"

"I swear," said Chi Po, and with that he trotted away down the mountain.

As soon as he arrived home, Chi Po told his mother and father all that had happened. Filled with anxiety, they watched him all evening to see if something strange would happen, like Chi Po suddenly leaping over the house, or sprouting horns. But he remained the same well-behaved little boy he had been before—even more so, for that evening he didn't grumble when his mother told him to go to bed.

And why not? Because he was eager for morning to come, eager to paint his majestic sorcerer. To be sure, morning began with school—the classics are evermore on duty—and explanations to his friends of yesterday. But at last the hour came when he was able to rub some of the inkstick into the hollow of his slab, mix ink with water, stretch a sheet of paper on the floor, snatch his coarsest rat-tail brush, and fall to work. In five strokes he painted Bu Fu large and thick and oppressive, sitting on a stone. Behind him was a tree and behind the tree, but to the left, a lofty cliff, much smaller, and paler, because Chi Po mixed more water into the ink, so you could tell the cliff was far away. Bu Fu looked (so Chi Po thought) as though he owned the world, but did not care whether he did or not.

Chi Po was satisfied, and his parents exchanged a knowing wink. To conclude, he wrote a poem down the upper left edge of the sheet, as follows:

> *A sorcerer, Bu Fu,*
> *and a bushy face*
> *make the world seem*
> *so small.*

And then he stamped his own personal seal on the page (a birthday present from his parents) with paste of red cinnabar.

The next day was the Holiday of the Lampions. Schools were closed, so Chi Po rolled up his painting and went looking for Bu Fu. Halfway up the mountain he met the one-eyed bulbul, who greeted him with great civility and flew ahead to guide him to the cave.

"Young one," cried Bu Fu through his beard, "stay fifty paces away until I call you. Poisonous fumes."

"What are you cooking in that cauldron?" Chi Po shouted across the fifty paces.

"I'm mixing the occiput of deranged lizards with crommaline and distilled willywater."

"What for?"

"To summon a few demons of my acquaintance."

This gave Chi Po an idea. "Can you summon a dragon?" he shouted.

"I can summon a gaggle of dragons!" Bu Fu flung back at him; but he was sorry as soon as he said it, because the fact is, whipping up dragons is a harder business than most people think.

"May I come closer now?" asked Chi Po.

Bu Fu sniffed to make sure all was safe and then said yes.

Chi Po skipped up to the cauldron and said: "Please, sir, do summon a dragon for me."

"To the point. Show me as agreed what you have there rolled up under your arm."

That was the painting, of course, and Chi Po unrolled it, expecting a great "Oh!" and a high compliment, because everybody was always kind to him. But Bu Fu only said "Oh?" And let me tell you, there's a great difference between an Oh sent abroad with an exclamation point, and an Oh followed by a question mark.

"Don't you like it?" said Chi Po, and his voice went up like a flute. "It's you, you know. My mother liked it."

"There's no accounting for mothers," Bu Fu answered. "I, at any rate, didn't own one."

"Not even when you were small?"

"I was never small:

> *I fell from a cloud,*
> *A lad six feet tall,*
> *Big as a barrel,*
> *Strong as a wall.*"

Delighted, Chi Po burst out laughing, but then his laughter scared him. Would it anger the mighty sorcerer? Not at all! Bu Fu began to laugh too, great hoo-hoo-hoos that rolled down the mountain and astonished the bulbul, who couldn't remember seeing his master so merry.

Eventually Bu Fu's laughter dwindled, and he looked sympathetically at Chi Po's scroll. "The painting," he remarked, "is obviously me; it is, indeed, glaringly me. Congratulations. But why in God's name am I larger than the tree, and even larger than the mountain? Surely even my bulbul knows that a tree is larger than I am (materially speaking, you understand), and a mountain, even a small mountain, is much the taller of the two. Now, my boy, what do you say?"

Chi Po had never thought of this, never in the world at all, and yet it was so very true. He sat down on a tree trunk fallen to the ground, a big tear growing in each eye. What a difference after all that laughter! "I shall never be a good painter, I know it now," he said sadly.

Bu Fu spat into the cauldron. A hissing cloud rose out of it, and the sorcerer spoke again. "The dash of the brushstroke is not bad, friend Chi Po; it shows an attempt not unworthy of a good apprentice to catch the essential breath of things. But wait for me. I shall allow you to gaze at something else."

Whereupon Bu Fu disappeared into his cave. There, in

the depths of its depth, he went scrabbling among a heap of mysterious objects until he found an album leaf painted by none other than Tao-tsi—an authentic Tao-tsi!—depicting birds and wisteria. I dare not tell you how and when he became its owner—but there it was. He brought it outside and showed it to Chi Po. The lad seemed to turn to stone. His eyes almost leaped out of their sockets. He said nothing. Time passed. At last, the two tears I have mentioned broke loose and came down his cheeks like little white snails. He repeated: "I shall never be a good painter."

"Stop sniffling and come with me," said Bu Fu after returning the Tao-tsi to its place.

Bu Fu took Chi Po's little hand into his huge palm, and they walked still higher into the mountain. The bulbul followed with a disapproving cackle, for though he liked emotions, he wanted no more than one of them a day. Bu Fu and Chi Po walked endlessly (so it seemed to Chi Po) through twisted paths and over rocks and roots, hearing the anonymous birds and the shuffling of small furry animals in the trees and the underbrush, and following upward the cold cascades, but all the time saying never a word, until they arrived at an overhanging ledge jutting into the void like a giant's elbow, and there they sat down in the cold air, and they looked into the distance, which lay before them in a white-cotton mist. Under their feet, the slope ran away into the mist, and as far as they could see it, it was all rocks, with tufts of grass, and a few prickly trees flapping their branches over the abyss and holding onto the mountain with their roots for very life. Behind their ledge sprouted the forest, and a few hawks made little holes in the sky, far, far away, but the sky was not blue but almost white, and you could look at the sun for a little while before it burned your eyes.

And there they sat, I don't know how many hours, until finally Bu Fu opened his mouth. "Because the Great Spirit made it all, you see, all unrolls into nothing, and nothing unwinds the trillioning all. Hey-ho, even sorcerers are tiny."

"Even sorcerers are tiny," Chi Po repeated, for that was the only part of Bu Fu's speech he had clearly understood.

Then Bu Fu recited:

> *These beautiful days in Hsiang-yang*
> *Make drunken my old mountain heart.*

"And now," he said, "do you see that the hawk is lighter, the cascade faster, the abyss more dangerous, and the mountain taller than I?"

"I think I understand," said Chi Po. "So, will you be my master and teach me the ways of the brush?"

"Perhaps," answered Bu Fu.

And from that day, Chi Po came to the cave as often as he was able, and even took the place of T'ing and Ling to carry Bu Fu's rice and marmalade. He also brought his inkwells, his inkstones, and his brushes into Bu Fu's cave and kept them neatly between the bulbul's kennel ("Cats stay away from kennels," the bulbul would explain to his simple-minded friends) and Bu Fu's logarithmic table, on which he kept a pot of dahlias.

The things Bu Fu knew! No wonder the villagers were secretly proud of him, old nuisance that he was. It was a downright comfort, after all, to tell yourself that when lightning struck your barn, or the wind walked away with your thatched roof, there was Bu Fu at hand who had done it all, and who could put an end to it if he had a mind to make the lightning or the wind leave off. It kept everything in the family, so to speak. And as for telling Chi Po how to paint, who could have done it better than the familiar of all Nature? The Kungs had sent *their* little boy all the way to Cheng-chou, at the far end of the world, where that old charlatan Qin Pai-yong taught painting in exchange for a greasy fee. He would let his pupils draw trees growing stiff as pikes out of stones, when everybody knows that such trees are all gnarled, as though they had struggled and twisted to rise out of the earth. Or he would praise the portrait of a mountain robbed of its river or its winding path—a dry, bony, grim, boring mountain. Why not paint an illiterate poet? But why talk about such a duffer? Bu Fu, on the other hand, could tell that two mountain peaks should never soar to the same height, or that you should interrupt and cover the course of a winding river if you wish to make it seem long.

"Tell me, sproutling," said Bu Fu at the beginning of an important lesson, "if your mother and father could give you anything you desired, what would you ask of them?"

That was a question Chi Po had often dreamed of himself, and had answered, too, in his dreams. So he replied without hesitation: "A new hoop and a pair of blue silken trousers for myself, a rocking chair for father, and jade earrings for mother."

"Excellent!" Bu Fu exclaimed. "I love, support, and admire that hoop, those trousers, that rocking chair, and those earrings. Excellent! What would happen to philosophy without them? But now, go sit at the door of my cave, watch the sky and the trees, take note of the inquisitive wind and the dignity of the clouds, observe how the squirrels and the rabbits live their lives without us, and dream of the brush and of your hand sweeping over the silk of your next painting."

With this Bu Fu pronounced several frightful gutturals, and abandoning Chi Po at the mouth of the cave, he went gathering acorns. Only the bulbul remained with Chi Po. He sat on a branch where he could watch the newcomer, and you could see by the tilt of his head and the angle of his beak that he doubted whether Chi Po could *do* it.

And it wasn't easy. Now that Bu Fu had reminded him of the good things he liked to dream about (and I haven't mentioned them all), Chi Po found it hard to send his thoughts into the trees and to keep his eye on the changing moods of the clouds. But the afternoon was warm, and Chi Po settled drowsily with his back to the cave, chewing on a pine needle as he sat. He watched a cloud leave the top of a cedar and edge cautiously over to the top of another cedar—"like a tightrope walker," thought Chi Po. And then he heard the wind: it ooooed against the rocks, frushled among the leaves, tickled in the pines, and then went loose above the earth. And on top of the wind went the snitting of the sparrows, the plak-plak of wild geese, the kris-kris of magpies, and above all, the strange lilling of the scarlet-throated winterwinch that one sees only when one is asleep.

All of a sudden Chi Po noticed an ant, a tiny ant, a baby ant, strolling on the ground. It strolled out of the shadow of a huge inch of a pebble and climbed onto a splinter of a twig. On the splinter it basked a while in the sun like Chi Po, then it nosed a larger ant with which it exchanged a friendly how-do-you-do. When this was done, it wormed its way down a hole, stumbled out again, and traversed a thousandth part of an old sandal Bu Fu had thrown out of his cave. Thereupon—

"Young one," said Bu Fu, returning with a basket full of acorns, "what is on your mind?"

"Oh," said Chi Po, a little ashamed, "nothing."

"Perfect," cried Bu Fu, his beard quivering. "You have understood my lesson. Now go home, because I have witchcraft in hand. Come back tomorrow. If your mind is still free of that clutter of hoops and rocking chairs—admirable clutter, don't misunderstand me, child!—I may allow you to paint a single dragonfly on a lonely lotus flower."

Whereupon Chi Po happily went home, doing his best to keep thinking of nothing.

As soon as he was gone, Bu Fu, whose walk had tired him, stretched out on the grass under the sun and went to sleep, snoring so loud that the echo answered deep within the cave. For this is how sorcerers live: they go for long walks, they throw a few spells around, and then they stretch out in the grass for a peaceful snooze, their hands clasped behind their heads.

S o," said Bu Fu the next day, when Chi Po came puffing up to the cave, "what of the clutter?"

"I hope I have left it behind, sir," answered Chi Po.

"For the time being?"

"For the time being. And my fingers are wide awake. Are they allowed to try the dragonfly?"

"Sitting on the lotus blossom. Have at it, lad!"

And Bu Fu told Chi Po why a dragonfly needs a flower, and why a flower needs a dragonfly, for the one stays in the ground and rises from the ground upward, while the other moves about and descends from the sky downward.

"Therefore," said Chi Po, "I must paint them where they meet, where down flows into up and up flows into down."

Bu Fu was proud of his pupil. He ran into the cave to fetch the Book of Quiddities, and opening it, he placed one of his thick hands on Chi Po's head and recited the following mystical formula:

> *No eel in your well,*
> *No hell on your hill,*
> *No fleck on your flock,*
> *No tick in your toque.*
> *The rite I wrote is right.*
> *Fare fair in your affair.*

When Chi Po heard this, he felt he could do anything. He hovered over his sheet of white paper and painted a lotus blossom married to a dragonfly. It was not one of your outrageously spread-out lotus flowers, big as a sofa, like those on which the sublime Buddha sits (for the sublime Buddha is of portly girth); no, it was a soft, small, half-closed bud, and Chi Po gave it a long, long stalk, all the way down the long sheet of paper. He painted it on the right side of the sheet, not in the crude middle, and all alone, without a companion. He was careful not to show any earth; the stalk just went down to the bottom of the sheet, and you guessed the rest. Then came the dragonfly, which Chi Po made with a whiff of pale blue. Its four wings were spread out, because only its thin legs touched the blossom, and it was past unrest and yet it did not rest. "If I make it rest," thought Chi Po, "people who look at my painting might fall asleep."

Most of the sheet was white, of course, so Chi Po took another brush and mixed more water with his ink to get a pale-gray color and drew some wavy lines from right to left across the page—"Quick, quick—that's the lake!" Then he took his dark brush and wrote on the right side of the page between the stalk of the lotus and the edge of the paper, in graceful characters: "Painted by young Chi Po on a sloping afternoon," and added the red seal that names Chi Po.

Bu Fu tried to conceal his satisfaction in order not to turn Chi Po's head. "The spirit is almost there," he said. And he said again, "Almost," because when you say "Almost" twice, it makes your listener twice as unsure of being sure as he was before. "Let me reveal, young one, that last night I burned two snails' horns on your behalf (because they are symbols of keen apperception), and the smoke rose straight to the moon. That is why I am not surprised at your mild but decided success."

"I shall do better, sir," said Chi Po bravely and bowed.

"Speaking of symbols...." And thus began Chi Po's second lesson. He learned from Bu Fu that the lotus is the image of fruitfulness and purity, that the chrysanthemum stands for good cheer, the bamboo for uprightness and dependability ("qualities," added Bu Fu, "which I for one have cultivated with particular assiduity"). He learned that the mushroom signifies modesty, the pine tree unbending nobility and mastery over all circumstances, and the peach tree long life and a tolerable marriage. And Bu Fu recited that fine old poem of Chang Ch'ao's:

The plum flower ennobles him who sees it,
The stork makes him dream romantically,
The horse teaches him heroism,
The orchid seclusion,
And the pine the dignity of the ancients.

Chi Po also learned that each season must be represented by its particular flowers and animals, that the flying bird is the image of freedom, the dragon the symbol of fertility, and the—

"You promised to show me a dragon!" said Chi Po, jumping in.

"The Eight Immortals confound you!" cried Bu Fu. "I have taught you secrets even the great Ku K'ai-chih only suspected, I have burnt snails' horns, discharged incantations, and twice postponed my dinner for your sake; I was about to overwhelm you with a prolix discourse on the meaning of emptiness and the emptiness of meaning; I am sacrificing my old age to your wavering talent—and for my reward you nag me with your 'Show me a dragon!' I ought to utter my lethal *'P'u!'* and reduce you to a smoldering heap of embers." Bu Fu's yellow eyes were blazing with anger.

You may fancy how frightened Chi Po was. "Do you mean that you don't know how?" he asked as timidly as he could.

Bu Fu almost split with indignation. He stood up, stretched out his arms and cried: "My bulbul!" and the bulbul flew into the thick of his beard. "You at least trust and love me," Bu Fu moaned. "*You* believe in me." And he tickled the bulbul's head with a fervor of affection. "Let us return to our seclusion, like the shy orchid," he moaned. The bulbul looked indignant.

"I'm sorry, sir, truly and honestly and cross my heart I'm sorry," Chi Po cried. "I promise to hold my tongue from now on. Don't I know that you can do anything in the world" ("outside it, too," Bu Fu remarked), "and that you are the greatest sorcerer of the universe and China?"

"Enough, enough, young one. I am satisfied that your
compunction is honest. But, you see, dragons don't grow on
trees. Listen to the story I am about to tell you. It will open
your eyes."

They sat themselves down on the knocked-over trunk.
Bu Fu still clutched the bulbul to his beard. (He couldn't
clutch anything to his bosom because his beard was in the
way.)

"The world," said Bu Fu, "is full of sorcerers and sorceries;
some sorceries are tiny, some sorceries are immense; you
can turn water to wine, which any apprentice sorcerer can
do, or you can bring a dead man to life again—and that,
of course, is quite a project. But to summon a dragon is
even harder than blowing the spirit back into a dead man's
mouth, because—think of it!—it calls for the undoing of the
unbeing of an uncreature. Now if you please, picture all
those sorcerers. One is making the rain fall in a drought;
another is sending a toothache to a wicked peasant; a third
is arguing with one of the Immortals. All this takes doing; it
takes a mighty dose of doing. And all that doing drizzles out
of the sorcerers and stays in the air. The air grows thicker
and thicker with the doing of sorcery, and who knows where
it will carry us in the end? I apprehend it, I fear it. Will the
world perish of utter bewitchment? Clouds of sorcery gather
over our despondent heads; each spell, each incantation,
adds its mysterious effluvium to the thickening atmosphere.
Where will it all end? Shall the world perish of irreversible
sorcerosis?"

The bulbul took refuge in a tree, while Bu Fu gathered
up his crucibles, his alembics, his trigrams, and his scrolls
and carried them to and fro in front of the cave, so that Chi
Po thought he could see evil clouds seep out of them, adding
their poison to the thickening atmosphere.

Bu Fu sat down again and continued: "Long before you
were born, we sorcerers held an assembly in the Valley of
Bones to explore the danger, and let me tell you that the
probability of our making the Earth uninhabitable to anyone

except demons and dandelions loomed not a little in our speeches."

"But," said Chi Po, "why didn't you *do* something about it, like banning all spells?"

"Because we couldn't agree," Bu Fu replied. "After prolonged debates, we divided into two hostile factions. The enlightened one (to which I belonged) wished to pass a resolution as follows: 'We view with alarm the strong possibility of universal contamination due to the uncontrollable effects of witchcraft, and propose that all spells be suspended for a duration of twenty years.' Thereupon the party of the narrow-minded threw a contemptible counterproposal at our heads: 'We consider with distress the likelihood of global poisoning attributable to the consequences of unlimited jinxing, and resolve that for a length of time of no less than two decades, a pretermission of all sorcery be imposed.'

"We showed that their proposal was one more proof, if any were needed, of their hypocrisy, their bad faith, and their ambition to subjugate all sorcerers. They, on the other hand, ranted about our headlong ruthlessness, our lies, even our imbecility. We lobbed objects both sharp and round at each other, and I myself, creature of peace and patience, took off one of my shoes and discharged it at a nearby head; I hope it was that of an enemy. Five or six sorcerers had to be dipped bleeding into a stream, and we adjourned full of satisfying hatred."

"But weren't those resolutions pretty much the same?" Chi Po asked, scratching his head.

"How wrong you are! Night and day! When you grow up to be a man, you'll understand."

"So nothing was done?"

"Wrong once more. We voted 522 against 313 that no sorcerer should ever cast a spell to get lilacs to bloom in springtime."

"But...lilacs don't need spells anyway, do they, in order to bloom in springtime?"

"A lucky fact that facilitated our agreement. But though

it was something, it was not enough. And ever since that time, the air has been thickening. Spell upon spell inspissates the frightened elements. Do you see now why I dread summoning a dragon? I should have to emit a spell of the fifth magnitude and, who knows, bewitch the world beyond recall, beyond even my own powers." Bu Fu closed his eyes in anguish and moaned.

There wasn't much Chi Po could answer, but the more dangerous the matter looked, the more he really longed to take a close look at a dragon, for he had convinced himself (only much later would he grasp how wrong he was) that he could never paint one convincingly unless he had seen it with his own eyes. So he kept quiet, but he decided that he would ask for a small dragon when Bu Fu was in good spirits.

Meantime, Chi Po went every week to the cave, and then he was twelve years old, and then thirteen. Bu Fu mixed a hundred potions to make Chi Po a noteworthy painter. He even cut open his thumb to shed three drops of his own blood into a hideous cauldron full of cinnabar juice, gliphons' livers, woodruff, and the intestines of infatuated spiders, with all of which he smeared Chi Po's brush-holding fingers.

Indeed, he was so busy now, that he stopped bothering the village. Otherwise Chi Po's father would not have allowed his son to go so often into the haunted mountain. As it was, the good Chi Huang-ju, prodded by the worried mother, had gone to confer with a village Ancient specially apt in affairs of wisdom. For a gift, he brought along a jug of superior wine. Here is what happened.

"Pai Tai-shan," said Chi Po's father, "should I allow my son to visit the old sorcerer to make him a good painter? The boy will bring honor to our village when he begins to adorn it with his brush. The sorcerer's spells cost me nothing, but mightn't they be dangerous to my only boy?"

Pai Tai-shan gave the question some thought, and then he replied, "Maybe so. Maybe not so. And then again, maybe

maybe so. Let us ponder the problem together, my friend, but let this jug of wine inspire us."

Chi Huang-ju agreed. When the jug was empty, and followed by another one brought in by Pai Tai-shan's second wife, the Ancient showed Chi Huang-ju three glass marbles, one of which was black, another white, and the third green. "Wisdom," said the venerable man, "sometimes decides to invite chance rather than wisdom to speak; and this is the course we shall follow today. The three marbles (toys my grandchildren play with) are now concealed in my two cupped hands. I will shake them, and then I will allow a single marble to slip between my slightly opened palms. If the black marble falls upon the mat, the answer is No. The white marble signifies Yes. And the green marble tells us that there is much to be said on either side of our question."

Thereupon Pai Tai-shan rattled the marbles inside his hands, and even looked sharply away so that no foul play could be suspected. After a little while, one of the marbles did fall from his hands, like an egg from a chicken, and it was white. "Fate's answer is Yes!" joyously cried the wise Ancient.

"Thank you with all my heart," said Chi Po's father. "That answer shall be my law." And after a variety of courtesies, he took his leave of Pai Tai-shan.

Stop! This is a tragic blow! My story is dead! We were going to hear the story of how Chi Po became China's most wonderful painter. But now the sage has said Yes, Bu Fu's spells will harm the boy. He will no longer be allowed to visit Bu Fu. Alas! Is he destined to daub the doors of low taverns and the carts of noodle vendors?

Truly it was a perilous moment. But fortunately the worst did not happen. For the question Chi Huang-ju *remembered* asking was, "Ought the boy to continue his visits to the sorcerer?" And the answer, thank heaven—but you have already heard it; it was a clear, white Yes.

As for the venerable Pai Tai-shan, who was very old, and easily waylaid by a jug (or two) of wine, he had forgotten the real question even more deeply than Chi Po's father, for indeed forgetfulness occurs in us in varying degrees toward perfection.

Be that as it may, Chi Huang-ju, fortified by the white marble, went home and gave his paternal blessing to Chi Po's lessons. The villagers grumbled a little about the danger to one and all, but inasmuch as Chi Po continued to bow respectfully to his elders and keep silent when they spoke, they gradually took to attending to other worries.

Bu Fu, on his side, became accustomed to seeing Chi Po run uphill toward the cave with a brush behind each ear. "If a sorcerer can't turn a giggling boy into the greatest painter of China, he might as well wash bed linen in his cauldron," Bu Fu confided to the one-eyed bulbul.

These were the months and years in which Chi Po began to love the classics, which, if one thinks about it, are not classics without reason. He liked to hear the words of Tsung Ping which Bu Fu often recited: *By living in leisure, by nourishing the spirit, by drinking the wine glass, by plucking the lute, and by contemplating the mountain in silence before taking the brush in my hand (gone, the gabble of gossip), I travel to the six cardinal points of the world although I remain seated before my silken scroll. I do not resist the influence of the heavens but respond to the call of the tameless, where the cliffs and peaks rise like fountains of rock, and the forests are shrouded in clouds like the wisdom that circles the philosopher's head.*

One day Bu Fu told Chi Po the story of Su Tu-po, who had been governor of Chou many hundred years before:

One day Su Tu-po's brother Hua-li rebelled with a great mob against his rule and entered the palace, where he killed Su Tu-po's attendants, all except a counselor named Cho Meng. Su Tu-po and Cho Meng fled with part of the treasury and built themselves a cottage on the slope of a mountain a thousand *li* away from their native province. But not a day went by without Cho Meng importuning Su Tu-po: "Why do we recline on our couches, doing nothing? Allow me, my lord, to ride to the Son of Heaven in order to apprise him of the fact that you are alive and thirsting for revenge." But Su Tu-po only answered "Hush" before taking his morning stroll, even in the rain. In the afternoon he painted, toward nightfall he played the flute, and in the evening, by candlelight, he read the Four Books, drinking wine between and sometimes in the middle of its remarkable chapters.

At last Cho Meng became impatient and rode away in secret to the capital. Because Su Tu-po was reading the Historical Annals of Sima Qian just then, he didn't notice Cho Meng's absence for three days. Then he looked up from his book and asked: "Where can that bundle of nerves have gone?" and straight away forgot Cho Meng again.

Meantime, the loyal Cho Meng lay at the Emperor's feet, crying: "Revenge!"

The Emperor gave him six thousand soldiers, with whom he reconquered Chou, killed all Su Hua-li's attendants, and threw Su Hua-li himself into the river, knowing full well that the rascal couldn't swim. Then he rode at the head of a magnificent company of horsemen and chariots to the mountain where his beloved master dwelled. When he arrived he threw himself at Su Tu-po's feet (Cho Meng felt truly happy only when he could throw himself at people's feet, or require others to throw themselves at his), saying: "I rode to the Emperor, whose wrath I kindled by my elo-quence. He gave me six thousand soldiers. I reconquered Chou and killed your unprepossessing brother, acquiring several wounds in the battle, wounds which I will show you by humbly removing my armor and hose."

"These gashes are splendid," murmured Su Tu-po after inspecting the wounds.

"In the name of my sacred scars," Cho Meng now cried while dressing again, "will you return to Chou, my master? The throne has been mended and repainted, and with the help of a charming tax I have devised, we can rebuild the palace, too."

Su Tu-po answered him as follows: "You are most

thoughtful, Cho Meng, but I am just now hoping to paint an iris, symbol (as you know) of reticent living. Will you rule Chou (if it isn't too much trouble) until I have finished my painting? When I am done I will rejoin you and take my place at the helm."

Thereupon he gave Cho Meng some healing herbs for his wounds and sent him away. But he never painted his iris. Instead he painted rhododendrons, wisteria, and weeping willows, continued to take his morning walks, and allowed the treasure to melt slowly away.

Cho Meng remained faithful to his master, however. Even though he enjoyed himself no end on the repainted throne, he sent a messenger to Su Tu-po twice a year inquiring whether the iris had yet been painted, and whether his Lord was ready to preside at last over the Reverent Cabinet. Shameless iris! The more Su Tu-po was asked, the oftener he replied, "Alas, I haven't managed to finish it." Sometimes the urge came over him to paint a blindingly withdrawn iris and conceal it from the messenger. But because he knew (said Bu Fu) that well-born persons never tell a lie, he lived out his life without ever creating his iris, and without presiding over the Reverent Cabinet. When the treasure box was empty and he had reached the proper age, he died and was buried near the edge of the lake. People came from near and far to linger a few minutes by his tomb, saying, "Here lies the painter Su Tu-po, the rogue who never finished the promised iris."

This was the story Bu Fu told in order to teach Chi Po the love of serenity which enables one to to listen devoutly to the Spirit and flee, by means of the brush, the horrors of the world. When Chi Po painted a mountain, or a pair of cranes, or a philosopher sitting in a skiff on a lake, Bu Fu would say: "The ambitious clever man can make a lake look so like a lake that the admirer believes his finger will moisten if he touches it. However, any mechanic can paint what is; only he who sounds the depths knows how to reveal that which is behind what is."

"But what may that be?" inquired Chi Po.

"The Spirit, which you cannot see, hear, feel, or touch. Should you see it, that is not it; and should you hear it, you heard something else. Yet it is also where it is not, because, formed before forms, it does not surrender to the rule of contradiction which is the rule of forms. So the mountain of your painting must abolish itself and, as it declines to nothing, hint at the Spirit which brooded it into being."

Chi Po felt rather dizzy, but he listened bravely, especially, to be sure, when Bu Fu told him all that he knew about brushstrokes and ink; how the brush must be swift but sure, avoiding knurls and stiffness, be at times light as a girl who dances to the sound of flutes, then as fierce as a warrior who hears the drum, sometimes as rough as a farmer breaking a stone, and sometimes as mild as a young doe; how it becomes, through long practice, like another finger rather than a dead tool.

Once a week Bu Fu repeated the ancient precept: "Before you paint, old fool, dip your brush in your heart and your thought."

Bu Fu taught Chi Po the way of ink: black for things that are near, and watered for things that are far; the lovely colors in which the boy delighted; and the spaces where neither the dancing of the brush nor the music of the ink are allowed, but all is white, nothing disturbs, the pale ink fainting toward the void, distance beyond distance, incalculable, deep deep for the mind to sink into.

And then Chi Po was fourteen years old, and then fifteen. He painted, quite prettily for one so young, *Water Buffaloes in the Rain, A Plum Branch, A Tadpole, The Pure Serenity of Green Bamboo, Nine Egrets, Brief Melodies for the Barbarian Flute, Gentlewomen Amusing Themselves in a River, A Sassy Sparrow, Bees, Cicadas,* and *Bamboo Shoots,* and a number of landscapes, each with its own poem. Here is one of these poems:

> *He rested in his skiff when he came*
> *To the middle of the lake,*

And the cry of time
Was like a white gull that sits
on the shore.

Here is another:

I paint the four seasons
Any three seasons, but Spring
(Do you blame me?)
Takes breath and brush away.

And another:

Who knows where the sky begins?
Therefore I can say, the pine tree
Puts his head through the sky.

And finally:

The boulder in the stream is a great despot.
The drops of water are many
But they are small. Therefore
They lick his feet
And run.

But he never did paint a dragon, as all respectable painters do. And why not? "Master," said Chi Po, "you make me paint egrets and ladies I have never seen but will some day without a doubt, but I will never see a dragon unless you show one to me."

"Stubborn wretch," cried Bu Fu every time Chi Po brought up this subject. And that was pretty often, because by now he had lost much of his fear of the old sorcerer, and even the horrid beard did not trouble him anymore. On the contrary, if Bu Fu had shaved it off (the Immortals forbid!), Chi Po would have fainted dead away.

Finally, Bu Fu began to intimate that he might hint a promise sometime in the future; when the future came (as, alas, it always does), he hinted a promise; then he promised; and then—he made poor Chi Po wait, and wait a little more.

"Dragons," he would say, "don't grow on trees, you know."
Which, by the way, is not entirely true, for dragons do grow
on trees if they feel like it.

ne day, down in the village, something beyond anything happened. A man, dressed in red, blue, and gold rode into the marketplace on a Mongol horse, dismounted, and asked the villagers for a box. He mounted the box and read a scroll to the villagers who had come running to hear him:

"TO THE TREMBLING VILLAGERS OF THE ALL-HIGH. The All-High, mindful of his loyal and trembling children, and ever favorably disposed toward them, as well as inquisitive of their needs, is sending the Lord Director of the Multitude, Second Class, to visit this province, accompanied by a suitable retinue of fifteen thousand persons, who will eat, drink, and sleep in the houses of the villagers selected for this memorable honor. The Lord Director will listen to grievances, bestow honorable sinecures upon the deserving, and reassess the Imperial Tax on rice, roofs, and kitchen utensils."

After reading his scroll, the man jumped back on his horse, sent his spurs into the animal's sides, and flew off.

When Chi Po brought the news to Bu Fu, the old sorcerer first said with some little indignation: "Smartnose, do I need *you* to bring me this news? All you have told me my bulbul reported two hours ago, and indeed, I read it in the bubbles of my magic cauldron last night, before the emissary arrived. Be that as it may, your future is now assured. This morning you will paint the peach blossoms that we spoke of yesterday. By certain dark means at my disposal, I will see to it that it is the noblest painting of peach blossoms ever fashioned by human hand. You will take this painting to the Lord Director upon his arrival, and present it to His Sublimity, not without muttering an incantation I propose to teach you. As soon as he sees it, his eyes will buckle, his knees will roll in their sockets, his hair will quiver, and his lips will stand on end. When he recovers his normal calm, he will ask you—humbly ask you, my good Chi Po—to attend him to Chang'an in order to offer your services to the Emperor. And there, if the gods be willing, you will live like a rabbit in perennial lettuce, marry into nobility, and paint beautiful things from morning to night until old age dims your eyes."

Bu Fu went inside the cave, opened a chest, and brought out a long sheet of paper. "I have kept a record of my activities on your behalf. Let me read you the mere list of ingredients: Foal foot, betony, calamint, agrimony, and fetherfew—3 pints per week. Sacred pebbles—44 crushed into powder, leaving but a handful for my private needs. Toadstools (with or without toads)—over 100. Tearful salamanders' eyes—62. Snails' horns—78 pair (not counting several defectives). Sap of spiders—several pitchers. Vipers' thoraxes, with mortal danger to myself—18. Gliphons' livers, particularly hard to extract—126. My own blood—3 drops. Useful advice—about 800 hours. If this has not done it," Bu Fu concluded, "science is a lie and the sun is green."

"Then I shall have to leave my father and mother, and you too, master?"

"No tears, young sprout, but remember Bu Fu on the day a slave, mounted on a ladder, nails your peach blossoms to the wall of the best of the Emperor's palaces."

"Never, never will I forget you, you who have been my benefactor, my leader. I promise to return to you when I have made your name shine throughout the realm, and we shall eat rice and marmalade together again in your grotto."

"Now, I say, no tears," said Bu Fu, who, against his principles, was beginning to feel his own coming. "To work! Our blossoms must melt the Lord Director, though he be a very dragon."

Too late! The word was out. Chi Po's eyes gleamed, and Bu Fu was shaken—in vain—by a coughing fit.

"You will not send me to Chang'an without showing me a dragon I can paint!"

Cough, cough, cough. Vile catarrh!

"I must see a dragon."

Cough, cough.

"I *will* see a dragon, or else may your ancestors perish!"

Poor Bu Fu! He had to promise a dragon before the Lord Director's arrival. Suddenly, however, his cough cleared up, and—I don't know why—he cheered up again. "So be it," he exclaimed. "A thunderstorm happens to be coming tonight. Hurry to me, if you dare, at the peak of the storm. In the slit and clap of the seventh lightning after you arrive, I shall do the doing that summons a dragon."

I leave you to guess how happy these words made Chi Po. A dragon at last! So he went eagerly to work, while Bu Fu, bulbul on his shoulder, went off to gather the day's raspberries and blackberries.

And nowhere ever has a branch of the peach tree been painted by man or boy as Chi Po painted it that day. He meditated on the tree and its small five-petaled red blossoms as he had seen it many times in the valley below, until he seemed to become a branch himself and felt the sap making his body and his arms twist and grow and gnarl like a snake or like a river or like the lightning or like a complicated thought. And then he licked his brushes, first the black one and then the red one, and flung himself on the paper like a madman or like a wave that explodes on a rock. He dashed a thick line downward, and elbowed it up again a little, and then up some more, and then a thinner forking in two, angling this way and that, till he reached the other side of the sheet. By then the black line was streaked with white because much of the ink was gone, but Chi Po left it alone. He seized the brush again and made a half-dozen twigs that rippled down the page, with sprays leaping off in all directions. Then with his red brush, he daubed the petals on, giving them bristles of pistils with another thin black brush. Three were flowers and seven were only buds, and he placed one flower with two buds on the low right, for what is low is denser than what is high; and the lower-left-hand side stayed white for the flowers to look into and be dizzy. Then he wrote under the beginning of the branch, in that wild, windblown hand which, centuries later, everyone would recognize as his: "Time! Run thou headlong, nevertheless a brush shall hold thee still as when a buckler stops an arrow." Finally, he placed his red seal near a bud, so that it too looked like a flower.

When he had finished, he looked at his work, and asked: "Has this come from *my* hand?" for he had utterly forgotten himself, and what he saw was so beautiful that he thought he would cry. Though it was but a branch hanging out of nowhere—you did not even see the tree, or the soil, or the sky, or the meadow; only that one branch—yet you could tell the whole ravishing landscape without looking any further. "Only the piddling paint-slapper paints everything," Bu Fu had said. "*We* with a morsel express the banquet."

Chi Po held his painting up to the sun. Suddenly a bee appeared. It buzzed around the flowers Chi Po had painted, but without making a mistake, without trying to sip them. It knew! Joyfully it buzzed its wings near the scroll and then it went to dine elsewhere. Chi Po laughed. "Lord Director," he cried, "you will hear from me!"

When Bu Fu returned, Chi Po showed him the painting. An hour seemed to pass. Three minutes did pass. "It will do," said Bu Fu at last. Then he added what he had never said before: "It has the breath." He said it very slowly, and neither of them spoke another word that afternoon.

That same night a fearful storm broke out.

Chi Po was in his bedroom listening to the rain raining and the wind winding; thunder ran after lightning as though the dragons of the storm had been quarreling with one another besides drubbing the earth. Chi Po's parents trembled in their bed under a pile of covers. What to do? Should he sneak out of the house, and maybe drown in a river or be killed by a bolt? Rrrrrumble!—how it did roil and roll! But if he didn't go now, Bu Fu would never summon a dragon.

Open went a side door, on came the straw raincoat, and out slipped Chi Po. A blast of wind grabbed him by the neck like a strong hand and threw him three yards up the gravel path. He marched and stumbled and ran. Every now and then a moon flickered through the angry, fat clouds, but the lightning did the rest to light his way. The trees all about him bent as though they wanted to tear up every root they had in order to flee the storm that bent them, and their leaves roared like an ocean of pain.

Not a soul outdoors. Chi Po went slinking and hurtling past the last house, the rain washing his face and his feet plunging into mud holes. All this to see a dragon! Brave Chi Po! Never fear: run, but keep away, keep away from those dangerous trees that beg for lightning. Once in the mountain you will be safe, for the wild animals are crouching in their lairs.

As for Bu Fu, he lay on his mattress in the cave, snoring fit to split a rock. But his snores were not the blithe harrumphs of the Immortals. In his dream, the thunder had become a large crowd of wicked people shouting, "Jump, Bu Fu! Jump, Bu Fu!" Jump from where? From the roof of the village tavern, with the Lord Director of the Multitude behind him pushing him and shouting in unison with the villagers, "Jump, Bu Fu!" Suddenly the bulbul lands on the roof, holding Chi Po in his beak by one of his ears. Chi Po steadies himself and falls at once to tugging at Bu Fu the other way in order to save him, all the time weeping and asking, "What has my master done?" The crowd yells, the Lord Director keeps pushing, Bu Fu loses ground, he begins to slide off in spite of Chi Po's efforts, the crowd is delirious with joy.... Hang it! I wish I were erudite enough to interpret dreams, because something tells me that this nightmare of Bu Fu's was pregnant with meanings; but all I can report is that the Lord Director pushed, Chi Po pulled, the bulbul screeched, and the crowd bellowed, until Bu Fu lost his balance and—woke up. Poor Chi Po had been shaking him till his arms were sore.

"A demon!" Bu Fu cried, and jumped into a corner.

"No, Bu Fu, it's only me, Chi Po."

"What in thunder and lightning are you doing here? You're flooding my cave!"

"I came for the dragon, Bu Fu," Chi Po replied, "precisely *because* of the thunder and lightning!"

And sure enough, Bu Fu could see—for he was perfectly awake by now—that never had the rioting elements been readier for the appearance of a dragon. No more excuses, no more delays. "Into the rain! Into the heart of the storm!" he called out.

He rapidly swept up a hundred of his witchcraft commodities as well as an old, half-rusted gong; and then both hurried out of the cave, their heads butting the rain and wind.

"You count the lightning bolts!" Bu Fu shouted over the clamoring weather. And he began to dance in front of the cave, wailing, clapping his hands, and wagging his head in the strangest way. The bulbul peeked from his kennel and looked on in astonishment. This was the first time in the bulbul's memory that his master had quitted his mattress before the hour of marmalade.

A terrible light crackled. "One!" cried Chi Po.

Bu Fu stopped and recited the first verse of the Dragon Dragooned backward. There were so many awful words in it that Chi Po became very pale.

"Two!" whimpered Chi Po. Should he have stayed in bed?

Bu Fu, soaked from head to foot, his beard wet as a mop, recited the last verse of the Dragon Dragooned forward. It spoke of unlimited pachyderms, of tidal waves eating mountains, and of sharp-toothed concatenations that hide in corners to tear children into nibbles and devour them.

"Three!" piped Chi Po, gasping for breath, he too wetter than a fish.

The wind roared, the thunder outroared it. Bu Fu poured dust of chalcedony from a retort to the muddy ground and threw a pound of dead worms into the twisting wind, a dozen of which almost blinded Chi Po.

"Four!" This time Chi Po, who could no longer see much of anything, shouted at the top of his voice.

Bu Fu's hoarse voice made its way through the storm. "Did you see him beginning to take shape?" shouted Bu Fu, whirling wetly three times around the soaking cake of chalcedony.

"No, I didn't see anything. Oh! Bu Fu!"

Crash, crash went the rampaging thunder.

"Don't faint, don't whatever you do faint dead away when you see the first coil."

"F-f-f-five!"

"There it is! The first coil! You saw it! Oh dragon, be merciful to us!"

"I'm scared, I'm going to be sick—"

"Silence! Keep counting!"

Bu Fu, still dancing like a wild Siberian, beat on the old gong with all his might and sang the strange Canticle of Inexistence. The wind, the thunder, the rain, the dance, the gong in the night drove Chi Po out of his senses, but he was able, after all, at the moment of the next lightning bolt, to groan out: "Six...."

He held on to the protruding root of a tree, sure that a blast of this pitiless wind would hurl him down into the village chopped into bits of Chi Po.

Bu Fu went into a fever, a delirium, a frenzy, a crisis. Still whirling, he drew the image of the Great Polyhedron in the air with a pointed stick, after which he howled, "Haoooooooh!" and resumed his beating of the gong.

The bulbul became even more interested. He flew clear of the kennel and perched on a branch nearby, while the sorcerer foamed at the mouth and danced and leaped and shrieked and gesticulated like a puppet in the hands of a maniac. "Watch, watch, watch!" cried Bu Fu, while the darkness growled and Chi Po thought he would fall and die.

"Seven!" shouted Bu Fu and yelled "Dragon, seven coils!" while the lightning came and went. He fell on the ground with his beard in the mud.

Well! The bulbul only said, "Quack!" (for bulbuls are not unrelated to ducks) with the most ferocious air he had ever worn, and flew straight off into the night.

And where was Chi Po? He was so terrified, he hadn't seen anything. Or had he? He had been blinded by a terrible light, and in the light—something—a scale? A fang? Maybe— he couldn't tell; maybe he had fainted—he didn't know. How he hated himself for being such a jellyfish of a boy! All he had seen for sure was the bulbul flying away.

Bu Fu untwisted himself. He staggered back to the cave, followed by Chi Po, and sat drenched on his mattress. "My dear disciple," he said in a limp voice, "that was quite, quite a dragon. Seven magnificent coils! And the head of a—what shall I say?—of a, well, of a dragon. I'm still weak from the effusion of witchery I caused for your sake. I hope you are finally satisfied."

"I—I am grateful to you, sir," stuttered Chi Po, altogether abashed.

"Good. Did you notice that dreadful tongue of his flickering like a gigantic salamander's? "

Chi Po couldn't lie. "I—I didn't see the dragon at all."

Bu Fu struck his head four times with both fists. "It... can't...be...true! I must be dreaming! Aren't you ashamed of yourself? All this nocturnal fuss, this danger to my health and to the cosmos, and you didn't see the dragon? Don't you dare ask me for another one!"

"Maybe I was so scared, I closed my eyes at the wrong moment. I'm such a fool. All I saw was the bulbul flying away."

"The who doing what?" roared Bu Fu, leaping up.

He ran to the kennel. The kennel was empty.

"Stefan!" cried Bu Fu (that was the bulbul's Christian name). "Where are you? Come back, come back!"

And he ran again into the loud rain calling his bulbul, who had never but never left him before. "Yang-yang," he cried (that was the bulbul's nickname), "where are you, my son? Come back! Your kennel is warm and dry! Come back!"

Leaving Chi Po dumbfounded at the mouth of the cavern, he ran here and there in the mountain, hours and hours, calling and calling, tripping and stumbling, crying, "Come back, come back!" and sometimes adding, "Forgive me!" (I shall tell you why in a little while.) When the storm drifted away and the dawn began to bring color back to the sky, Bu Fu was still running.

Chi Po waited patiently in the cave for Bu Fu to return, but at last he went home, dried himself, and slipped unnoticed into his bed, where he fell asleep before dawn after passing in review the misfortunes of that grievous night.

The sun was drying the village out when Chi Po woke up. "How much I don't want to go to school today, how sleepy I am and how melancholy. That dragon! The bulbul! And Bu Fu in a state! Let the sun go about its business, I'm going back to sleep."

Which he was set to do when he heard his schoolmate Fee Sh'ing calling through the window. "No school!" Fee Sh'ing shouted. "They've sighted the Lord Director arriving ahead of time in a big cloud of dust. Instead of school, all the upper-grade boys are tacking the bunting on the Magnificent Golden Residence of Noble Visitors. Get up at once and come along." And a great drumroll in the street proved that Fee Sh'ing was not playing a practical joke.

For a couple of hours, Chi Po climbed up ladders and tacked bunting on the Magnificent Golden Residence. (My honesty compels me to say that this was nothing but a huge barrack decorated with a scattering of gold spangles, yet all the same it was the pride of the village.) The smaller boys swept and picked up nails. But Chi Po felt so worried about Bu Fu and the bulbul that at last he slipped away—everybody was too excited to notice—and hurried up the haunted mountain to Bu Fu's cave.

Wretched Bu Fu! He was squatting outside against the wall of the cave, holding a half-eaten bowl of rice and marmalade in one hand, wringing the tears out of his beard with the other, and sneezing like a geyser every ten seconds.

"Alas, I see that the bulbul didn't come back," said Chi Po.

"He left me," Bu Fu replied sepulchrally, "and me like a brother to him, a father. The ingrate up and left me."

"Did the dragon scare him? That must be it. The sight of

that dragon made him lose his head."

At these words, Bu Fu began to sob and sneeze twice as loud as before without answering, and you shall know why very soon. Meantime, Chi Po had a wonderful idea. Since Bu Fu was such a great sorcerer, why not use a spell to recall the bulbul? A small object like a bird wouldn't require a great expense of ingredients.

"Bu Fu," said Chi Po as gravely as he could, "you who send your image to the dreams of men, who cursed the village by saying '*P'u!*,' who made Mi Fen's cow bear a two-headed, one-legged calf, who made the wicked rich man whose name I forget disappear, who can throw thunderbolts, flood the valley, and above all summon invisible dragons, rise up now and recall the bulbul with one of your horrendous spells."

But Bu Fu only went on weeping and fretting his breakfast. Chi Po could see that something awful was welling up in Bu Fu's chest. The lad ran into the cave and brought out the trigrams, the crucible, bottles of lotions and potions and notions, and he even tried to carry out the logarithmic table, but that one wouldn't budge.

All in vain. Bu Fu kept on crying and blubbering. "Bulbul, bulbul." Nothing seemed to interest him.

There remained only one thing to try, namely the set of the Four Ordained Pyrolitics, which Chi Po had been forbidden to touch on pain of having his fingers burnt right off their knuckles. "Let them burn," Chi Po thought. "I must save my old master."

It turned out that they didn't burn him at all; in fact, they were rather damp and *very* mouldy. "Here they are," he said, laying them before Bu Fu. "Now you can force the bulbul to appear, just as you did the dragon."

When Bu Fu saw that the Four Ordained Pyrolitics hadn't burnt Chi Po's fingers, and heard that accursed name "dragon" again, he broke into a howl, sank his head on Chi Po's shoulder, put his arms about Chi Po, and wailed like a wounded baby. "Boo-hoo," he went, "I'm a fake, I'm a charlatan, I'm tinsel, I'm guff and blabble! Boo-hoo, I'm a hollow mockery. Let the whole indignant world know it. Boo-hoo!"

"Venerated master," cried Chi Po, who did all he could not to break down with Bu Fu, "what are you saying? Everybody knows you're the greatest sorcerer in the world. Didn't you make the wicked rich man disappear?"

"N-n-n-o," Bu Fu sobbed, "I didn't. I met him in my mountain, all shredded, and groaning, 'My books are unbalanced and I am unhinged!' I never saw him again."

"But didn't you make Mi Fen's cow bear a two-headed, one-legged calf?"

"N-n-n-o, that wasn't my doing; maybe another sorcerer did it, boo-hoo."

"But don't you send your image to visit people in their dreams?"

"And what about theirs in mine, boo-hoo-hoo?"

"But what about the dragon?"

Bu Fu tore out several of his hairs. "There wasn't any."

"No dragon?"

"None."

"And that's why the bulbul flew away! He understood! He understood it all!"

Alas, Bu Fu knew it only too well, and the tears plunged to the ground and streamed downhill. "I'm a cheat, I'm a failure, I'm a crook, I'm an extortionist."

"An extortionist?"

"Yes. I made you carry all that rice and marmalade, boo-hoo, for those spells, boo-hoo, that never did anything."

But Chi Po wasn't beaten. "Didn't you say '*P'u!*' to the village?"

"Yes, I did."

"And didn't a terrible storm fall on the village that very night?"

"Well—yes." Bu Fu brightened a little. "It did, didn't it?"

"Of course. So you see, all isn't lost."

"But my bulbul saw through me, evil old throttle-throat that I am; he couldn't swallow that dragon."

"Oh, well, birds have such consciences. In a way, it's all my fault. I shouldn't have been pestering you all these years. I can imagine a hundred different dragons all by myself."

"Then you're not angry with me?"

"Well, I don't know. Is it really true, horse your cart and mope to fry, that you are a humbug?"

"I don't know! Isn't it awful, but absolutely repulsive, when a man can't look downright into his mirror and say: 'Look here, my friend, you're a humbug'? Of course, I haven't got a mirror, but oh, my friend, the trepidations, the misery, the insomnias, wondering whether one *is* a humbug or not. Because I did say '*P'u!*' without the shadow of a doubt. Not to mention the abundance of mischief that goes back to my beginnings."

And Bu Fu wiped a straggling tear off his nose.

"What made you go in for sorcering in the first place?" Chi Po inquired. He was now grown-up enough to wonder about other people (this is a curiosity that comes to us little by little), and, as far as Bu Fu was concerned, he felt at this moment that he could ask him anything. He felt ripe and serene. After all, *he* hadn't pretended to see a dragon, and *he* had never mixed slop and chaff into a cauldron.

"What made me go in—? I'd rather not say."

"But you must; otherwise I shall never trust you again. And this time you must tell me the truth."

Bu Fu was offended. "I don't *always* lie, you know," he said, and wailed a little.

"Did you have a supernatural vision?"

"No."

"Did an old sorcerer take you in as his apprentice?"

"No."

"Well?"

"I—one day—I was working in an artificial-potato factory—"

"What is an artificial potato?"

"It's a potato made out of bark and stuffed with chocolate. It's much handsomer and better-tasting than real potatoes. You put a few in your potato field and the crows like them so much that they leave the real potatoes alone."

"But if they're handsomer and better than real potatoes, why not keep them and let the birds enjoy the real potatoes?"

"That is a striking idea. If I had thought of it, I would have mentioned it to our overlord, and then I might have become a respectable citizen instead of...instead of..."

"Now, now, now..."

"...a bamboozler!"

"But what happened?"

"For three years I spudded artificial potatoes from morning till evening. One man stuffed, the other spudded. I spudded."

"And then?"

"We did so well that we won prizes. The real potatoes multiplied in the fields. It was lovely. It was useful. But it was not enough. Stirrings, young one. Dreams. The soul craves. Sundays I studied, I painted, I wrote poems. A fermentation in my being, a soaring, an utter transcending of potatoes. In short, I grew ambitious. I wanted to equal the achievement of the noblest philosophers."

"And what is that?" asked Chi Po.

"To be unemployed. When I heard of a mountain which, in spite of its suitable character, was untenanted and un-haunted, I hesitated no longer, vowed never to touch another potato, and settled in this very cave, whence I began to practice the thousand devilries which made the village mine. And I succeeded! I had been right about my soul, my genius. For fifty-three years I have eaten the village's rice and marmalade and quaffed its best wine gratis!"

"But you *were* a humbug all that time," Chi Po pointed out.

Bu Fu's beard trembled. "I have done my best to be a conscientious sorcerer," he moaned, "but now you'll denounce me to the village, you'll renounce me. I must leave my cave and starve, unless the wrathful villagers cut my throat, if they can find it. So be it. I deserve no better, old scuttleful of sins that I am."

"You who were going to give me an incantation to take to the Lord Director! And I who wanted to be a true painter and to be worthy of a tiny place in Chang'an, by means of the slop and chaff in your cauldron, the right incantation you were about to give me, and all and all. No wonder the bulbul left you. And I too trusted you so!"

Bu Fu leaped up and clapped his hands together. "You shall have your incantation. By the great dra—by heaven—I will squeeze the whole extent of my sorcery into a single dense spell, rub it into your peach-tree branch, make it cling to the Lord Director, see you applauded in Chang'an, and, consumed with happiness, burn my trigrams and retire."

"How can I believe you?" Chi Po sadly asked.

"Believe in me, young one. I am still Bu Fu. When is His Sublimity expected?"

"Tomorrow. I was helping with the bunting this morning."

"Magnificent! I stake my tarnished reputation on this spell."

Bu Fu shook his fist at the sky. "And *you* will be sorry," he shouted, hoping the bulbul would hear him and be sorry.

Then he turned to Chi Po. "We must allow the Lord Director two days to unpack and receive the first wave of dignitaries," he said. "On the evening of the second day, he will be stupefied with bowing, toasting, visiting the mill-wheels and model rice paddies, pinching horses and babies, studying charts, listening to complaints, and drinking to every villager's health. On the morning of the third day, you will dress in your holiday clothes, present yourself to me, receive your bewitched painting, and memorize a magic chant of my making. While the spell on your work is still fresh, you will produce it to the man, chant the chant, and then—you shall see wonders."

All—well, nearly all—happened as Bu Fu had foretold.

On the morning of the third day, Chi Po, though dubious but dressed in his finest silks, received his spell-endued scroll and learned by rote the chant in question. In my opinion, this chant was not truly of Bu Fu's own making. I

believe that he had distilled it instead from the most hermetic
pages of the Holy Palimpsest. (Hermetic pages are those
specially written by scholars for their own edification.) I
have changed a few of its words, lest it singe the paper of
this true history and draw upon myself and the reader some
surprising misfortune:

> *Hail, O cutlets and tripes everlasting,*
> *Anchovies and syrups, foes to fasting!*
> *Mind does not mind if matter matter,*
> *While carrots grow longer and cantaloupes fatter!*
> *Roasts shall float by in drifts of spina,*
> *And wines be bibbed of charming vintage!*
> *What matter to mind if mind be matter?*
> *Bananas, grow longer, and onions, fatter!*

Silence. Chi Po's mouth was wide open. Then, brave as
always, he dared ask, "What does it mean?"

Bu Fu looked to the left and to the right before answering.
"It means itself," he whispered, "like a bridge that arches from
one shore to the same. But now, my boy, close your mouth,
fold your ears, pinch your eyes, tame your breath, silence
your stomach, and memorize the words. After you have used
the chant, pulverize it utterly in your brain, on pain of being
obliged to eat it for your breakfast every morning as long as
you live. Memorize it, I say, and then recite it with dramatic
gesticulations the moment the Lord Director (Second Class)
directs his first glance at your scroll."

Chi Po was so bright a lad that within half an hour he
was able to recite the incantation forward, backward, and
even on its side. He bowed to Bu Fu, tucked the scroll of the
peach blossoms inside his garment, and, three days later,
presented himself at the Magnificent Golden Residence.

f course, it is easier to go *to* a grand place like the Lord Director of the Multitude's temporary residence than it is to go *into* it. For instance, two very large, ferocious-looking men were standing on either side of the entrance carrying clubs. They had been specially trained from childhood to snarl, and to do it in rhymes. One would snarl to the other: "How were your breakfast eggs, dear fellow?" and the other would snarl in reply: "White around and inside yellow." But most of the time they just guarded odd gates, browbeat strangers, and saluted humbly whomever paid their wages.

"Will they ever let me in?" Chi Po reflected. "I don't suppose I should waste my incantation on them. Bu Fu didn't tell me how many times I could use it. Oh, they're looking at me. Forward, Chi Po, with a pure heart and an unclouded countenance."

He took the scroll out of the pocket of his tunic and climbed the four steps to the entrance. "Greetings, my lords," he said in his most mature voice. "I should like to see His Sublimity the Lord Director of the Multitude in order to present him with the gift of this scroll, freshly painted, and follow him to Chang'an as a student in the Imperial Academy."

"Where's your invitation?" snarled the first guard.

"Your authorization?" snarled the second.

"Your documentation?" resnarled the first.

"Your validation?" resnarled the second.

Unfortunately, the only document Chi Po possessed was his scroll, and so the door remained shut in his face while the clubs took on a menacing aspect.

"But may I wait on the pavement for the Lord Director to come out?" asked Chi Po.

"What's the pavement to powerful old me?" snarled the first guard.

"I *trample* on your pavement, don't you see?" snarled his rhyming colleague.

So Chi Po sat down on the pavement with his scroll, only a few yards away from the gate. People he knew walked by and asked him why he sat there in his holiday clothes. Chi Po answered vaguely, "I am waiting."

By and by he noticed four or five tall strangers who walked to and fro near the Magnificent Golden Residence. Every time one of them spotted a villager, he slunk after him and, coming up from behind, tapped him lightly over the head with the flat of his hand. Being taller than most made it easy for him to tap other people's heads, and wearing padded sandals kept his footsteps silent. The tapped villager turned around pretty angrily, of course, but he realized at once that the man belonged to the Lord Director. Besides, the tall fellow muttered "Official business" and apologized. So the villager walked away in a state of astonishment, rubbing the top of his head. Was this a custom of the distant capital? As for the official, he scribbled furiously in a little notebook and when done, went looking for the next villager.

After a while, one of these men saw Chi Po and came over to tap him on the head. Since Chi Po had been looking at him, there was no way of sneaking up on the lad from behind. But the tap was rather light, and the tall man smiled pleasantly as he muttered "Official business" and scribbled hastily on his pad.

"Why are you doing this?" Chi Po asked, rubbing his scalp.

"How kind of you to talk to me" was the answer of the official, who immediately sat down beside Chi Po, bending his long legs so he could rest his chin on his knees. He seemed happy to be speaking to a layman. "I have a right to ten minutes of rest every hour," he said, "and during that time I love to chat with people. What is your name, my boy?"

"My name is Chi Po. I am fifteen years old and a painter."

"Mine is Li Fang. I am forty-one years old and an official with a wife, two concubines, and six children. It's a hard life and people aren't very friendly."

"Maybe it's because they're not used to being struck on the head. They are quite used to painters, however, and they are friendly to *me*."

"That is not surprising. They know that painters don't signify."

"Tell me though. Why do you hit people on their heads?"

Li Fang leaned over and whispered confidentially into Chi Po's ear: "To keep in touch."

"I don't understand."

"Well, our Lord Director likes to understand the common people, especially when he travels. And since nothing is more common in China than common people, he employs a number of informants, of whom I am humbly proud to be one. We walk about the streets and tap as many sources of information as we can. Then we take notes and give them to the Deputy Secretary."

"But are they accurate notes? You don't seem to talk to anyone."

Li Fang leaned over confidentially again and chuckled. "It's true, isn't it! And yet our notes are *noticed*, and that, my boy, is what matters."

"What does the Deputy Secretary do with them?"

"He puts them in alphabetical ideogrammatic order and sends them up to the Chief Secretary with his recommendations."

"And then does the Chief Secretary give the notes and the recommendations to the Lord Director?" Chi Po asked.

"How did you know?" Li Fang exclaimed, his eyes and mouth opening wide.

"It seemed reasonable to me."

"It is! And yet that is precisely how we have been operating ever since the present Lord Director assumed his post. Thank heaven, the dear man has remained calm; a great soul; he strides every morning past a mountain of notes and recommendations and carries on with his old unshakable firmness. Look here! You're wide awake for a mere peasant boy. Would you care to be apprenticed as an informant? I could introduce you and drop a kind word on your behalf."

Chi Po declined, but he felt that Li Fang might be willing to help him. So he told the informant why he was sitting on the pavement, why he wanted to see the Lord Director, and how the two guards yonder (pointing discreetly) had kept him from entering by snarling and waving their clubs.

"Nothing is easier than mollifying guards," said Li Fang, "and as for our Lord Director, he is the most approachable person in the world. He will see anyone. Go to the corner of the street and come back with a springy step. Leap up the stairs to the entrance. Say casually: 'I'm sent by the Honorable Chou Tieh,' and walk in."

"Who is Chou Tieh?" asked Chi Po. "I don't know anyone by that name."

"Neither do I. Perhaps there isn't any Chou Tieh. You might say Tsu Ching instead. Any name will implement your ingress. It depends on the tone of voice."

Chi Po was amazed. "But," he said, "the guards already know me and they know I wasn't sent by any Chou Tieh or Tsu Ching. Anyway, you've talked so loud I'm sure they've heard every word you said."

"It doesn't signify. I strongly advise you to take my advice. But stop! My ten minutes are over and I must get in touch with the people again. Thank you for this delightful conversation."

So saying, Li Fang tapped Chi Po on the head again and then blushed and cried out in great confusion: "Oh, excuse me, I already have your views. You favor the conscription of invalids into the Emperor's salt mines."

"I do not!" Chi Po exclaimed indignantly.

"It doesn't signify at all. Things balance out, you know," said Li Fang enigmatically, and he hurried away on his stork's legs looking for a suitable villager.

Chi Po was doubtful what to do, but it was almost

noon and, really, he had no better design for seeing the
Lord Director than the one Li Fang had given him. So he
walked to the corner, returned with the springiest step he
could organize, breezed up the stairs like an official bent
on serving his beloved country, and announced: "I'm sent
by the Honorable Chou Tieh and Tsu Ching." He thought he
might as well double his chances.

Both rascals bowed, tucked in their clubs, opened the
door, and let him in.

What an uproar of bustling, once Chi Po found himself
in the great hall of the barrack. He hardly knew which way
to turn his head. The hall was full of vociferous gentlemen
crossing every which way, bolting from rooms, vanishing
into rooms, chatting a few moments when they met, calling
across the hall, and dropping papers and portfolios as they
ran from one end of the hall to the other. All Chi Po could
hear was a snitch of conversation here and a snatch of
conversation there:

"Has the Lord Director seen the report on reports?"

Or: "His Sublimity says he will attend the ballet tonight."

Or: "The delegation of landless villagers has just left,
thank goodness."

Or: "Is there a good laundry in this wretched village?"

How was Chi Po ever to find the Lord Director?

"Oh, Bu Fu!" he thought, "I don't know what to think of
you, but don't abandon me now. You swore you would send
me to Chang'an."

He decided to tug politely at the sleeve of an official who
was resting on a bench. "Sir, could you tell me where to find
the Lord Director of the Multitudes?"

"Nothing is easier," the official replied, "because the
Lord Director will see anyone."

The man led Chi Po into a small antechamber where an
official sat at a desk with a long scroll before him. There Chi
Po was asked to state his name, his address, the purpose of
his visit, and the last time he had caught a cold.

"We do want to keep His Sublimity from catching colds,"

the registering official said.

"May I see him right away?"

"In principle, yes; but when a man like the Lord Director is willing to see anyone, he is of course very busy. So will you please step into the next antechamber?"

In the next antechamber, which was larger than the first, Chi Po saw some thirty villagers sitting on chairs and benches. He knew almost all of them, but they were very quiet and pale, so Chi Po sat on a stool in a corner, clutching his scroll, and kept still.

Suddenly he heard someone shout: "Boot him out!" in still another room, followed by two slammings of a distant door, one of them a slam-open and the other a slam-shut. Presently a door into the antechamber opened and a clerk said in a sweet voice: "Whose turn is it, gentlemen?"

One of the villagers, pushed by the others, rose from his seat with a nervous smile and disappeared into the adjacent room. A few minutes later, the voice shouted again: "Boot him out!" and the door-slamming recurred.

This continued until there were no more villagers in the waiting room except Chi Po. "Each one of them," thought the boy, "believes he has a good reason for being more cordially received than the one before him, but I, thank heaven, have my incantation," and he repeated it under his breath to make sure he wouldn't stumble at the critical moment.

At last his turn came—the last petitioner before the noontime repast for all the officials. The clerk led him before a great desk, behind which was sitting the Lord Director (Second Class). To the right of his master stood the Deputy Secretary. Chi Po knelt in front of the desk. "Your name and the purpose of your petition, if you please," said the Deputy Secretary.

"I am Chi Po, your lordship. I wish to be taken to Chang'an as a painter in your noble retinue, and I humbly solicit your honorable protection for my endeavor to enter the Great Imperial Academy. I have brought a depiction of peach blossoms for your lordship's condescending consideration to support my most respectful petition."

The square face of the Lord Director showed that he hadn't heard a word of what Chi Po had said. He was waiting to hear from the Deputy Secretary. The latter spoke: "Subject: Chi Po. Object: attendance at Great Imperial Academy. Substantiation: image of peach."

Then the clerk who had opened the door for Chi Po repeated in a loud voice: "Subject: Chi Po. Object: attendance at Great Imperial Academy. Substantiation: image of peach." For the Lord Director wanted everything in duplicate.

"Submission of substantiation granted; final decision pending," said the Lord Director, whose square face rounded benevolently. He turned to a lackey whom Chi Po had not seen, as he was standing in a far corner of the room. "Delivery of refrigerated beverage urgently requested." The lackey left, and returned presently with a lemonade.

Having received permission to rise, Chi Po unrolled his scroll on the spot where he had knelt. It shone, red and black and white, like the spirits of Yang and Yin exuded by a young demon in the foaming meadows of high summer. The Lord Director rose from his desk. Surrounded at a small distance by his Deputy Secretary, and at a slightly supplementary distance by the clerk and even the lackey, he bent his honorable eyes to the scroll. At that moment, bold as he had proved himself on the day of his first encounter with the sorcerer, Chi Po delivered his incantation with utter precision:

> *Hail, O cutlets and tripes everlasting,*
> *Anchovies and syrups, foes to fasting!*
> *Mind does not mind if matter matter*
> *While carrots grow longer and cantaloupes fatter!*
>
> *Roasts shall float by in drifts of spinach,*
> *And wines be bibbed of charming vintage!*
> *What matter to mind if mind be matter?*
> *Bananas, grow longer, and onions, fatter!*

When he saw the unearthly expression on the Lord Director's face, he could not help thinking in triumph: "This time, dear master, you succeeded!"

"What did I just hear?" croaked the Lord Director.

Now this was an unexpected poser for the Deputy Secretary, who was more at home with the likes of "My neighbor's trees are shedding their leaves on my side of the fence!" than with noble, hermetic texts. As he didn't know what to report, he decided it was best to become indignant. "Oh Sublimity," he said, "you have been listening to scurrilous and satirical verse directed against your own somewhat portly person. Let roasts float by in drifts of spinach! Did you capture the hint?"

"By all means," said the Lord Director. "Roasts, spinach— ha! As you were saying..."

"Are these not hints of malfeasance in office? Bribes received in kind? Administrative gluttony? And spinach— is anything more insulting, more common? Spinach, sir! Almost cauliflower, if I may allow myself the word."

"Nothing of the—" was all that Chi Po succeeded in crying out.

"Boot him out!" roared the Lord Director.

Two hands, attached to two arms, seized Chi Po by the armpits. He felt himself lifted in the air, and a most experienced and propulsive kick—

The *Lives* of this great painter, all of them understandably reticent concerning this particular episode of his career, do not tell us to whom these hands and the propellant foot belonged. To the lackey of the lemonade, whose limbs were certainly free now that he had served the beverage? To the clerk, known for his frequent visits to the unsavory districts of Chang'an? Or even, perhaps, to the Deputy Secretary who, in a case all but worthy of the scaffold would have wanted to assume his share of the action? The answer to this question awaits further scholarly investigation. Instead, it is known for a fact that Chi Po was momentarily transformed into a missile. A door opened, he flew across it, and he landed in an empty room (except for the portraits of half a dozen emperors hanging on its walls), one of whose other doors opened on the alley in which the honorable tubs of garbage of the Magnificent Golden Residence were kept, and another that led back to the very hall into which Chi Po had made his entrance.

The wretched boy, crying "My painting! I've lost my painting! They've taken my painting from me!" and staggering he knew not where, opened this latter door—not the one that led to the fetid alley but the one leading back to the great hall. By chance, say some; because the Immortals were watching over him, say others.

In spite of the hunger that was beginning to gnaw at his vitals, Chi Po sat himself on a bench—the very one on which he had found the helpful official—lowered his head, took it into his two hands, and wept, but wept silently so as not to disturb the world. He mourned over his failure, of course, and Bu Fu's last lie, but above all he sorrowed over what he felt was the death of his beloved painting, for he imagined it on the floor of the Lord Director's office, trodden upon, laughed at, torn to shreds. Yes, its death...I believe that Chi Po ripened greatly that day and became almost a grown man.

A few minutes went by, and then Chi Po felt that someone was standing over him. He lifted his head and, indeed, a dignified official, wearing a double gown of the finest silk, sleeves elegantly wide, bonnet of a scholar, his face adorned with a nicely trimmed gray beard, was curiously watching him. Chi Po wanted to rise at once, but the mandarin kept him seated by placing a hand on his shoulder and seating himself on the bench next to the lad whose face, he saw, was awash in tears. "Tell me everything," he said, "I have a son your age."

He needn't have asked twice. Chi Po told him his woeful story and sobbed his very heart out. "And Bu Fu gave me an incantation, and he cheated me again, it's the dragon all over, I'll explain, but my beautiful painting is gone!"

This official happened to be the Emperor's Edict Compiler, who was traveling side by side with the Lord Director of the Multitudes. (In fact, the Emperor had charged each to keep an eye on the other.) His mission was to inspect the provincial archives and rid them of dust and parasites. He didn't understand much of what Chi Po was saying, but he pitied the little man and wondered if he was a hungry orphan.

"Lift your chin, dry your tears, and blow your nose," he said. "Inasmuch as your painting is bound to be filed with the other petitions, nothing is lost, and in the meantime, if you will be so good as to recover your spirits, I shall treat you to lunch."

Sadness, we have seen, does not banish hunger. Chi Po was only too glad to leave the Magnificent Residence, which he hoped never to enter again, under the wing of an important mandarin whom the two guards saluted at the exit as though the Emperor himself were leaving the place; glad, too, to sit down at the table of a nearby inn.

During the plentiful meal, the Edict Compiler noticed that Chi Po was intelligent and, for a provincial, quite well-mannered. He didn't talk too much, he listened to his superior, and he was neither cringing nor arrogant toward the waiter.

"I have it!" he exclaimed, waving a strawberry at the end of their lunch. "We will engage you as a page and take you back with us to Chang'an, where you shall dine on suckling pigs, the fatted calf, and groaning boars."

This was a happy turn at last, but Chi Po explained that he was no famished orphan; he had parents who must give him permission to leave the village.

"Your parents will burst with joy. Since you are a boy with a brain—see how cleverly you roped me to your side—you will go far in Chang'an, and you'll enrich your parents. Take my word for it: the mayor will bow to them when he passes them in the street."

The Edict Compiler had guessed right. Chi Po's parents

gave their humble assent, for ever since the boy had been taken on as Bu Fu's very particular apprentice, they had in their secret thoughts been cladding him in a vestment of respect. However, they did not burst with delight, that would have been fearful; rather, after giving Chi Po a new gown, kissing him on both cheeks, recommending that he be forever wise and respectful, and not to forget to send them as many gold pieces from the rich city as he could spare, they wept hot tears when they saw him walking away, and he, you may be sure, did so as well.

Before taking leave of his parents, Chi Po spoke as follows to his father: "Father, go to the mayor the moment I am gone. Tell him to send T'ing and Ling from now on to the sorcerer with wine, rice, and marmalade, because it would be dangerous for the village to deprive him of his rations, and not to forget the change of garments every Holiday of the Lanterns." Need I tell you that Chi Po no longer believed in any danger from the prevaricator on his mountain?

And need I tell you that he didn't return to the cave for a last farewell? He abandoned his paintings, his sheets of fine paper, his brushes, his inks, and all the rest. Was he not going to spend the rest of his life buried in the archives of Chang'an? His heart was broken, and he was angry too. The morning he left the village, he stood up in the cart where he had taken his place with the other pages, clerks, scribes, assistants, and assistants to the assistants and looked back toward the mountain where he had spent four years with the old bamboozler. And these were the thoughts that ran through Chi Po's head—thoughts he would sometimes share with his disciples in old age:

"Bu Fu, you lied to me for four years, and you failed me when I needed you most. You were not a sorcerer at all, but a lazy old clown who took advantage of a little boy. And now you have made me lose the most beautiful painting I ever created, and I am being carried away to Chang'an as an empty page and not as a glorious student. Keep all my other scrolls in your cave. Look at them now and then, and every time you do, may your conscience bite off another piece of your soul."

That was how bitter Chi Po was, while the cart, drawn by a pair of oxen, its axles creaking, rattled away from the village, taking him away from his home, his family, and his childhood.

nd then Chi Po was seventeen years old. He still lived in the palace of the Edict Compiler, where his first duty had been to carry huge tomes of ancient edicts to the Compiler whenever the latter needed to consult them.

Every time the Emperor launched an edict, the Edict Compiler went looking for any past decree that might perchance contradict the newborn one, and if he found one, he crossed it out with a thick line of ink. Done with his search, the good Edict Compiler added the new edict to the last volume with a much-admired fine hand.

Because 3,784,459 edicts had been launched since the days of Fu Hsi, the work went slowly, but the slow pace did not alarm him. He often said, while thumbing an old tome, "There is no hurry, no hurry at all, time takes its time in our timeless empire."

He was not sorry about asking Chi Po to work for him, for the boy was a quiet, reliable lad, reporting to work every morning, and friendly to one and all. Life in the country had made him strong enough to carry even the heaviest book of edicts without complaining. Soon he was entrusted with the Book of Decrees of the Emperor Hsuan-tsung, who, during his rule of forty-four years, had rained so many attractive edicts upon his land that his Book was now the heaviest of them all. But not only was Chi Po able to haul it up and down as if it weighed no more than a common brick, he quickly mastered its contents as well, so that if the Edict Compiler needed to ascertain whether Hsuan-tsung had ever proclaimed an edict concerning stray dogs (he had, in fact, sent out sixty-eight edicts on this subject) or concerning clogged gutters (a mere thirteen over the entire reign), Chi Po could put his finger on the desired rubric within the week, to everyone's astonishment.

As a result, from a lowly Blank Page, Chi Po quickly rose to the level of a Rough Page, and he was now a Title Page. At dinnertime he was allowed to help himself before the other clerks. He longed to be allowed to enter the Great Imperial Academy, but in the meantime, most evenings he stayed quietly in his own two rooms. He read the classics, devised passionate poems, dreamed of lakes, waterfalls, meadows, and hills—and, yes, he secretly painted them, for he had procured all the materials and tools he needed so that his destiny should be accomplished.

Other evenings—not very often, I hasten to say—he frolicked about town in the company of his fellow clerks. This merry band was usually joined by the lads who worked at the Ministry of Religious Rites, and all these happy-go-lucky nobodies strolled along the beautiful promenade called the Avenue of the Purple Bird, which is frequented by the no less beautiful ladies of the city and the fearsome officers of the Imperial Guard. Afterward they went drinking and dancing in more modest side streets, and there—but enough! Let us leave these gentlemen to their amusements; they are none of our business; and I know that you, dear readers, wish me to stick to the noble incidents of Chi Po's spiritual and courtly life. Chi Po himself, when he wrote to his parents—he sent them a letter punctually once a week—did not trouble them with nonsense. Instead, he shared his emoluments with them like an earnest and loving son.

He wrote to them, but he never asked about Bu Fu. When the old sorcerer came to his mind, it was only to remind him of the fatal incantation, and the peach blossoms lost, torn, or buried in the archives of the Lord Director of the Multitudes.

Chi Po had gone more than once to the offices of the Lord Director in order to find out once and for all what had happened to his scroll. Thanks to the influence of the Edict Compiler, he even succeeded one time in talking to the Lord Director in person. The latter blushed, whether in shame or in anger, and shouted, puffing his cheek, "What! Pillage the files?" and "Why didn't you make a duplicate, my little man?" The Edict Compiler was fond of his Title Page, but not wishing to make an enemy of the Lord Director, he asked the young man to be patient.

But in the end, the narrow-minded Lord Director could do nothing to keep Chi Po from being a painter whose name we speak almost next to that of Ku K'ai-chih. And it all happened because the Edict Compiler and the Lord Director both liked to eat clams for a snack at the office between meals.

One day the Edict Compiler ran out of clams and sent one of the rough pages to his colleague the Lord Director to beg three or four mouthfuls, "not without promise of amicable reciprocation in any similar contingency."

"With pleasure," said the Lord Director. "What shall we wrap them in?"

Oh Chi Po, you are innnocently carrying the Edict of Hsuan-tsung concerning the Amortization of Usufruct on your shoulders, and your mind is on the excellent wine you drank last night with your crowd at the Tavern of the Yellow Cat, and just now the Lord Director has asked, "What shall we wrap them in?"

"May I suggest this blotter, Your Eminence?" a secretary suggested.

"Will suck up the clammy juices," the Lord Director objected.

"May I offer my own bonnet?"

"I do not wish to see anyone without his bonnet in my offices."

"Oh! here is the gazette of the day."

"No; there's a cross-ideogram puzzle in it that I haven't even begun."

"Well, sir, perhaps we could rifle the files for an insignificant scrap of something."

"Files don't like to be disturbed. However, anything for a colleague.... Do it, man, but discreetly."

"Let me see. Here is the Urgent file; here is the Stagnant

file; here is the Dying file; and oh, ah, here is the Forgotten file."

"But is it permissible to open the Forgotten file, my dear secretary? That is very much like unforgetting it."

"Why, sir, we could assume our most distracted air and seem to be discussing an administrative problem while I fish out a scrap of paper for the clams."

"'Fish out something for the clams.' Heh-heh-heh," laughed the Lord Director, whose square face turned almost round.

"Ho-ho-ho, ha-ha, hee-hee, very good indeed, sir, you are a wit," said the secretary (who was no fool), pulling out poor Chi Po's painting. "Here is a daub of—I believe they are almond-tree blossoms. It will do very well, if I may allow myself the expression of a private but subordinate opinion."

"You may, my dear secretary," said the Lord Director, "and furthermore, I concur with you. Now let us choose five of the choicest clams and give them to this young page for our respected colleague."

The rough page naturally carried the package to his superior, Chi Po, who took it to the Edict Compiler, and no sooner was it opened than Chi Po said "Aah!" and fainted.

The Edict Compiler was surprised. "These clams are quite fresh," he said, smelling the clams, "why did Chi Po faint?" He clapped his hands. Two pages arrived and carried Chi Po outside, into the fresh air, on one of the larger compilations, while the Edict Compiler seized the first clam between two delighted fingers and opened his moist eyes on the succulent item.

And he saw—what *could* he see but the painting? Undamaged by the clams (thank heaven!) Chi Po's peach-tree branch glowed softly in the office of the Edict Compiler, and the ancient must and dust on the vellum all about him, and the frittered leather covers everywhere, seemed—was the Edict Compiler dreaming?—to receive and surrender a fragrance of country blossoms when the west wind fondles them. The Edict Compiler—the clam still suspended between his two fingers—recalled a pretty girl with raven hair he had kissed and pursued in—ah, how long ago! He thought of a pail of milk he had carried from a cow at the age of—long, long ago. He remembered romping in a meadow and doing cartwheels on the clover, that day—oh when, oh when? "Where am I?" asked the Edict Compiler, dropping the clam and looking about him as though he had just caught sight of a tomtit where his books of edicts lay.

He clapped his hands weakly, and two blank pages appeared. "Reactivate Chi Po and bring him to me," said the Edict Compiler dreamily.

Presently Chi Po entered, a trifle pale. "It is my painting," he said. "There is my seal."

That same evening the Edict Compiler served tea and almond cakes at his house, and he asked Chi Po to wait on his guests. He had invited the Subdirector of the Court of Sacrificial Worship, the Minister of Titles of Nobility, the Supervisor of War Machines, the High Commissioner of the Imperial Waters and Forests, and three young Advisors to the Grand Eunuch, all three full of waggish logogriphs and carriwitchets.

"I have purchased," said the Edict Compiler casually after the cups of fine porcelain had been filled a few times, "I have purchased a new painting to decorate my country house; quite a charming one, and, in my opinion, a bargain, because I believe it to be an authentic Li Tang." And he winked at Chi Po, whose hand was shaking as he poured fresh scalding water into the teapot.

" 'Authentic' is easily said," observed the Subdirector of the Court of Sacrificial Worship.

"Not as easily as 'real,'" retorted the wittiest of the young Advisors.

"However," said the Supervisor of War Machines, "it is imprudent to pass judgment upon an object before one has taken a personal view of it. I cite the thirty-third aphorism of Confucius."

Whereupon the Edict Compiler asked Chi Po to clear the table and unroll his scroll upon it.

"Bizarre!" cried the Minister of Titles of Nobility. "I find it very odd that a man should paint one branch of a peach tree and leave out the tree itself. It isn't natural, you know, for, as everyone knows, a branch is attached to a trunk. Still, if one *must* paint a single branch, I think this one is pretty enough, and if you didn't overpay your dealer, you will not disgrace your wall by hanging it. Myself, when I spend my money on art works, I insist on abundance. The more expensive the painting, the more things ought to happen in it. For instance, I should like to see a nest of birds in this branch, a few clouds behind it instead of all that white space which cost the artist nothing, and (I hope I do not shock you) perhaps a toothsome young girl playing the flute underneath, sitting on the grass. But I say again, if you *must* have a single peach-tree branch, this one will do."

"Unimpeachable, in fact," tittered the wittiest Advisor.

"It is true," said the Subdirector of the Court of Sacrificial Worship, "that one ought not to judge the value of a work of art before knowing its price. As I am too polite to inquire into the cost of this one, my dear Compiler, I must be allowed to withhold my opinion lest I should be thought an innocent for overvaluing a cheap painting or a vulgarian for undervaluing an expensive one."

"I agree," said the second young Advisor, who was less witty than the first. "And you?" he asked of the third one.

This third one was a timid youth. He blushed, and said, "I like it, I like it very much," and blushed even deeper.

Then they all fell to looking at the painting a little more, while Chi Po stood by, looking at *them* and wishing in his heart to call them fools, all except, of course, the timid one.

He hadn't noticed that one of the guests had not spoken— namely the High Commissioner of the Imperial Waters and Forests, whose name was Po Yang. The man had only smiled and stroked his beard. What a surprise when he finally opened his mouth! "My dear Edict Compiler," he said, "you are a rogue. This branch was not painted by Li Tang, but by a young living man, a remarkably gifted young man. It will be the pearl of your excellent collection. And now tell me who the young painter is, so that I may take him to my bosom one of these days and salute him."

Before the Edict Compiler could say a word, Chi Po had set down his teapot and flung himself at Po Yang's feet.

"And here he is indeed," cried the Edict Compiler, delighted to see the thunderstruck faces of his guests. "My discovery, gentlemen, let no one forget it. Without me, this village boy would still be milking cows."

"In my opinion," grumbled the Minister of Titles of Nobility, "all the boy has done is imitate the manner of Li Tang."

After that, all settled down to a respectable degree of merrymaking, including Chi Po, who had to sit beside Po Yang (himself a notable poet) and answer a hundred questions, but who didn't forget to thank the youngest Advisor and to promise him (in a whisper) a painting for his alcove representing a swan among the geese.

The very next day Chi Po became an Imperial Scholar at the Great Academy. Needless to say, its professors could teach him little concerning the ways of calligraphy and the depiction of nature. On the other hand, he had much to learn about the classic texts of the Empire. By applying his intelligence and the capaciousness of his memory to the tasks, he passed, not without glory, the examinations by means of which even a son of villagers can become a scholar and mandarin. Thus the Edict Compiler's prediction came true: the mayor of Chi Po's village began to bow to the lad's parents when he crossed them in the street, a bit overdressed, he couldn't help thinking.

quarrel full of refined courtesies broke out between the Edict Compiler and the High Commissioner of the Imperial Waters and Forests as to where the newly graduated twenty-two-year-old Chi Po should now take service: with the Edict Compiler again, at a level suitable for a freshly ordained mandarin, or with the High Commissioner, amid waters and forests. In the end the good Edict Compiler surrendered to the argument that the young man would be better off breathing fresh air than among even the most dustless compilations of edicts of the realm. The Empire too would benefit if Chi Po renewed himself far away in the countryside, just as, long ago, the little boy had stopped to study a dancing squirrel in the haunted mountain.

Of course, Chi Po made a present of the peach-tree blossoms to his benefactor. This scroll disappeared from view a few centuries ago; we know it only, alas, through the admiring descriptions made of it in its own time.

Chi Po now wore an embroidered gown with the widest possible sleeves and the bonnet of a Scholar of the Empire. He lived in a little house in the district of Eternal Harmony. Mornings he worked under the direction of Po Yang, afternoons he painted, or else he strolled in the gardens of Chang'an, studied the motions of monkeys and tigers in the Imperial menagerie, rested under a cherry tree while watching the ducks in the pond of the Forbidden City, and read the poems of Li Po or those of his director Po Yang. The latter often sent him on tours of inspection far from the city—there where the Spirit, which is everywhere, to be sure, is the least disturbed by our snorts, our grunts, our growls. I will not pretend that the waters and forests of the Empire made great advances under the direction of Po Yang and Chi Po, but the young man's brush took new vigor from their manifold music. Little by little his fame spread all over China, and this happened without bribing, flattering, lying, boasting, or slandering rivals—no, simply by painting well; for such a thing can happen in a place that is really far away from us.

Most marvelous of all, his name reached the ears of the Emperor, though it ordinarily takes thirty years for a commoner's name to travel from the Forbidden City to the Inner Palace and the Privy Closet.

When this happened, even the Edict Compiler began to speak deferentially to Chi Po. But nothing spoiled the young man. His words and voice were as sweet to the youngest page as to the mightiest minister. He loved long and peaceful conversations. When he was no longer the youngest at the table, certain disciples began to write down his thoughts—he himself has left us nothing in writing. Let me quote a few of them. "By planting the chestnut tree one makes the wind visible." "This sky is a blue skull, and I am the thought it has." Regarding the paintings he gave away to his friends: "Think of it! I am a guest in a dozen households at once." While the Emperor's generals levied armies, built walls, demolished them again, overthrew cities, plundered the enemy—and sometimes friends too, undoubtedly by mistake—Chi Po said, "Seeing what it is you see, I hasten to paint what it is you should prefer to see." But the only saying we find more than once, indeed again and again, in the notes of these disciples—hence it must have been dear to him—is this one: "World! I and my brush are thy contrary."

Finally, the Emperor even *saw* one of Chi Po's paintings. It was his *Weeping Willow Bent over a Pond*, a black and gray painting full of vanishments, mysteries, and unappearences. The view of this picture had instantaneously turned two minor officials of the court into monks at a distant monastery, where to the end of their days they led lives devoted to holy abstinence and brooding. I must also report that a princess descended directly from the emperor Yao, on seeing this picture, sent a venerable crone as marriage broker to Chi Po, even though the lad was a commoner. But he dared decline, and wrote her as follows in his best hand: "I owe your kindness, dearest lady, to the poor skill of my humble brush. But were I to possess the perfection of your beauty, I would forsake my brush, content to gaze upon you by day and by night. And thus, divine princess, in obtaining your favor, I should lose your favor, which alas, I esteem more than my very life." Which was not altogether true, but he remembered one of Bu Fu's aphorisms: "Truth is like a stranger knocking at the door. Be sure he means well before you open." Be that as it may, Chi Po sent the princess his *Sparrow Swallowing a Worm*, which has remained in the palace of her descendants to this day (I saw it hanging there during my last visit); for, although the lady was brokenhearted, the chronicles report that she married the Lord General of the Hinterland that same year, giving him in due course five future warriors and four ladies-in-waiting to be.

This *Weeping Willow* of Chi Po's bore another result. The view of it caused the Emperor to raise his left eyebrow. As Po Yang confided to Chi Po later, if the Emperor had raised *both* eyebrows, Chi Po might have been decapitated without further ado as a man too likely to cast a shadow on the monarch. Shortly after the eyebrow abated, the Emperor summoned the young artist to an audience in the presence of the full court; and Chi Po, who was after all a mortal like you and me, and who had left his village not so very long before, began to feel a little tremulous, for he was more comfortable with his brushes and his inkstone, and maybe a goldfish or two, than with exalted rulers.

And yet, although Po Yang was right, and a man might be decapitated now and again, the Emperor himself was a most amiable monarch. When still a boy—he was now in his fifties—his father had given him the Annals of the Empire to read, but the young heir had smiled and said: "Why should an emperor be arrogant and read books (especially books without pictures) when most of his blessed people cannot read at all?" This retort was repeated all over China, and the people began to love their future emperor even then for his modesty.

When he succeeded his father on the throne, the new emperor became famous for his skill at playing Folgo. This is a game you play with a stick, held in your hand, which ends in a little wooden tongue set at a right angle to the stick. Thus equipped, you strike a little ball into any one of several holes some distance away on the lawn. If the ball falls into a nearby hole, you score a few points; if it falls into a distant hole, you score a great many points; if it falls into no hole at all, you lose.

The Emperor played Folgo with his Privy Council, announcing his administrative decisions between one ball and another; for instance: "We will take your report under advisement," or "A commission is to be appointed at once." Of course he made edicts and laws and rules and decrees at other times too—in his bath, for example—but never so wisely as when he was playing Folgo and his nostrils were filled with fresh air.

On the day Chi Po arrived for his audience, he was received under the enormous tent which, when the sun shone, was stretched over the lawn where the Emperor played. The majordomo asked Chi Po to stand on one side while the Emperor attended to the day's business. His Majesty was surrounded by a number of courtiers and counselors who occasionally took their turns playing Folgo, taking care not to lose so very lamentably as to rob the Emperor of the glory of difficult victories over them.

To make a start, the Minister of Home Troubles bowed to the Emperor and groaned as follows: "Your Magniloquence, the peasants of Kuangtung have just risen in rebellion. They demand to be paid for the rice we have condescended to separate from them in order to feed our army. They have killed 366 lords, burned seventy-six palaces, and lost 26,000 of their own while running into our swords."

"Tell them on both sides," answered the Emperor, "that

in times of imperial stress, when the enemy knocks at our gates, we should all stand side by side, work hand in hand, march shoulder to shoulder, see eye to eye, bury our differences from coast to coast, and smile from ear to ear."

So instructed, the Minister of Home Troubles made way for the Minister of Foreign Troubles, who rushed forward and cried: "Master, the Siamese are marching north!"

"Why," asked the Emperor, "shouldn't they march where they please?"

"But your Magnipotence," replied the minister, whose tears were rolling down his cheeks, "*we* are north!"

"So we are," the Emperor exclaimed. "Let us cut into little pieces the generals who didn't order them to turn around, and then name a new flock to replace them."

Next the Minister of Economic Resources came forward and sighed: "Alas, Your Immensity, the Si Kiang has overflowed again; the crops are destroyed, the people starve, prices rise, faces fall, nothing but mud wherever you look."

"We must pray to heaven," said the Emperor, "and exercise moderation."

He was about to add a few useful precepts, when a man on horseback appeared in the distance, galloping furiously. The man stopped his horse at the edge of the lawn, out of respect for the Folgo game, dismounted, and ran toward the Emperor.

"Who is this man?" Chi Po asked the majordomo.

"He is the Emperor's Listening Post in Kabul. I fear trouble!"

By that time the Listening Post had reached the Emperor's feet, toward which he sank, allowing his forehead to smite the grass.

"Speak, speak, for heaven's sake!" the frightened Emperor exclaimed.

"A revolution in Kabul!" cried the Listening Post, raising his head. "Oh my Master, they have hanged the Caliph and all his cabinet excepting only the Great Ghazi!"

The Emperor grew pale when he heard this. Is not a

caliph somewhat like an emperor?

"Bless my ancestors!" he cried. "What crime did the poor Caliph commit?"

"His crime, Oh Master—chalked on a tablet hung round his neck over his white smock as he dangled from the rope—was to have been violently overthrown, as he himself confessed."

"No more Folgo today," cried the Emperor, grasping his Folgo stick with a trembling hand. "Proclaim our grief to the world and make it known that we cannot allow this act of bestial lawlessness to remain unpunished. We propose to enforce swift and decisive reprisals, and we call upon every civilized nation to join us in the most drastic measures."

A murmur of satisfaction rose from the courtiers. Chi Po almost forgot his audience, thinking of the poor Caliph and how sorry one always is to die. But strange to report, the Listening Post did not appear to share in the general approval. He came closer to the Emperor and signified that he wished to speak into his ear. "Son of Heaven," he whispered to the Emperor, "the new Caliph of Kabul has charged me to convey his sincerest effusions of friendship for our nation. Indeed, after impaling several elements unfriendly to us as a gesture of goodwill, he has sent the people of China, embodied in your person, a priceless golden chain which their god Ma-Mon used to wear when he went into battle against other gods. The man who wears it is twelve times more likely than common mortals to live to the age of one thousand. I am keeping the necklace, my Lord, hidden in the pommel of my saddle. I say no more."

The Emperor turned toward his courtiers and ministers. "Nevertheless, I repeat that we Chinese have no intention of interfering with the internal affairs of other nations, and we urge our allies throughout the world (as I said before) to adhere to the universal principle which, let me repeat, I mean—in short, I order everybody to stay home."

As no one objected to this policy, the Emperor turned again discreetly to the Listening Post. "How is it," he asked, "that the Great Ghazi was spared?"

"For humanitarian reasons, Master," answered the spy. "He was too ill to stand execution. But he will be hanged as soon as he recovers."

Thereupon he was ordered to return to Kabul after a change of horses and delivery of the pregnant saddle to the Emperor's private chambers.

Now that the day's serious business was ended, the Emperor turned to the courtiers, ministers, and commoners who had gathered round him, and holding a Folgo ball in his right hand and the Folgo stick in his left, he spoke as follows: "Justice, gentlemen, will be vindicated. Mothers will be respected, artificial-potato factories will increase their output, and I trust that the entire world will be our friend, with the exception of our enemies. We are rich, yet we will thrive; we are forward-looking, yet always optimistic; courageous, yet full of confidence; and though we will hold fast to the beliefs of our fathers, we shall not surrender to newfangled and alien doctrines."

Applause flew round the Emperor like a lovely diadem. Then an outdoors throne was set on the lawn and the Emperor sat down to grant audiences to his beloved people. That day, however, Chi Po happened to be the only person privileged to be addressed by the monarch. The majordomo announced him. Chi Po groveled toward the throne as decently as it is possible for a person to grovel.

The Emperor spoke: "Loyal worm, we have allowed our exalted eyes to examine your piece of brushwork, and we have found it meritorious."

"Worms, Your High Altitude, thankfully rejoice in the warming rays of the glorious sun."

"Loyally answered. Tell us now, who, and what is your father?"

"He is but a poor carpenter, Your Magnipotence."

"A carpenter, eh? To look at you now, young mandarin, one cannot but conclude that he touched wood when you were born, ha-ha-ha!" This sharp reply put the Emperor in high good humor, in spite of the hanged Caliph.

"However," he continued, "as the son of a poor carpenter, how were you able to learn the ways of a noble art so distant from your low origins?"

"I—my Lord—I—I hardly dare admit."

"Dare, my boy, dare away. I am not *altogether* inhuman, you know."

"I—a sorcerer taught me, Your Beneficence."

"A sorcerer! So...so...so..." said the Emperor. "And how long did you stay with this sorcerer?"

"Four years, Your Beatitude."

"That—he-he-he—that was quite—ho-ho, haw-haw—quite a spell!"

When the Emperor saw his people laughing even louder than he—several of the younger courtiers went so far as to roll on the ground—he suddenly gave his face an angry expression. "Stop this unseemly hilarity!" he shouted, half rising from his throne.

A dead silence fell on the crowd.

"We find," he said harshly to Chi Po, "that you owe your condition of mandarin to the magic tricks of a sorcerer, and thanks to this same sorcerer you have all but become Inspector of my Waters and Forests. It has also come to my attention that princesses fight for your favors. And you have almost bewitched *us* into the bargain. Perhaps we had better have you and your sorcerer hanged."

The courtiers and counselors expected the Emperor to order his guards to arrest Chi Po on the spot. But not at all. The Emperor was playacting. The thunderstruck look on everyone's face tickled him. He would also have liked Chi Po to bawl a little. But the brave young man had decided to stay calm and still.

"Well," said the Emperor at last, "you are not what I should call a gifted conversationalist, but we can't *all* be as amusing as *some*, for Providence does not allot its gifts in equal measure to all creatures. Let us proceed and show you an example of *my* magic. Since I am a true emperor, and a generous emperor, the eleventh of my dynasty (may it rule for all time to come), I shall now grant you any boon you choose to ask for within the limits of respectability. Withdraw yourself from our fair presence—the time has come, in any event, for the imperial nap—and deposit your boon with us in a week's time."

Thereupon Chi Po kissed the Emperor's toe and groveled his way out of the Folgo tent.

ny boon! Even any respectable boon! Chi Po strolled about the gardens thinking deeply and came to rest in the Hibiscus Pavilion. "I could ask," he thought, "for a set of new robes, a title of nobility, baron perhaps to begin with, or the vacant position of Commissioner of the Imperial Storehouses, where I could lord it over two hundred feverish workers. But if I ask for new robes, I shall have to buy a wardrobe to hang them in; if I buy a new wardrobe, I shall have to move to a house large enough to hold it; if I move to a house large enough to hold it, I shall have to employ servants in order to—enough! This is clutter, and Bu Fu always said: 'Clutter is good, but clear your head of it.'

"As for becoming a baron—I? Son of nobody? Everybody would laugh at me. Besides, did not a princess fall in love with me without a title? True, a title might impress the daughter of Po Yang, who is so beautiful but oh so cold to me, but I want her to love me as I am: nothing but a humble official and scholar with thick and thin brushes in his hand, who pours ink on blank scrolls. Did Bu Fu boast a title? Baron Bu Fu! What an amusing idea, though!

"What a horrid idea, instead, that of asking to become Commissioner of the Imperial Storehouses! I shall have to cringe to a superior, as I did to the clown who rules us; and what is even worse, I will see the man below me cringe to me, before he calls *me* a clown to his wife at the dinner table. As for storehouses, they are full of items of every description, and items of every description are the clutter that Bu Fu respectfully disdained.

"Furthermore, I would be in some danger of working and working and working, which is, according to Bu Fu, an undesirable condition, since, unlike cows, men and women do not need to eat all day long. It is true that a man who has both inferiors and superiors can refer most of his work either to the latter (for further decisions) or to the former (for implementation), and I am sure that I could become tolerably successful either way, but would it not be simpler not to become Commissioner at all? Am I not comfortable in the Waters and Forests? I have time enough to meditate in these Hibiscus Gardens, paint when the mood takes me, do a little good when I can, and spread no evil ever. To be sure, Bu Fu received his rice and marmalade for doing nothing except tell the village a few fibs, but then he is older than I and has had much practice at being idle.

"The Emperor threatened Bu Fu. 'Perhaps we shall do well to—' Alas! How could I have defended him? Didn't I myself thrust him from me? Didn't I curse him? And why? Because he was a mischievous, lazy old fibber. Mischievous, lazy, old? These are good things. Fibber? Not so good. Still, who made the village proud to have its own mighty sorcerer in the mountain? Who told me to empty my brain of clutter? Who gave my brush the Spirit? Who mentioned to me the fullness of emptiness and the emptiness of fullness? Oh, let the Emperor threaten! It is you, Chi Po, you who are much to blame. Who tormented Bu Fu into summoning the dragon? You did. And he tried to summon the unsummonable because he wanted to please you.

"And then the bulbul flew away. Do you remember Bu Fu's face (what you could see of it) when you told him that the bulbul had fled? And his poor tears when he confessed the terrible truth about himself? Perhaps he is dead, and you were not beside him to say thank you, my master, thank you, Bu Fu, greatest of sorcerers, you who made a little, stupid boy paint the spirit of the peach-tree blossoms...."

That is how Chi Po dreamed away the afternoon, sitting amid stones, plants, and breezes, and shaded from the sun. He bowed distractedly to the officials and the swans who passed near the pavilion, but he did not really see anything, not even the end of the day and the coming of night. He kept thinking about Bu Fu, who had been his master in spite of everything, and then he fell asleep in the pavilion without having had any supper, for Bu Fu had told him: "Supper will come round every day, but a thought to which you do not immediately attend may vanish forever."

By and by Chi Po dreamed of Bu Fu, whose eyes were now gray and whose hair was unlustered. Bu Fu said in this dream: "A young man should call on his old master before he goes on a long journey, and he should utter a courteous farewell," and he was shaking his head very slowly. Chi Po saw himself as a boy of eleven again, dancing before the squirrel as Bu Fu arrived, and this time when the sorcerer appeared Chi Po held out his little arms, but Bu Fu just kept shaking his head. Then Chi Po heard himself cry, and almost sob: "Master, master, thank you!" and that was not in his dream at all!—he had really said it aloud, so loud in fact that he woke up with a start. "Bu Fu is the greatest sorcerer after all," he cried, "and I have been a blind, ungrateful scoundrel!"

As he said these words, he heard a whistling in the garden. It was midnight. The courtiers, swans, horses, and cats had gone to sleep in order to be smilingly fresh for the Emperor's awakening tomorrow. But here was a whistling— none of your expert, delicate whistlings, but a good sturdy back-country sort of a tune—and here was a black shape flying in the black night—and here was the one-eyed bulbul landing on Chi Po's shoulder with a great flapping of wings.

The bulbul didn't look a bit aged, except for a few wrinkles and a gray feather or two. Perched on Chi Po's shoulder, he whistled like the wind through a crack in a door while Chi Po stroked his feathers, kissed his beak, and called him his old friend. "And now," said Chi Po, "we must return to the cave, for everything our master foretold is accomplished."

A week later, on the promised day, Chi Po presented his petition to the Emperor, who granted it even before the Folgo party was over, for he suspected everybody of knowing all about Ma-Mon's chain and was mortally afraid that Chi Po would ask for it. Of course, like any Emperor deserving of the name, he pulled a long face, scratched his august brow, and diddled with the Folgo ball before granting his boon. "My dear Chi Po," he said, "you have a talent for extraordinary difficulties. Where shall I find the means? However, when I bring to mind again your matchless 'Philosopher afloat'— afloat, I forget in what—I am ready to give you sun and moon." All the while, he was fondling the gold chain hidden under his tunic and thinking, "A thousand years on earth!"

But what of Bu Fu? How many years had it been since we last saw him? Is he still alive? Poor Bu Fu! He lay in his cave, moping the years away, so sad that he even stopped scaring the village, except for an occasional nightmare or a trifling curse. Since he had become innocuous, the village cut his ration of victuals in half, so that his mighty bulk diminished and his hair grew unlustered. His only true accomplishment in all these years was to consider the possibility of planting a few vegetables in a patch near his cave. But mostly he moped, and he longed for his bulbul and for Chi Po.

Now that he received but half his ration, T'ing came to the mountain alone; Ling stayed home. This way, Bu Fu had only half the news about the world. But still he heard that Chi Po had become a great man whose friends and enemies were only the best people, and that he sent a piece of gold to his father and mother every week.

Bu Fu had secretly broken, torn up, or scattered his retorts, alembics, trigrams, and cornucopias, and he had even squashed the Nine Amulets of Wen Ming without a squeak of protest from them. He kept only his fine Tao-tsi and the scrolls Chi Po had left behind. Whenever he unrolled them, he felt, as light as gauze, something of the Nameless Essence touch him, but altogether he was so lonely that he grew ever thinner and paler.

"What a calamity I have been!" he sighed now and then, and occasionally he spoke with a few birds, but they were pretty unintellectual compared with the bulbul.

However, one morning Bu Fu heard a distant sound of

drums, trumpets, cymbals, and bells, and then he saw a long caravan of richly dressed courtiers riding on magnificently caparisoned horses up the crooked path that went from the village to his cave. Who could this be? They must be from Chang'an, for no one in the village owned such golden robes, such silver headgear, such interesting horses, and such fabulous musical instruments.

On rode the caravan, with the happy fanfares making such a to-do that the mountain thickets stirred and the leaves shook their heads. At the forefront of the caravan flew the one-eyed bulbul, beating the rhythm with his wings, until, becoming impatient with the slow horses slouching uphill, he made straight off for Bu Fu and fell into the old sorcerer's arms.

"Miscreant, I forgive you!" Bu Fu cried, dancing with joy and almost flying off with the bulbul in sheer ecstasy. He rushed into the cave to bring out the very kennel the bulbul had always slept in. The bulbul too, beside himself with happiness, made a hundred delighted circles around Bu Fu's head, whistling like a dry hinge and stroking Bu Fu with his feathers. How pleasant reunions are! May you and I too meet again those we have lost!

But of course that was only the beginning. A gaudy cataphract was the first to appear before Bu Fu. He whipped out a long trumpet and blew into it as hard as he could, in case he might not have been noticed. Then he addressed Bu Fu. "Are you the sorcerer Bu Fu of the cavernous haunt?"

"I am he."

"Do you confess yourself a loyal subject of the Emperor, willing to shed your last drop of blood for him?"

"My *last* drop of blood is unstintingly his to command."

By this time the rest of the caravan had arrived. They all dismounted their horses and made a circle about Bu Fu, who wondered whether they were going to carry him off to be beheaded. "Oh, I deserve it," he managed to think between their questions, "but is that reason enough?" As for Chi Po, he kept himself hidden behind the courtiers.

"The Emperor," the horseman proclaimed, "having vouchsafed to hear reports of certain successful though widely misapprehended deeds of a preternatural character wrought by yourself, hereby appoints you to the post of Prime Sorcerer of the Empire. Signify your acceptance by kissing the Imperial seal at the bottom of this scroll."

Well, poor Bu Fu was all but dismantled by this speech. The bulbul looked knowing. Bu Fu stared at the man, the man stared at him, and the courtiers stared at each other. One might have heard a single one of the bulbul's feathers drop to the ground, had he lost any.

"He accepts!" thundered Chi Po, running to Bu Fu, who at first didn't recognize him. To be sure, it was the strangest morning that had ever dawned on the world. Chi Po fell on his knees before Bu Fu and cried out: "I am Chi Po. Your ungrateful disciple Chi Po. But now I have come to take you to Chang'an to be Prime Sorcerer and my master forever if you will forgive me!"

Now Bu Fu was no longer the sturdy terror of the village he had once been, so he sat down on a log and took Chi Po's head into his lap, while the bulbul squatted on his shoulder as he had been wont to do. "I am glad I am alive," he said, touching Chi Po's head. He was as pleased as he was old, and he was really stupendously old. Then he fell into a deep silence. The courtiers held their breaths. Here and there a horse neighed. But at last Bu Fu seemed to hear something for the first time. "Prime Sorcerer?" he asked. "Who?"

"You, Bu Fu, and no one else."

But Bu Fu looked at all the courtiers with alarm, and he leaned down to whisper into Chi Po's ear. "Can it be you, my dear Chi Po, you, my pupil, who urge me to become useful? Tell me rather your secret advice. My hearing is dull, but my nerve is keen."

Chi Po smiled, and placed his mouth over Bu Fu's earlobe. "Master, you shall be as useful as you desire."

"I accept!" cried Bu Fu, devoutly kissing the seal. All the courtiers applauded, the cataphract pranced, and the music started again. Mandarins bowed, trumpets shattered, horses harrumphed, drums caroused, the bulbul whistled, and Bu Fu was standing now, leaning on Chi Po and granting mankind his first official consideration.

Presently a bundle was made of Bu Fu's tattered belongings, the Tao-tsi and Chi Po's scrolls. The sorcerer was placed on a large, good-natured horse, and then the company took the road to faraway Chang'an. All sorts of ideas bounced around in Bu Fu's head. Now and then he stole a look at Chi Po to make sure that this elegant young man was really his little pupil. "My dearest wish, good Chi Po, is to continue to look after you, and indeed to guide you once more. For if the incantation I lent you took a little more time than even I, to speak quite honestly, expected, behold and admire its power, delayed but decisive! A pity I destroyed my faithful trigrams."

"You will have new trigrams in Chang'an, silver ones, too."

"Who knows? I've aged, my good Chi Po."

So they rode on a few miles. Chi Po took a detour to visit his parents, and then he rejoined the company. Bu Fu made him tell all that happened to him in the years gone by, until a few rather dark clouds appeared in the sky.

"Are there many storms in Chang'an?" Bu Fu inquired.

"Very, very few. Why do you ask, Bu Fu?"

But the sorcerer only looked thoughtful. Who can tell what he was thinking? Sometimes Bu Fu himself paid surprisingly little attention to his thoughts. He was not one for pushing thoughts to their conclusion on every occasion. Now and then he simply allowed them to go wherever they pleased. Be that as it may, after a while he opened his mouth again. "My noble friend, know that the unreality of dragons is essentially provisional and tentative. A dragon can, at the appropriate moment, choose to renounce the condition of not being. But what and when is that appropriate moment? Only a sorcerer—however, this is not the time for tedious arguments; I shall simply say that I remain at your disposal."

The harness bells jingled, the bulbul sang "Sweet Daisy of My Heart," the caravan marched on, and whenever they passed a village, one of the retinue blew into his trumpet or slammed his cymbals to show that while there's life, there's noise. But Bu Fu was mumbling all the time and allowing his horse to do the admiring of scenery.

"I might try my hand at an earthquake," he was grumbling among other things. "In an empty field, of course. At first." And he looked like somebody who thinks, "Have a care, citizens, I may decide to pulverize you a little with a bolt of lightning," and rather enjoys it.

Many days passed with the most amiable conversations imaginable, until they all arrived in Chang'an, where, amid celebrations possible to conceive but hazardous to describe, the All-High confirmed his nomination and gave Bu Fu the kiss of peace.

Though the chronicles fail to report whether Bu Fu ever did launch an earthquake, even a small one, it is known that he lived for many years thereafter, that he was the laziest minister anyone had ever seen in China, and that the bulbul grew shockingly fat. The Emperor, I am afraid, expired one afternoon when he mistook a Folgo ball for a large marshmallow, which proves that Ma-Mon was nothing but a ruffian. Fortunately, another Emperor took his place who extended his protection to Chi Po and Bu Fu. Of course, Chi Po continued to paint (I hope you have had the happiness to admire a few of his works), and even after his marriage to the daughter of Po Yang, every afternoon he and his old master drank tea together. They talked about everything in the world, and quite a few subjects *out* of it, but they never mentioned a dragon again.

APPENDIX
CHI PO AND THE SORCERER
1961-2014

Sometime in my thirties, on a train between New York and Washington DC, I was leafing through a little German book I had picked up I forget where and when—a modest Piper Verlag publication containing a set of vivid reproductions of watercolors by the great Ch'i Pai-shih (the current spelling is Qi Baishi), who died in 1957 at the age of ninety-six. "High the transport, great the joy I felt" as in the jostling train I looked at the pictures of blossoms and insects and wavy waters. The illustrations were followed by the briefest of biographical notices, but it reported that, growing up in a remote province of China, Ch'i Pai-shih had been taught, not by a prosaic brush-master but by a sorcerer. A poet's attention could not be but arrested.

I had long had a spotty knowledge of, but much feeling for, the arts of the Far East and the principles that govern much of it. I had spent a year in Japan, written an imitation of a Kabuki play (*The Monk Who Wouldn't*), and looked hard at beautiful Far Eastern things whenever the occasion offered itself; but even earlier I had fallen in love with Zen-inspired scrolls, refined porcelains, screens, inlaid lacquer boxes, and the like. I remember, for instance, an exhibit held in the lobby of a cinema in New York, on 57th Street, at which I stood motionless heaven knows how long, and how transfixed before the black-gray-white rendering of a snowy egret. I never could get enough of these birds and insects and flowers and monkeys and tigers, these tiny wise-bearded men floating in faraway skiffs on half-perceived lakes, these cascades more vapor than cascades, these white absences and vanishments, so alien to the art of my grosser culture, which, even in its most religious outpourings, revels in the solid and abundant good things of material life, and believes, in good thrift, that every nook of a canvas ought to be gratified with paint.

Be that as it may, several years went by before Chi Po (as I decided to call him), the sorcerer, the paintings, my bulbul, and certain half-serious, half-mocking views concerning "the world" harmonized and crystallized into the present tale. Written in a loft in Lincoln, Nebraska (a most un-Chinese place), the typewritten text began its life, rather oddly, as an extract in the December 1961 issue of *Harper's Bazaar*, sent there by the William Morris Agency, which (in those good days) represented me. I noted in my ledger that I was paid $350, minus $35 for the agency.

The little book itself was published by the firm of Charles E. Tuttle (Tokyo and Rutland, Vermont) in 1964, in a strikingly beautiful edition designed by Meredith Weatherby, with scroll-like illustrations by a Hong Kong artist, Lo Koon Chiu. I accepted the subtitle *A Chinese Tale for Children and Philosophers* suggested by the publisher.

The Tuttle edition remained in print for about ten years. In the decades that followed, I revised, revised again, and again revised the text, but without touching the beating heart that gave it life from the start.

I translated the text, now fully matured, into French sometime after the year 2000. *Chi Po et le Sorcier : Un conte chinois* was published by the Editions de l'Herne in Paris in 2004. Lo Koon Chiu, happily discovered to be as alive as the author, kindly gave the publisher permission to photocopy the Tuttle illustrations. As a result, the French edition bears a close physical resemblance to the *princeps*.

The History of
SIGISMUND,
Prince of Poland

Yo, acudiendo a mis estudios,
en ellos y en todo miro
que Segismundo sería
el hombre más atrevido,
el príncipe más cruel
y el monarca más impío,
por quien su reino vendría
a ser parcial, y diviso,
escuela de las traiciones
y academia de los vicios.

PEDRO CALDERÓN DE LA BARCA, *La Vida es sueño*, I, 708–17

This time, I shall tell you the strange history of Sigismund, son of Casimir V, king of Poland, such—more or less—as I had it from the mouth of Jan Modrzewski, antiquary in the town of Rzeszow, whose father had been the great childhood friend of mine. Jan told me the story over three evenings we spent in a modest restaurant not far from his shop. Now and then he would add a few observations of his own concerning this story. I have faithfully transcribed the ones I happened to remember.

The land, in those times of long ago, was the prey of infinite woes. Wherever you looked, the peasants were abandoning their fields to battle their lords with rakes and pitchforks, and to massacre them before being themselves slaughtered. From the south, the Turks, masters of Hungary, where they were busy compelling the Christians to convert to Islam, threatened to invade Poland. In the north, another threat came from Livonia, occupied by the Swedes, whose ambition was to impose their abominable heresy on all of Europe.

More than once, if truth be told, the king had thought of becoming a Muslim himself and allying himself with the Turks in order to chase the Swedes, or else to turn into a son of Luther in order to fight the Turks alongside the Swedes. He did neither (the Lord be thanked), but the great man felt capable of selling his soul to the devil, so mighty in him was the love of his country.

And yet, these disasters were but a foretaste of those that fell on Poland at the birth of Sigismund. After twenty-two years of efforts and goodwill, Queen Ludmila succeeded in giving birth to a big and pretty baby, but she died in childbirth despite the help of physicians, surgeons, midwives, astrologers, and the prayers of the archbishop of Gniezno, friend and confessor to the queen.

No sooner had the newborn uttered his first cry on earth than frightful prodigies were seen throughout the kingdom. A man was changed into an ass, blades of wheat sprung from the ears of a farmgirl, the waters of the river Warta leaped into the air, the earth shook from one end of the realm to the other, several roofs of churches fell on the parishioners, crows were seen carrying live coal in their beaks and setting fire to many a house, and fish began to walk in the streets.

The king thought he would go mad. But little by little his reason reasserted itself, and he summoned the dean of his astrologers, the celebrated Zbigniew of Grodno. "What do the stars say, Zbigniew, "what have you seen? Don't spare me. I am a soldier."

"Your Highness," replied the astrologer, "wise protector of Poland and the true faith, the steeple of the cathedral of Tarnow has collapsed, killing a crowd of the faithful who were praying for those killed by the collapse of the belltower of the cathedral of Lwow. Furthermore, little Sigismund, may God bless him, tore off with his teeth one of the two nipples of the countess Mathilda, who has the honor of breastfeeding the dear baby."

"And only twelve days old! I sense new disasters for our land," cried the king. "What do the stars tell us? Why don't you speak?"

Indeed, the astrologer seemed to be avoiding the mysteries of which he was the undisputed master. But in the end he was obliged to reveal what he knew. "Alas, alas!" he moaned.

"What does that mean?"

"Misery!"

"They're dethroning me."

"Curses!"

"They're murdering me."

"Horror!" cried Zbigniew, "bloody meteors crisscross in the sky, the most cruel conjunction is at hand, that of Saturn and Mars in Capricorn in their most fatal exaltation, while in the Crab, a constellation in the image of a dragon has appeared out of the void—"

"Enough allegories" shouted the king. "Tell me what you saw, and speak to me in plain Polish if you wish to keep that head of yours on your shoulders."

Offended, Zbigniew rose to his full height and spoke in the gloomy voice of a prophet: "Rising Sigismund shall torment Poland with justified plunder, virtuous rapine, and noble massacre. Moles shall grow wings. Eagles shall hide in ditches. And the prince shall thrust the king into the dust."

Having said this much, the astrologer resumed his normal voice and manner. "Pardon me, my Sovereign, pardon me, because those were the words of the planets, the comets, the stars, and of my sacred books!"

He thought that his last hour had struck. But the king looked blank. He seemed not to understand. He demanded that the astrologer repeat the message word for word, which the poor man did, trembling in all his limbs. "Pardon me, your Majesty—"

"Silence, rascal!" cried the king. "This flummery of virtuous rapine concerns some Sigismund past or future; it has nothing to do with me, no, not with me."

Hurt in the pride of his science, Zbigniew grew bolder. "And the earthquakes? And the fallen belltowers and steeples? And the fish walking in the streets? No, all-powerful Majesty, shy away from illusions, I beg you."

"So be it," retorted the king. "I'll rebaptize the brat. It was Ludmila who gave him his name. Didn't I tell her, just before she drew her last breath, 'Good heaven, my best, nowadays every second prince in Europe is called Sigismund!' It must have been a premonition. If necessary, I'll call him Jesus, and we'll baptize him a second time."

These blasphemous words could not appease the astrologer. "Beware of illusions, your Highness, beware of illusions! The stars don't like quibbles. Unlike the Sybil, they speak clearly. Sigismund or Je—or Charles—the baby they designate is ours whether we like it or not."

"In that case I'll kill him. Let him try to thrust me into the dust when he's dead! Go. Have captain Teczinsky come to me."

Terrified, Zbigniew threw himself at his lord's feet. "Do not blacken your soul with yet another crime, my king! Do not heed advice sent to you by Satan!"

Another crime? What was the astrologer thinking of? Alas, Casimir knew it only too well. Excommunicated by the pope because of the too swift departure from the throne of his predecessor—from his life too perhaps; so rumors had it— but why stir up old stories? The king had dipped generously into the public treasury to offer fine gifts to the pope's nephews and nieces, which had allowed him to receive the Host once again. Needless to say, the king had understood the astrologer. He wept as he answered him. "Oh my sins, my sins! In spite of the churches, the abbeys, the convents and the hospitals I founded, my soul is no better than a cesspool."

"Imagine, in that case, my lord, the murder of a newborn who has but one nipple on his conscience!"

The king was still weeping. "My little Sigismund, my pretty babe! What to do?"

"Always do what is good, and think of your soul's salvation."

"And the salvation of Poland? Is that not more important than my own? Virtuous plunder! Noble massacres! I who detest guessing games! Explain! Interpret in God's name!"

Zbigniew was making the gesture we are all familiar with, that of raising his shoulders while stretching out his two arms with upward palms, when a stunning thunderclap and an uncanny lightning bolt struck the castle as though from nowhere, for there was not a cloud to be seen in the darkening day. It was, obviously, a divine manifestation. The two men rushed to the royal chapel and fell on their knees before the altar. Thunder and lightning doubled in strength.

"Zbigniew!" suddenly exlaimed the king as he raised his head. "The thunder comes from the Tatras.... Something is looking for me from those mountains.... Mary Mother of God, pray for us.... Let us pray, Zbigniew...."

They did so. A terrible stroke of lightning ran through the chapel, followed by a yet louder clap of thunder. But after that, only a strange grumbling sound was heard. It seemed to say something to Casimir. "It is a message from the caves of the Tatras," said the king. "I hear it.... I understand it.... Yes.... We must spare his life yet bury him...."

All of a sudden the heavenly growling ceased. The chapel became stiller than still.

ittle by little, as time will have it, King Casimir grew old—old but yet vigorous (he still led the boarhunt), and, for the rest, remaining an excellent ruler, especially for the nobility. He still mourned his beloved Ludmila, and a groan escaped from his throat when he thought of the child he would have loved to hug. For he had borne no other. No lady of the court (nor none other) had gratified him with a baby—a bastard, to be sure, had such a child been born, yet unquestionably a prince. The only object of his paternal tenderness was his niece Estrella. As for the good Zbigniew, alas, he was no more. The king's chief astrologer had fallen backward from a ladder in the royal library while trying to grasp, on a high shelf, the eloquent *Nobilissimus liber de arte moriendi* of Johannes Nide. He lost his balance, and his skull fatally struck the marble floor.

After his death (allow me, said Modrzewski, a short detour not devoid of intellectual interest), a loud quarrel divided his many admirers and his three or four enemies. Zbigniew had prophesied, in November, that he would die the following summer. He fell from his ladder on the ninth of June. His detractors concluded that he had misread the stars ("as usual," they added under their breath), but his admirers argued, to begin with, that the distance between the ninth and the twenty-first of June was not worth mentioning, and furthermore, that the weather had been abnormally warm in early June. Be that as it may, the astrologer's prediction had given his wife ample time to prepare, with suitable discretion, widow's weeds that were judged in the best taste by the court.

I return to Sigismund. A false funeral had been held for the babe. He was kept carefully away in a pavilion not far from Cracow, and the rumor was spread that the child was, perhaps, the fruit of an illegitimate passion between a distant parent of the monarch (who was not named) and her butler. When this affair began to be forgotten (albeit this sort of forgetting is seldom complete, and the guilty make a mistake when they put their trust in it), Sigismund was carried to the foot of a forbidding cliff at the frontiers of the land, and chained to a cave. The gentleman charged with this mission was the baron Szymon Klotalski, lord of Zakopane. The few trusted men whom the baron employed had no reason to doubt the scandalous romance; the like happened so often!

So here is Sigismund, in his twenty-first year, dwelling in the land of wolves and bears, chained to his grotto. The chain was long enough to enable him to take the air, and even to walk about a little. At one end it was thrust deep into the stone wall of the cave, at the other it clasped the young man's ankle. By means of a sinister key, it was changed once a month from one ankle to the other, but in order to do this, four soldiers were not one too many to compel the prince, for he struggled mightily during the minute or two it took to shackle him once more.

Indeed, the prince had grown into a colossus. Michelangelo would have admired, perhaps loved him. He exercised powerfully every morning. I mentioned bears, because they were abundant in the surrounding mountains. Well, I do believe that Sigismund could have wrestled down the biggest of them. At the same time, this giant was a cultivated man. Casimir had no intention of turning him into a savage. Klotalski had given him the Gospel to read (he knew it by heart by the age of eighteen), together with the most edifying saints' lives, the best works of history (especially, of course, the glorious history of Poland, without, however, coming too near present times), collections of poetry and romantic tales of adventure, lives of great men, treatises of military and diplomatic strategy, and (needless to say) the finest texts that Athens and Rome have bequeathed to us.

The chain was a long one, as I said, and on sunny days Sigismund read his books, seated on a bench, his elbows resting on a long, rough pinewood table. Nearby a brook of the purest water ran over the stones. Father Radim, like Klotalski a man to be trusted, celebrated mass for him every Sunday, and took his confession twice a year. I said he was a man to be trusted, but he too knew nothing, or wanted to know nothing. He did not care whether Sigismund was the offspring of an illicit passion, or a princely baby-hostage seized from the Swedes. It was enough for him that here was a soul that needed to be groomed for paradise. Hence he had seen to it that on a tree trunk near the cave were nailed a great wooden crucifix, a splendid image of the Virgin, and the portraits of several saints whose regard is worth securing. As for Klotalski, he had caused to be nailed, on the next tree, a superb full-length portrait of the king—in full regalia—recently painted by the Venetian Tomaso Dolabella.

Clad in skins, kept in good health and well nourished, the young man's body naturally began to feel other needs. To satisfy these, Klotalski, as soon as he became conscious that the boy had become a man, brought in a woman—the only woman, presumably, he would ever see in the flesh (many girls and ladies stared at him from the engravings of his books). Her name was Layla. She was a chubby Turkish slave, cheerful, not too young, not too fine looking, who undertook to play all the needed roles. She was mother, mistress, nurse, cook, barber, chambermaid, and, in Sigismund's eyes, something of a sorceress. For, although the herbs, roots, leaves, flowers, and stalks that she gathered in the forest and mountain did wonders for his meals, his fevers, and his scratches, he couldn't help being a little afraid of her. "Medea!" he would throw at her head when a bizarre flavor tickled his palate—though without hurting the poor woman's feelings by explaining who that wicked creature had been. Also, it was obvious to him that she avoided Father Radim as if he (saintly man!) had been a sorcerer.

To be sure, she couldn't have answered him, because

she was mute. Oh no! It was not the Christians who had perpetrated this cruelty. I am sure it was not. It is simply not believable. Fortunately, being dumb didn't prevent Layla from making herself understood. Together with her grimaces and her gestures, her hm, hm, hm translated quite effectively her wishes and her moods. "I'll baptize her and marry her," Sigismund often reflected, "as soon as I've shaken off this damnable chain." Of course, he knew from his books as well as you and I that there lived in the world women more beautiful than Layla. But so it was. He liked roundness, and he had read, in I don't know what philosophical text, that the sphere is the perfect form. I believe that Layla would have laughed at the notion of marrying Sigismund, but she wouldn't have refused him, because the virile young man knew how to please her. For the time being, however, she counted rather on Klotalski's promises, which included a mound of ducats and a gilded coach to take her home to Turkey as a lady.

It goes without saying that Sigismund had learned how to use a sword. His master was Klotalski himself, an old hand, whose age no longer allowed him to spit Cossacks and Tatars, but who brought to his pupil the experience of a lifetime.

At some distance from Sigismund's cave (and the narrower one in which Layla lodged), a royal patrol saw to it that no one would ever come near the mysterious prisoner, on pain of death if he tried. The distant sound of a trumpet regularly announced the arrival of Klotalski and his escort (with or without Father Radim) and the welcome new supplies for the two hermits. That was the only music known to Sigismund, except for the Turkish ballads Layla hummed on many an evening, accompanying herself on an old half-broken lute or a cracked tambourine.

One fine summer day, when nothing in the air hinted that destiny (if you'll permit me the use of this pompous word) was preparing tremendous changes in Sigismund's life, that same trumpet brought him out of his cave, rattling his chain. "Layla," he shouted, "where are you hiding, you heathen trollop? Nosing about the forest to pick more poisonous plants? Come back and prepare a snack for Klotalski, his ruffians, and myself."

Presently the master of Zakopane made his appearance through the trees at the head of a squad of soldiers and flanked by a grim-looking personage, holding a whip, whose title was Master of Peasant Discipline. The men, though well armed, were carrying a load of supplies which they took to Layla's cave, as they had done many times before. Afterward, they and the Master of Peasant Discipline sat down at a table nearby.

"Greetings, my son," said Klotalski when he arrived, hugging Sigismund, "let's sit down."

The truth is that the compliments that passed between the two men were not of the same nature. For Klotalski, Sigismund was a precious charge, a symbol of the crown's trust in the provincial nobleman he was, and almost a son. Instead, Sigismund felt a mixture in his soul of filial attachment to and hatred of his jailer, a feeling of respect and a feeling of contempt, in a complex of emotions hard to disentangle.

"And how are we today?" asked Klotalski cheerfully.

"Ask me *what* are we today," was the gruff reply. "We are a prisoner. Worse than a wretched caged lion."

"You don't look wretched to me, my boy. You look as vigorous as a lion with a goat in his belly. Enough banter. Have you read your Hecataeus?"

"I have. And I have a high regard for ancient history; but I prefer the current one. Did the crown assessor stop at Zakopane to see you? What did he say? What's new at court?"

"Gently! Yes, he did me the honor of sleeping in my house, and he did pass on a bit of gossip. It appears that the tsarevich Astolof, who left Moscow two weeks ago, has arrived at Lwow perfumed from bonnet to boots in order to please our Princess Estrella."

"A toyshop prince," said the young giant disdainfully. "Besides, everybody knows she has been Bogdan Opalinski's mistress."

Klotalski pretended not to have heard these last words. Sigismund knew too much about that traitor against his own class, that noble rebel, lover of the mob, whom as a child the king had dandled on his knees. "Perfumed or muddy, better that the Russians marry us instead of joining with the Turks against us."

To which Sigismund replied: "Poland would be better off if, instead of hiring a mincing prince, it launched me, Sigismund, to crush the Turks."

A mere bystander would have felt that a prince of the blood, unaware of himself, was saying these words. So at any rate, thought Klotalski, not without a grain of secret pleasure which I will be explaining to you in a while. "That's all very well," he said, "now recite Hecataeus."

"One moment. First tell me: is Opalinski approaching Cracow at the head of his bands?"

This time Klotalski became angry. However, Sigismund gleefully noted in the baron's face not only anger but also fear and helplessness.

"Don't meddle with what doesn't concern you!" Klotalski thundered.

But Sigismund stood up from his bench and shouted: "Long live Bogdan Opalinski! Death to the oppressors! Oppressors like yourself! No more chains!"

And he rattled his chain like a bell that sounds the coming of freedom.

"It's been two months," said Klotalski, "since you felt the whip," while, from the other table, the Master of Peasant Discipline made as if to take that instrument from his belt, and the brawny soldiers of the escort got ready to turn their hands into fists. Fortunately Layla arrived in time with a mighty tray of soups and wine for everybody, and the Master and soldiers sat down for their refreshment.

"Greetings beautiful lady and thanks!" said the baron

with a chuckle. He patted her backside and slipped three zlotys into her hand.

"Hm, hm, hm," said Layla, who had a happy disposition with or without zlotys, before returning to her grotto.

The two men began to eat and drink. "And now," said Klotalski, "recite."

Sigismund was in no hurry. He lifted his spoon. "Who am I, Klotalski?"

"Always the same question!"

Sigismund held his eyes on the baron's. "Son of a king? That one's bastard son?" And he pointed his spoon at Casimir's portrait, which stared at them from his tree. "Kidnapped by gypsies from my cradle? Or by yourself, traitor I'll strangle the day I discover your crimes!"

"Blusterer! The whip is too mild for you. I don't know who you are." (Klotalski didn't mind lying.) "I know only that my orders are to keep you alive and far from the world—and we both know the reason for *that*. I obey my superiors without asking questions. Did you or did you not study your Hecataeus?"

"Book fourteen. I have it by heart. 'The night when Palakus, king of Scythia, received the Abyssinian ambassadors, he offered a banquet of a splendor unknown outside of Egypt. A hundred dancers—'"

He was interrupted by Layla's return with a dessert of blueberries and cream, which pleased the baron. He asked Layla to sing. The Turk went to fetch her lute, on which she tinkled as best she could an ancient Ottoman lament, humming all the while almost melodiously, while Sigismund recited. "'The ambassadors were dazzled by a hundred dancers of both sexes, an orchestra of innumerable harps, trumpets, oboes, and drums, and a feast that lasted till dawn. At sunrise, as they were leaving the table, with their dignity intact—for they had eaten and drunk prudently, fearing that their reason might founder—'"

"I interrupt you, my boy," said the noble tutor, "in order to urge you to admire that coolness of mind of the ambassadors, which no man who serves the State should ever lose."

"Do you believe everything Sir Greek tells us?"

"Perhaps not, but what counts is the moral idea behind his tale, whether quite truthful or not. Go on. You are the owner of a prodigious memory. I wish I had a fifth of yours."

"Tell me, tyrant, when will it be my turn to hear the trumpets and the drums and the harps? I who hear nothing but the howling of the wolves in the mountain, and *this* music, *this*?"

And he furiously rattled his chain. The escort and the Master looked and listened.

Klotalski's only reply was: "Are you raving or do you continue?"

"So be it. 'Leaving the table' and so forth, 'the king of Scythia spoke as follows: the luxury of which you have been partakers, gentlemen, this pomp, this magnificence, all this is but vanity. When you return to the emperor of Abyssinia, tell him above all that in our Scythia all men are equal–'"

"What?" Klotalski interrupted again.

"What do you mean, 'What'?"

"What you've just recited, are you pretending it's in Hecataeus?"

"Where else, damn you? Do I have it from Layla?"

She had stopped singing and plucking her lute and was listening. Klotalski turned sharply to her. "Get out of here," he shouted, "go back to work!"

"Don't bark at Layla," Sigismund cried out, "and listen closely to what the Greek has to say."

Sigismund stood up from the bench, and leaning on the table with his two hands, his head close to that of Klotalski, he continued from memory: "'No unjust taxes are extorted here from the people, the farmers own their land and eat when they are hungry, our artisans are honored and well paid, our kings are elected by the entire population, and those are the reasons we sing and dance; and I myself, king that I am, on the day our good Scythians name my successor, I shall mount my horse and become again the simple scout I was before they chose me for the throne.' "

During this speech, Klotalski had remained at first as though stunned; then he grew red with rage; his cheeks seemed to swell. At the last word, he struck the table with his fist so hard the bottles, glasses, and dishes danced, and he too stood up, nose to nose with Sigismund. "Damn God and Christ if you're not lying!" he yelled, though at the same time he crossed himself because of his blasphemy.

Sigismund's voice rose as high as the baron's. "Nobody dares accuse me of lying," he cried, and he would have tried to throttle Klotalski had not the Master of Peasant Discipline come running from the other table (followed by the soldiers) and struck Sigismund in the back with his whip.

Looking around, Sigismund saw that he must yield. He sat down again and brought his voice down to a growl. "Long live Hecataeus," he brought out. "He will be my tutor when I become king. No more chains! As for you," he said, turning around to face the Master, "I will have you cut into small pieces."

The Master smirked and went back to the other table.

The altercation between the older and the younger man had not been the first one in their lives, far from it. But both calmed down as quickly as they flared up.

"Show me the book."

Sigismund and his chain dragged back to the cave, whence he returned with the offending work.

"Open it where I placed the bone from the chicken I shared with Father Radim."

Klotalski skimmed the famous fourteenth book. He shook his head. "This translation was made by a traitor. It is false. Don't ever forget that a king is a king and a peasant is a peasant. The Holy Ghost was not elected by kings, and peasants will never elect kings. Enough."

Sigismund's voice became soft. "Klotalski."

"Yes, my boy."

"You must be *somebody* in the capital. A governor. A minister. Perhaps you are my father."

"Alas, I have never been married," said the tutor naively. "It's one of my lifelong regrets."

"So...who am I? Tell me this at any rate: do you know who I am?"

Telling the truth is commendable. Obeying the king is more so. Klotalski had to lie once more. His voice was now as soft as Sigismund's. "I swear to you that I don't know. And I'm not *somebody,* my lad. I'm only a minor provincial nobleman. I was chosen to guard and nurture you because they knew, up there in the capital, that I was covered in debts. Because of you, I've been able to repair my roof. So there you have your tyrant's portrait."

Part of this speech was no lie. Thanks to the king's great obligation to the baron, the rain no longer penetrated Klotalski's ancient castle. It penetrated, at any rate, much less.

An immense sadness took hold of Sigismund. "Birds, wolves, butterflies, fish, the river itself are free. Why am I, a being made in the likeness of God, highest in creation, why am I held by a chain? What have I done? What is my crime, other than that of having been born? But that's a crime I share with all of you, and yet you are free!" And he gestured toward the other table, though he spoke too softly to be heard by the soldiers.

Tears came to Klotalski's eyes. "Need I remind you, my poor child, that at the moment of your birth, a voice coming from Heaven, and countless prodigies on Earth, declared that, whoever you might be—the king's son, a peasant's baby, the offspring of a Jewish peddler, what do I know?—you were destined to inflict the most frightful calamities on Poland? I tremble when I remember that the king's astrologers foretold, looking at the firmament, that you would make our monarch himself crawl at your feet. A clamor rose that you must instantly be killed. But Christian charity prevailed. The child was brought to these mountains. And that is all."

"That is all," repeated Sigismund softy, his cheeks in his two hands, weeping.

How often had he not heard this story! But he didn't believe it. He, son of a peasant, a peddler! He who felt capable
of defeating Alexander!

He dried his tears, but his voice continued soft—the voice
that moved Klotalski more than what he heard when the
young man bawled and menaced. "You were afraid to beget
a monster, yet in chaining me to that cave you created that
very monster. For that is what I am. Resentment and hatred
fill my soul; they frighten me. The voice the king heard,
Klotalski, was not divine. It was the voice of Hell. It tempted
the king and he succumbed to it. Had that child been treated
with love from the day of his birth, his virtues as a man
would have driven the Devil to despair."

I believe that Klotalski was about to reply that a good
Christian has no business troubling himself with theological
speculations, when, suddenly, the shrill blast of a trumpet
put an end to the conversation. Neither man could guess
that, from that moment, everything was going to change for
Sigismund, everything was about to end, and was about to
begin.

"Let me go, ruffians, beasts, take your hands off me, leave me to going on my way!"

Such were the outcries of Agafya, a young woman I haven't the time to describe to you just now because of the hubbub of her arrival. In unison with her, two of the king's soldiers, who were holding her in their clutches, were yelling, "Shut your mouth, woman, you're standing before the chief!" While behind them, another soldier was leading by its bridle a large horse, the kind one imagines more readily hauling a barge along a canal than prancing in the Viennese ring of the Habsburg. The poor horse was adding to the confusion by neighing his distress with all the might of his humble lungs. The young woman, on her side, who is more easily imagined at the tiller of that same barge, pipe beween her lips, than sipping a chocolate at a Habsburg afternoon, kept screaming, struggling, and babbling in broken Polish. Sigismund and all the others looked properly amazed, as did Layla, who came running, a kitchen towel in her hand.

In a few seconds, Klotalski took hold of himself. "Silence, woman, peace," he shouted, "and you, soldiers, give me a full report."

"My lord," said one of the men, "this here prisoner was comin' down the mountain like somebody what wishes to see us. We pulled her off her nag—specially Kristof here who is the strongest, because the woman's a fighter, no joke! and so we brung her to you, and here's the knife that was tucked in her belt."

While the soldier was telling his story, Agafya twisted and wriggled and yelled, while now and then turning around to blow a reassuring kiss toward her horse. But how can I describe all this aloud, one event after the other, when five or six things were happening at the same time? I would draw a picture if I knew how!

I may as well interrupt this turmoil to tell you that the first thought in Sigismund's head had been: "How skinny she is!" followed by an appreciative glance toward his Layla. But in fact, Agafya was a handsome, robust girl, with blue eyes, a sturdy bosom, strong-muscled legs, and a merry round face, surrounded by a mane of blond hair covered now with dust. Her ruddy cheeks suggested a state of unassailable health, her rugged hands that of hard work in the fields since childhood, and her coarse, restitched garments that of modest means at home. Her only jewel was an ivory cross she wore around her neck. Why was this foreign young woman riding a horse alone across the most remote Polish mountains? Might she not be a spy disguised as a peasant?

"Who are you?" asked Klotalski in his best voice of judge of the peace of his province. "What are you looking for in these parts? Where do you come from? Know that you are about to be put to death."

Indeed, the two soldiers who held her fast were now training their pistols at her head with their free hands. She wasn't flinching, however. But she couldn't hear the Master of Peasant Discipline whisper into the baron's ear: "Right. She must be shot without speeches. You know our strict orders, my lord."

Sigismund did hear. "You hurt that girl, scoundrel, and you'll weep the rest of your life."

"Keep your tempers, all of you," said Klotalski, and he repeated his questions.

"It's easy," said the young woman. "My name is Agafya Matveyevna Kulkova, and I come from my dad's big farm near Pochinok. My mare, she's called Bialik, at your service, and don't nobody be daring at hurting her."

"What is this Pochinok of yours?" Klotalski inquired.

"She's a town in our holy Russia, may God bless her," proudly replied the girl.

"How is it you speak such good Polish?"

"Because I had a Polish grandmother what teached me before dying at seven years old."

"And whither were you riding when we caught you? Speak the truth."

"That's easy too. I was on my way to Cracow."

"To do what, peasant-girl?"

"Yes, peasant-girl, my lord, but with my honor which was besmirched and which I'm to Cracow traveling to avenge."

Sigismund became agitated. "You're a victim! Like me! Look!" And he made loud the dismal music of his chain.

"I seed it, and I'm all goose-pimpled to see what I see. It ain't natural. Where am I anyway?"

The Master of Peasant Discipline was growing impatient, but Klotalski's curiosity prevailed. "You're in your grave, girl, if you lie to us. Speak. Tell us your story."

"Damnation," shouted Sigismund, striking the table, "how can the girl tell her story with two pistols aimed at her an inch away from her head?"

"All right, all right," said Klotalski, who had already understood that the girl was no spy. "Let her go, men, and let her breathe."

The moment she was freed, Agafya made a little curtsy, thanked Klotalski and Sigismund, kissed her cross (proof that she was not a bad girl), rubbed her sore arms, and went to stroke Bialik's muzzle before returning to her interrogator. At that moment, Layla appeared with a bowl full of milk. Agafya drank it thirstily and hugged the Turk. "You're a kind one, you are!" This sent to Sigismund's heart another wave of sympathy for the intruder.

While this was happening, Agafya, no fool she, reflected that talking about her grievance and grief might make helpful friends of these people.

"We're listening," said Klotalski.

"Somebody besmirched my honor, sir. Sure I'm not the first girl that ever done the wrong thing, but like my papa said, I had to saddle Bialik and go find justice in Cracow."

"From your farm all the way to Cracow! Not bad! So

then, a handsome visiting Pole betrayed you?"

"No, sir, one of our own, a true Muscovite, one that's visiting Cracow; and I can tell you he ain't awaiting for me!"

She enjoyed all these men hanging from her lips, as they say, including the soldiers. Only the Master of Peasant Discipline looked grim, for he saw that the most absolute royal command, namely to kill any intruder on the spot, was being more largely ignored by the minute.

"I gather," said Klotalski, "that one of the tsarevich Astolof's followers is the guilty party."

Agafya burst out laughing. "Followers, ha, ha, ha! The one that's doing the following is me what's standing here!"

Nobody understood.

"Perhaps," ventured Sigismund, "the lass doesn't know what a follower is."

"Yes I do," retorted Agafya. "I'm not a cretin. I can read. We own three cows and five pigs and almost no debts. I know a follower when I see one, and mine is none of them and it's up to you to help me in order to comsempate me for the fright you've done me and Bialik."

"You're not a little crazy, woman?" This time it was the Master of Peasant Discipline who spoke.

"Yes I am, sir whip. Crazy. Crazy about Prince Astolof! Yes, it's him, it's him! That knocks you down, don't it?"

Indeed. Like a cannonball. A circle of open mouths. Agafya exulted, and she repeated, "Yes, it's him, it ain't no follower, it's him!"

Sigismund was the first to recover, so to speak, from this *coup de théâtre.* "I believe you!" he cried. "Compel the tsarevich to marry you! And after that, come back and unshackle me!"

The Master of Peasant Discipline had another whisper for the baron's ear: "A bullet through her head, because the girl is going to provoke a scandal in Cracow."

"True," grumbled Klotalski, but the idea of a scandal in Cracow had a quite contrary effect on him, an effect that would have dumbfounded the Master had he guessed what was going round in his chief's head.

In the meantime, the loquacious Agafya chortled. "Yes, let him marry me, but I'll see to it that he gives me at least a rich boyar to patch up my honor. Oh, when I think of it! My blood boils. Not a flower he gives me. Not a pair of earrings. After three months. Four months. 'How dare you, trollop!' is what he flings at me next time I catched him riding his horse across the fields. 'You've been dreaming, my lass! Your lover he put powders and stuff in your wine, and you thought you'd slept with a prince.' Well! It's him that will think he's dreaming when he catches sight of me in Cracow!"

Her words delighted Sigismund. "Go, my beauty, and jump at him while he's courting the heiress."

Klotalski said nothing, because the crafty lord of Zakopane was dreaming too.

"Silence!" he said at last. "Listen, Agafya Matveyevna Kulkova, "there seems to be a bit of truth in the story you've told us. Enough, at any rate, for me to take you along with me to Cracow, where it so happens that I need to go. And if you behave, I might even present you to the king."

Agafya could not thank the baron enough, and Sigismund, rather surprised, congratulated him. "For once a semblance of justice," he said.

The Master of Peasant Discipline thought that his chief had gone mad. More so when Klotalski returned the prisoner's knife to her.

"Is that a purse hanging from your belt?" he asked.

"Yes, my lord.

"Full of golden ducats?"

Agafya burst out laughing. "I wish! But never mind. I've got kopecks enough in it to keep from starving to death. Besides, where I'm coming from, we're used to not eating much."

This didn't keep Klotalski from slipping the girl a fine gold coin. "With this you can rent lodgings and buy diapers for the tsarevich's little heir, if the need happens to arise."

Agafya had a sense of humor. "Don't worry," she said,

"I like to joke too," and the coin went diving into her purse.

Now the baron took Agafya a little to the side, out of hearing of the others, who could do nothing but look on and wonder. "Tell everybody you meet in Cracow loud and clear what has been done to you. It will help your case. And I do not object at all, in spite of certain threats you've heard, if you talk about everything you've seen here. Hush. That's between you and me."

Turning back to the group, Klotalski gave orders to the king's soldiers to take Agafya to their encampment, allow her to wash, feed her and her nag, and, in short, treat her like the next queen of Muscovy.

After offering to kiss the feet of Klotalski and Sigismund, Agafya left with her escort and Bialik. She had almost vanished into the forest when Sigismund shouted after her, "And tell the king that Sigismund is waiting for him!" She turned to him without understanding, of course, smiled and waved, and disappeared.

Klotalski brusquely ordered the Master of Peasant Discipline and the other men back to Zakopane (the scoundrel promised himself to send an eloquent denunciation to the king), and remained alone with Sigismund and Layla.

"Do you really intend to present that Amazon to the king?"

"Perhaps."

"What are you hiding from me, you old fox? All of a sudden you're a friend of Casimir."

"I have told you a hundred times that I hardly know him, and that he knows me almost wholly by my reputation. But while the girl was babbling away, I kept thinking, why not combine matters—my autumn instructions concerning yourself, a lawsuit that's been dragging for years, and the grievance of that poor peasant-girl. Casimir is just. If she's not lying, he will be magnanimous to her, if only to protect Astolof from a scandal that would be bothersome at the time of his betrothal to Estrella. And then, damn it all! she will be grateful to me. I would like that."

This last phrase surprised Sigismund. "At your age?!"

"Laugh at me if you will. However, I assure you that I'm a man built just like you. True, I've turned fifty (he was sixty), but that's not old. You have your Layla, I have no one."

Layla took Sigismund's hand in hers.

"Away with you, heathen!" shouted the lad with a laugh. "As for your honor, only you and God know who was the first to besmirch it!"

But as Layla, laughing heartily, was returning to her cave, Sigismund grew serious again. "Baron, you can't hide from me that you're a schemer. I don't know what wiles you're dreaming up just now, but something has happened since the coming of that Agafya. I see it in your face. Tell me what it is." He expected no answer.

"Sigismund," said Klotalski, and then he paused. The young man's eyes opened wide. Klotalski spoke gravely. "If our monarch deigns to let me approach him, I shall fall on my knees and beg him to set you free."

Klotalski saw Sigismund's lips tremble, tears swim in his eyes, his body shudder, and one of his hands grasp the edge of the table, as though he might faint.

ack in his Zakopane manor house, two hours on horseback away from Sigismund's cave, and having placed Agafya in the hands of the old housekeeper, Klotalski gave himself up to a deep meditation, sunk into the leather chair in front of the fireplace which was his best thinking-spot. Summerlong it was the cat Popiel who occupied the place of the logs. Klotalski looked at him without seeing him. Agafya appearing out of nowhere had clarified in him ideas that had nothing of Venus in them—a Russian peasant-girl, excuse me!—ideas of a political cast which had been rolling idly in his head for a year or two, purring as it were like Popiel half aslumber, but which now spoke to him with a voice of thunder. The promise to Sigismund had been unpremeditated and spontaneous, and yet that year or two of thinking, and the coming of Agafya, made its utterance at the same time fated, inevitable.

"Bring back Sigismund," he thought. "Away with Astolof! Agafya's denunciations will cover him with ridicule. Her chatter about what she witnessed around the cave will help revive the rumors which have never died about a certain prisoner shackled in a faraway place. A few retired guards have blabbed, in spite of their oath, and wondered aloud, in this or that tavern, about the identity of the mysterious prisoner...."

Indeed, the opposition exploited these rumors, for it disliked the plan of a union by marriage between a Polish niece of the king and the son of a tsar. The opposition! Here Klotalski's ideas turned black. This was no longer a matter of sticks and rakes. Today, led by the greatest traitor, the unspeakable Bogdan Opalinski, an army was on the march, an army that cackled about charters, representation, unjust

privileges, redistribution, equality before God and king—
incredible!—and the honor of the poor, like that Russian girl
born in the mud who talked about her besmirched honor;
should one weep or laugh?

"So be it," he mused. "She will help us discredit the
stranger who wants to head our armies and marry our
princess, and who may some day want to succeed Casimir
and subject Poland to Russia. Never! Sigismund! Sigismund
shall lead our armies. Prince and later King Sigismund!"

Klotalski saw himself in conference with the king, whom
he knew, need I tell you? far, far better than what he reported
to the prisoner. Popiel was surprised to see lips moving
without making a sound. For the lord of Zakopane was
rehearsing in petto the speech he intended to deliver to the
king. "Sire, Sigismund will be twenty-one years old this year.
Call him back to you. The time has come to defy the oracles.
I do not deny that at the hour of his birth, they frightened
us all. I myself, a youthful counselor at the time, stood out
among those who wanted the baby put to death. But those
years were an age of darkness. Who believes anymore in
oracles and prodigies? Our lackeys, our peasants! Great God!
We believe in our own Kopernik. Our neighbors of Bohemia
admire the other one—I forget his name—Klepper or Pekler.
People of any rank feel at ease with the constellations—they
spy on them with lenses! Furthermore, may I remind your
Majesty that the Church never trusted astrologers? Bring
back, bring back your only child, your beloved son, place
him next to the throne, place at the head of our army a
colossus from our own earth and blood. Returned from
the dead, he will appear before the people as a miraculous
being, one who will reanimate our demoralized troops in our
struggles against the Turks, the Swedes, the Cossacks, and
above all against that murderous philosopher whom I do not
wish even to name. And allow me to remind you that over
the course of years, I have filled your son's spirit with ideas
suitable for a young prince, haughty and imperial ideas that
shall make of him Poland's eagle."

Klotalski noticed that Popiel was eyeing him. His lips stopped moving and rising from his ample chair he walked to the window ("Aha! Another broken pane!") in order to be quite alone with a few other thoughts. He, tutor, guide, guardian to the prince and benefactor to Poland, trusted advisor to the monarch, was he destined to remain for the rest of his life the plaything of chilling drafts on his Zakopane estate? Certainly not! A nobler fate awaited him in Cracow. But silence! Klotalski told his thoughts to be still, because sometimes it is best simply to know that they nest in the spirit's depths, ready to render service, without the bubble and babble of "in so many words."

So Klotalski knew what to do when, a week or so later, he arrived in the capital with a few retainers and Agafya, newly dressed in a pretty red and blue garment sewn for her at Zakopane. But a great surprise awaited him at court. Although the tsarevich had yet to arrive (he was detained by the ceremony of the opening of the first bridge ever built over the Dniepr), the king fretted over the marriage he and the tsar had projected. In his mind he dismissed some minor worries, to wit that the tsarevich was known to be *coquet* and overly amorous, not to say downright lecherous, and that Estrella was still in love with the renegade Opalinski. Incidentally, she made no attempt to conceal this attachment, but fortunately she was not a doll, she had told him in plain words that love is one thing, marriage another, especially for a king's niece. One did not sacrifice the chance of ruling Muscovy for the sweets of a romance. No, what worried Casimir was precisely what bothered Klotalski (and many others), namely the notion of an alliance with Russia which, in the long term, might prove fatal to Poland. Especially in the absence of a Polish heir. And yet, a Polish heir existed. In secret. Dangerous. But who else should be leading the Polish armies and ascending the throne?

Seated at his table in the Hall of King Piast, the king received Klotalski, who still wore his travel habits, and, in the distance, near the door, an unknown girl. In spite of her boldness, Agafya felt a little intimidated by the capital, the castle, the salons, and now, before her, the king. What a distance from her farm! All the same, the thought of confronting Astolof gave her the courage which only a conscience at peace can provide.

From afar she curtsied to King Casimir the way a girl

does to the mayor of Pochinok. Klotalski, on his side, rushed up to the king's feet, or rather to that of his desk, but the king rose, went round the desk, and took the baron in his arms. He hugged his old friend and comrade, but his look was somber.

"You are too kind, your Majesty," said Klotalski. "I deserve punishment, not love; I disobeyed your commands; the girl standing over there..."

"Come, my old friend," answered the king, "let us sit here, and tell me quietly."

The two men sat themselves in an alcove.

"My lord, the girl saw and heard the fettered prisoner, and I spared her life. Require mine; it belongs to you."

As I said before, this interview was going to astonish Klotalski. Well then, to begin with, instead of rising in fury, the king showed no particular emotion. He listened without especial interest to the story of the Pochinok peasant-girl and Prince Astolof. Still, he signaled to the young woman to come near. She did, and, motioned by Klotalski, knelt before the monarch.

"I hear that the son of the tsar has taken advantage of you, young woman."

"Yes, your Highness. I'm but a sinner, but he is worse."

"And you would not be ashamed to tell your story before my noblemen and before the bishop?"

"No, your Highness, I will tell everybody everything until justice is done to me."

"What about the strange man you saw in the cave? What are your thoughts about him? Tell me the truth."

"He is so handsome and so good that he deserves being your son."

Klotalski grew pale, but the king responded with a sadness that struck his vassal. He said simply, "They know how to turn a compliment in your Pochinok."

"It's the truth what I said to you," answered the girl.

"Good."

The king called a page, to whom he entrusted the girl. "Tell mistress Wanda that this girl is under my protection.

Let them give her honest work to do for the princess, lodgings under the roof—in short, all that is needed. And you," added the king, looking at Agafya, "trust me, you shall have justice."

The king and the baron remained alone. The king drew a letter from his pocket which he had nervously crumpled. "Read," he said.

God almighty! Klotalski learned that of the five thousand men sent by Casimir to crush Opalinski, half had gone over to the rebel and the other half had fled before his hordes of peasants. General Chodkiewicz had been made a prisoner and beheaded by one of the peasants. Six castles had been burned to the ground, their noble owners executed, their land distributed to the villains.

Klotalski remained speechless. The king's whisper sounded as if it came from beyond the grave. "I am bringing Sigismund home. The disasters predicted by the stars are nothing to those that are befalling us today. I consulted the bishop. He says: 'Let the firmament go about its business; you, be virtuous and defend the Church against heretics and rebels.' In short, I am bringing Sigismund home. My blood calls for my son. I want to hold him in my arms. I want to beg for his forgiveness. He is my heir. Let Astolof marry Estrella, but that is all. I shall welcome him, he will learn from us what is Polish courtesy, but it is not for him to lead our armies. To do that we need our own hero, a Polish hero. You and I are taking the road together to Zakopane, and from there, to the future Sigismund III. May God forgive me. May my son forgive me...."

The king did not notice Klotalski's stupefaction. The latter could only mumble, "I too, I too..." as he kissed the king's hand.

Needless to say, he felt a touch of disappointment, you can guess why, but he was about to suppress it as a loyal subject when he heard his lord say, "As for you, you will not be forgotten. Not forgotten, lord of Zakopane and Count of Transylvania."

Klotalski burst into tears.

Sigismund was tall, powerfully muscled, and fierce, but he was also as sensitive as an ailing child. The sudden appearance of Agafya and what had happened from that moment kept him awake all night. He rose in the morning unwell, unable to exercise and pray, incapable of study. The air was too warm, too humid. The chain tormented him. He wanted to escape into the forest, over the mountain, to Arabia, to the Indies. Layla watched him wandering to and fro, rattling his chain, and muttering menaces, promises, prophecies. Now and then he stopped to fix his gaze on the portrait of King Casimir nailed to a tree, as if to discover a resemblance—for, naturally, there *was* a resemblance! That evening, a fever laid him low. He was shivering in spite of the warmth that remained in the air. Worried, Layla wondered, should she look for the soldiers, those coarse and wicked killers of Muslims? Why, she knew far more than they and their doctors! So thinking, she went into the forest looking for the curative plants her people had given her as a child. She didn't remember them exactly, but she trusted her instinct, not understanding that instincts can deceive.

Returning with I don't know what roots, leaves, and herbs, Layla made Sigismund drink a concoction, which, seeing that it seemed to make him a little better, she strengthened the next day. And again the day after. Sigismund became pleasantly calmer—and drowsier. A good sign, thought Layla. In the end, he sank into a motionless sleep that lasted two days and two nights. Layla watched him in terror. What if he died? She herself would perish of grief and remorse before Klotalski's men could cut off her head. Fortunately, Sigismund rose out of his sleep cured of his fever and as hale as he had been the week before. Still, all during that sleep, he had been possessed by a fearful dream that shook him to the roots of his being. I shall tell you this dream as honestly as I can. But the question remains, was that dream sent by Lucifer, who seldom forgets us, or by the Lord God, who sometimes remembers us?

Ah the ribbons, the lacework, the gold embroideries, the feathers, the crimson silks, the shining velvets, the neat moustache, the lovely sword (it must have cost the Russian state the worth of a year's fieldwork of twenty peasants), the breast-worn brilliant Grand Cross of the Virgin Girdle, and, needless to say, the perfumes! The impression Prince Astolof makes on the Princess Estrella is, shall we say, odd as he showers compliments upon her. Estrella is beautiful, as befits a princess, but her aspect is sober and severe because she wears a dress of a coarse fabric partly gray, partly brown, and partly black. For the young woman is four times in mourning: first for her father, the second for her mother, the third for Bogdan Opalinski who has forsaken her in order to make war on Poland, and the fourth for that very Poland, bleeding from many wounds.

Estrella stares at Astolof's moustache, whose wings extend far to the right and left, terminating in the finest of points. She watches the moustache bob up and down as the tsarevich speaks. "How sweet is your name, Estrella, for it means 'star' in Italian! Howsoever, my pretty compliment fits only half of you, since your eyes are *two* stars that shine with a celestial light. Thus, Princess Twin-Stars, at your approach, trumpets and drums are heard, while the birds and the fountains greet you as if astonished, the birds becoming fountains of feathers, and the fountains turning into liquid birds. All rejoice: the drums because you banish night, the trumpets because you spread your wisdom over the land, the birds because you soar above all other women, the fountains because of the swiftness of your mind. But better than all these, behold a prince at your feet, and this prince is I Astolof, yearning to exchange Muscovy's harsh steppes for the ravishing enchantments of mighty Poland."

The princess will not be left wordless, and she knows how to keep, as they say, a straight face. "My heartfelt thanks, Prince Astolof. The elegance of your speech, of which I am unworthy, suggests that Muscovy, far from being as harsh as you judge it to be—albeit I beg you to note that I have not enjoyed the privilege of traveling to the east of Poland—you are perhaps aware that I come, on my mother's side, from an ancient *Spanish* family—"

"—of the purest Christian blood!" interjects the prince.

"Hence," continues Estrella, "I have journeyed only in the contrary direction. Nevertheless, the delicacy of your compliments reveals a court deeply penetrated by the humanities and sensitive to the light of high culture. Never again will I believe the reports that your worthy father impales his prisoners."

"Oh my princess! Your words fill me with joy. A glorious future rises in my imagination. You, heiress to King Casimir, I, young Caesar—for, allow me to inform you, Tsar and Caesar are one and the same word. I and you, united in a single kingdom, shall vanquish the Swedes and the Turks, heathens who refuse to believe in God, we shall terrify the Habsburgs, Prussia will beg us for alms, and I would myself become a shining estrella were I not troubled by the miniature of a man hanging against breasts which, I am sure, eclipse the whiteness of the swan. During the splendid feast given in my honor last night, I was going to beg you to dissipate the mystery when the Governor of Cracow interrupted us. Does this image, the fiery lover who speaks to you must hope, represent a deceased brother, or a regretted cousin?"

"Tsarevich," replies Estrella, "my duty forbids me to keep secrets from you, and if our respected Governor had not—but here comes another interruption, for my uncle is joining us."

As she speaks, the royal guards open the double door for the king. The latter affectionately embraces the two young persons. "My dears," says he, "I count on you to distract me from a most painful session with my counselors."

"Secret matters, dear uncle," asks Estrella, "or concerns that you can share with us?"

"Considering," adds Astolof, "that shortly—what I mean is, sooner or later, or rather, as I hope and pray, not before a hundred years from now—I and Estrella will have the sad duty of taking these matters into our own hands."

"Of all my worries," says Casimir, pretending not to have precisely heard Astolof, "the worst is due to the gentleman you wear so proudly round your neck."

"At last!" cries out Astolof, "at last I will know who my rival is."

"A penniless exile," answers Estrella. "This portrait is but a relic, a vestige of my childhood. We were both sixteen years old. It is the woman who marries you, my lord, not the child."

"I bend, but I do not break before a miniature," proclaims the tsarevich. "Furthermore, I hope that my ardent kisses and burning caresses—"

"Sir!"

"No, no, I insist. My kisses and caresses—preceded, need I say it, by all the rites of religion, for I am punctual in the exercise of my devotions, in Moscow, every Sunday—but where was I?"

The king is about to pick up the thread of the prince's discourse when the assistant to Gedko, maître d'hôtel of the royal house, enters, announcing that dinner will be served in one hour.

"One hour!" cries out Astolof, growing pale. "Allow me, sire, allow me, princess, to withdraw so that my valet and my hairdresser may have time to refresh me for the royal table." He kisses the tip of two fingers, sends them the kiss, and flies away.

Uncle and niece look at each other with a sigh. Each waits for the other to speak. The king sighs again and says, cheek in hand, "The tsar forgot to inform me that his son is an idiot."

"*You* forget, dear uncle, that one doesn't need a brain in

order to be prince."

"And yet you, my girl, you are at one and the same time princess and wise, except when it comes to the miserable outlaw you nurse at your breast."

"The outlaws are outlaws because our laws think of them only to make them suffer."

"Have you forgotten how many noblemen he has killed? How many Jewish merchants? How many artisans? How many serfs, yes serfs, who were defending their masters?"

"Cost what it may, the wars of the downtrodden are just. No more chains!"

"Principles! They excuse anything!"

A painful silence follows. Then: "Tell me, my dearest uncle—"

"What, my love?"

"Is he near Cracow by now?"

"Perhaps. If so, will you run to him?"

"Never. I shall do my duty."

"You are sublime! But what else can I do? Have I another choice? Who will help us against so many enemies, if not the tsar? If you knew, oh if you knew.... I dream of ending my days in that humble cell the good Cistercians are keeping for me at Oliva, where you can see the Baltic spread almost at your feet. I would abdicate, like your august relative, the great Carlos of Spain. Prayers and rest.... Astolof will prance on his horse across Poland, spreading perfumes on the way, and you will vanish into the forest with Bogdan and make him forget, by means of those ardent kisses and caresses mentioned by the tsarevich, the massacres he has in mind."

"Bogdan no longer believes in love," says Estrella sadly.

"Another idiot."

Estrella tries not to be angry. "Let me go dress for dinner too."

"Wait," says the king.

But he keeps silent for a long minute. Estrella looks anxiously at him. Finally he speaks in a low voice. "Perhaps what I did twenty-one years ago was a crime. Perhaps? No. It *was* a crime."

Estrella doesn't know what to say. She does better than speak. She takes the king's hand in hers and holds it tight. Casimir continues. "I can yet undo this crime. My son is alive and God forgives. That voice from the stars came not from Heaven, it came from Hell. It tempted me and I succumbed. I want to take back my son. I want to give him the crown."

"That son of yours," says Estrella, "is fated to make you crawl at his feet."

"I consent," replies the king in a voice infinitely weary.

Thereupon, a servant announces the unexpected arrival of the baron Szymon Klotalski, accompanied by a young woman. To Estrella's surprise, the king suddenly looks radiantly happy. The reason is that for him, the sudden appearance of the faithful tutor is a clear sign of the divine will. Were he not king, he would run into Klotalski's arms instead of merely rising from his seat to welcome him. "Come here, my friend, come here!"

Klotalski approaches the king and at the same time signals to Agafya to stay in the background. The king won't let him kneel. He clasps the baron in his arms. "Welcome, welcome! But is our Sigismund well?"

Klotalski now kisses the princess's hand. She too greets him with pleasure. "Something is troubling you, baron," she remarks, however, more attentive than the king to the visitor's mien. "No bad news, I hope?"

"Sigismund is in the best of health," replies Klotalski, speaking to both, "but all is not well, I do not deserve your welcome, I disobeyed orders, I must be punished." And he points to Agafya, standing near the door through which they entered. The king questions Klotalski, who tells him all that has happened near Sigismund's cave. The baron both accuses and excuses himself for not having had the girl executed on the spot. He had pitied her. "She is a simple peasant-girl, talkative, but devoid of malice. She was coming alone from Pochinok and riding toward Cracow when we caught her tumbling down a mountain on her horse."

"What was she looking for in Cracow?" asks Casimir, who would have been disturbed by this tale in the past. Now, at this critical moment, it has left him nearly indifferent.

"She is looking for compensation for her besmirched honor, your Majesty."

"And who was it who besmirched her honor?"

"I hardly dare tell you, my lord."

From afar, Agafya, who has heard nothing precise, but who understands that they are talking about her, cries out: "I done nothing bad!"

At just this moment, Prince Astolof, twice as elegant and perfumed as before, returns to the salon. Agafya utters a yell that is heard in the cellars of the palace, a yell seconded by that of the tsarevich, but that one in a register of utter bewilderment: "Agafya here!?"—an imprudent exclamation!

"It's him, it's him," cries Agafya, throwing herself like a tigress at her seducer. The astonished king has no more than a second to order, with a gesture, two guards to keep the girl from tearing at Astolof's cheeks.

While she struggles and spits a hundred accusations, the prince screams: "Go away! Take her away! I don't know her!"

More amused than surprised by the dramatic scene she is witnessing, Estrella cries, "But, prince, you yourself just named her!"

Astolof mumbles and stutters. He would to vanish from the salon, but he dares not move and must listen to Agafya continuing to vociferate: "Liar! I looked for you and I found you! Not even a flower! Promises! And I'll make you pay!"

"Come to me, my poor girl," says Estrella, and you (addressing the guards), let her go, let her breathe."

She has Agafya sit on a low stool at her feet, and calms her by caressing her hair. "Justice will be done to you, never fear. What did the prince promise you? Tell me everything."

"He was going to marry me off to a boyar at least," whimpers Agafya.

"A boyar!" cries the king, "the girl is mad. Why not the

tsarevich himself? She needs to be locked away."

"Thank you, sire," says Astolof, "and chained to the wall."

Agafya is really weeping now, and Astolof feels encouraged. "Princess," he says, "do not allow these sordid stories to soil your ears. Stories of peasant-girls who attempt to break out of their base rank by inventing—whatever they can think of. It is truly nauseating."

"He is lying, lying, lying," utters Agafya between sobs.

Estrella is still stroking her hair. "Indeed," she says, "I feel a kind of nausea mounting in my soul. And I announce that from now on, this girl is under my protection."

King Casimir shrugs his shoulders. He has more important matters to think about. It is Klotalski, silent up to now, who responds to Estrella. "Entrust the girl to me," he says. "I shall keep her at Zakopane. She will be well taken care of, very well taken care of, in my home, at my table, in my—in short, she will have no regrets."

Astolof, who has moved closer and closer to the door which leads to his suite, looks relieved, but the others seem a little embarrassed. "At your age?" asks the princess. Needless to say, her remark pleases neither Klotalski nor the king. Estrella blushes. As for Agafya, she turns to the princess with a grimace. Not for her, the baron's proposal!

"Would you like me to take you into my personal service?" asks Estrella. "You will serve me breakfast, and my chocolate every afternoon, and you will speak to me in Russian, so I can begin to learn that language, which, it appears, I shall be needing presently. You will be well paid, your life will be far sweeter than it would be were you to marry one of those drunken boyars—they all beat their wives—and after two years of service, I propose to send you back to your country with a fine dowry which, assisted by your beauty, will fetch you a solid husband adorned with *genuine* qualities."

She accompanies these last words with a meaningful look at the tsarevich.

"Madam," says the latter, who does not understand

meaningful looks, "you shall be but coarsely served, and you will learn a Russian spoken only by clods."

"My heart goes out to clods."

"I shall teach you *our* Russian."

"When the time comes."

"So be it," says the prince, and, turning to Agafya: "Are you happy now?"

"I am, but no thanks to *you*."

Agafya, in fact, has decided that by remaining in the palace she will be able to pursue her campaign against Astolof. As for serving chocolates to the princess, why, she had rather take the road back to Pochinok.

Diplomatically, she expresses her gratitude to the princess, not without an embellishment: "Take care, madam, that he don't hoodwink you like me, you're too good for him."

On her way out, held fast by a halberdier, she springs free of the soldier, runs at the terrified Astolof, and hisses "I ain't finished with you!" before the soldier catches her again and pushes her out the door, cursing at her between his teeth.

Astolof feels that a speech from him is wanted. "Your Majesty, Princess, and you, sir, whoever you may be, I assure you that the farmgirls of our country are not in the habit of complaining about gentlemen who deign to notice them. I blush at the carnival you have witnessed, for it has given you an undeserved picture of our people, so submissive by nature."

To which the king replies: "I hope, my son, that a dinner enhanced with good wines will soothe your spirits. I mention it because for the past ten minutes I have watched with one eye Gedko in person by the door signaling discreetly but with despair in his countenance, that the meats are losing their taste. Let's go! You, my dears, precede us two elders. I have a few words to say to my faithful Klotalski, and then we shall join you."

Astolof offers his arm to Estrella, a trumpet sounds, and they walk together to the dining room set out for intimate repasts.

Klotalski expects to be severely reprimanded, not only for his failure to keep intruders away from Sigismund but also for having provoked a scandal, in the presence of servants and guards, that belittles the Russian prince. He is opening his mouth when the quicker king speaks.

"Your sudden arrival is a sign of God. A sign added to the others. I defy the stars. I am bringing back my son."

Klotalski is too overcome to answer.

"Are you listening to me?"

"My entire soul is listening to you, sire."

"Let what happens happen. At dawn tomorrow you will return to Zakopane. You will have received from my doctor a satchel filled with a powder that Medea would have recognized. You will pour it in Sigismund's jug of wine at suppertime. During supper, you will speak to him of the glorious victories of Casimir Jagiello over the Teutons. Of the heroes of Antiquity chronicled by Hecataeus. Of the passages in the *Iliad* in which Achilles kills the enemies of the Hellenes but shows himself full of pity for old father Priam. Of the love of Telemachus for his father Odysseus, and the latter's love for *his* father—I forget his name, you will find it for me. Of pious Aeneas for his father Anchises, whom he carried on his shoulders through rubble and ruin. Gradually Sigismund will fall asleep. His sleep will be long, nothing will be capable of disturbing it. So sleeping, you will bring him to me. We will put him to bed in a sumptuous apartment. When he wakes, he will be rendered the homage due to the heir to the throne. He shall be told, however, that everything that is happening, everything that he sees and hears, might be but a dream. We will observe him. We will draw conclusions. If, after all, the stars spoke true, if the horrors they predicted do manifest themselves over Poland and over my own head, a second potion, kept by my physician in reserve, will plunge Sigismund once more into a profound sleep. He will wake up chained to his cave again. He will remember his brief princely life as the strangest dream ever staged in the theater of the human brain. Do you pledge yourself, Klotalski, to serve me in this enterprise, as you have served me in all my others?"

The baron throws himself at the king's feet and takes his hand. "I am yours body and soul. May God bless your virtuous design."

"Tonight," says the king, "I shall inform the tsarevich and the princess. Tomorrow morning, knowing that you are on your way to the Tatras, I launch a solemn proclamation from my balcony, addressed to the people of Poland. The Muscovite will have to wait. We will encourage him to conquer as many ladies and maidens in our palace as will allow themselves to be vanquished. If my colossus of a son vanquishes our enemies, we shall no longer need the tsar nor his boy, and Sigismund will marry Estrella."

"Amen," says the lord of Zakopane. "Amen."

On their way to the dining hall, the king, his arm around Klotalski's shoulders, whispers to him: "And in a month or two, I will send you the Russian girl."

"You are too kind, my liege," replies Klotalski, who cannot foresee that destiny laughs at his aging concupiscence.

igismund is dazed and dazzled. He thinks he is dreaming. Can that be himself reflected in the great mirror before which he stands? He is dressed as magnificently as a prince of the blood should be. The rose-hued feather that rises a foot above his cap makes the colossus even taller. In the same mirror, a step behind him, he sees a tall thin gentleman, mature but not elderly, whose hat is also plumed but whose feather, red rather than rose, must consent to rise to a somewhat lower altitude than Sigismund's. At a respectful distance, the prince perceives several courtiers, guards and servants—few people, for the prince, just now awakened from his mysterious slumber, and just now dressed, must not be alarmed. In truth, Sigismund's sleep still lingers in his brain.

"You.... Who are you? I've already forgotten," he says, staring into the mirror.

"I introduced myself, Prince, the moment you opened your eyes. I am Poland's chancellor, Florian Zamoyski."

The chancellor does not like having someone say (in a rude voice, besides) "Who are you?" but he hides his displeasure and hopes that the others in the room have not noticed the rudeness, nor the absence of resentment on his part. As for Sigismund, all he has really heard is the word "Prince," which he now repeats, "Prince, prince...." After that, dreamily, he touches the mirror and murmurs: "Layla's is so small...and the other day it broke...."

He feels his garments, his hat and its feather, fingers the tip of one of his boots. The men all look at him looking at himself, and in the mirror he looks at them looking at him. His sword in particular delights him. He turns away from the mirror. "Is it truly mine?" he asks, inspecting the sword.

"It is yours, my lord; it was given to you before your

birth by the prince Gabor of Hungary."

"It is finer than the one I had...in my...there...."

Now he walks around the room. It is called the Blue Bedchamber, and indeed almost everything in it is blue: the heavy drapes that frame the windows, the cloth on the armchairs, the canopy over the grand bed, the quilt over it, the cushions, and even the ceiling, upon which an artist, no doubt Italian, has painted a Maytime sky dappled with a few amusing clouds. The prince runs his palm up and down one of the bedchamber's walls. "These walls," he marvels, "these walls are straight."

"Poland," boasts the chancellor, "makes a point of employing the best architects."

And now he contemplates the bed. "This is where I woke up not long ago, after having...after being.... Is this where I will be sleeping every night?"

"Yes, my lord; the Blue Bedchamber and the rooms that appertain to it are yours."

"Soft pillows," says the prince.

"Upholstered with the finest Chinese down."

Sigismund vaguely remembers that several men in livery dressed him as he woke. From his bed he had seen the marvelous chandelier he now admires, with its twenty-four branches in gold and silver upon which numberless candles await the night. Of course he has seen the likes of it in his books, but what a difference between the picture in a book and the object itself!

Gently the chancellor and his suite lead Sigismund along an ample corridor to the grandiose Hall of Victories. But from now on the prince will be concealing as best he can his wonder, feeling that it diminishes him. For the first time, his tone is firm: "I have understood," he says, "that I stand in Wawel Castle."

"Indeed, my lord, and the king your father will soon appear before you."

Again Sigismund walks around the Hall in order to see and to touch. By now he has recovered his full lucidity. "Why

all these banners?" he asks, pointing to the impressive number of these trophies hanging from the ceiling, some of them
rather torn up.

"Prince, these are some of the banners the armies of
Poland have captured from enemies over the centuries. We
are expecting, your lordship, that you shall be adding many
more in the near future."

"Leave it to me."

He steps toward the doors of the Hall that lead to the
balcony and stands in the open, looking at the city. It is a
beautiful morning, the sun is shining without hindrance.
Below he sees the paved courtyard of the palace. In the near
distance, rising above the gated palace wing opposite the
balcony, he sees a church tower surmounted by a steeple.
"And that?" asks Sigismund, pointing with his lifted chin.
To which the chancellor, still a deferential step behind
the prince: "Our magnificent cathedral, founded by your
ancestor, Boleslaw the Brave." And he adds, with especial
gravity: "That is where we anoint our kings since the year
of our Lord 1363."

Standing on that balcony, Sigismund suddenly has
the presentiment that an event terrible in nature will
be happening soon. But this passes in an instant, and he
returns to the Hall of Victories, where a large tapestry meets
his eye. "That?"

"A cloth, my lord, woven in Brussels. It represents
Jupiter, just emerged from his cave on Mount Ida, about to
strike down his father Kronos by means of the lightning bolt
pictured in his right hand."

"And that?"

"A Flemish harpsichord, gift of the Elector of Branden-
burg to your late mother."

"My mother in heaven," murmurs Sigismund. "Her name
was Ludmila. I know everything."

Now he stops before a mantelpiece, where he caresses
the soft coolness of the marble.

"This mantelpiece is priceless," says Zamoyski, "it was

crafted by Antonio Lombardo in person."

His hand on the marble top, Sigismund suddenly laughs and cries, "I'm hungry!"

"This is hardly surprising, my lord," says the chancellor with a smile, "after the long fast your royal highness has endured since your departure from the mountains. Our good Gedko, the king's maître d'hôtel, has prepared everything. Kindly sit down."

"On this bench?"

It is now the chancellor's turn to laugh. "This is not a bench, it is a *fauteuil*."

"I don't like laughing," says Sigismund roughly and reddening with anger.

Zamoyski's face twitches, but only for a second. Prudent, and conscious of his duty, he pretends not to have heard. "Kindly sit down, my lord," he repeats. A servant moves the armchair so Sigismund can sit down in it.

He examines the rock-crystal glasses, the pewter, the silver pieces, and drops a glass on purpose on the stone floor. "It broke," he says, while a servant hurriedly sweeps up the pieces.

"This is nothing, my lord," remarks the chancellor, "you own hundreds of these."

"What are they made of?"

"Bohemian crystal, my prince."

"To be sure. And that, of course, is silver."

"Massive silver from Würzburg, my lord. And the saltcellar in gold and silver was made for us by a pupil of Cellini. But here at last is your dinner."

A feast is served by a row of servants, headed by Gedko. Soups, fowl, game, fish, the most refined sauces, exotic vegetables of every color and shape, a pyramid of fruits of every perfume, a half dozen bottles of wines which the Frenchman Henri of Valois brought to Poland when he became its king and left behind when he took flight in order to be assassinated in his own country—our colossus joyously makes the most of it all.

His happiness increases at the entrance of a troupe of Abyssinian dancing girls, as beautiful as they are naked, summoned to season the feast with their sinuous glidings to the sound of tambourines they strike with their hands. Zamoyski whispers into the prince's ear that these ladies are unanimously disposed to obey him in any task he wishes to impose on them. Sigismund's happiness rises again.

As he is savoring some Persian mangoes, Gedko announces the Master of Royal Music, Wenceslas of Szamotuly. The latter, after a pretty bow to the prince, begins to play a melody on a harpsichord that moves the prince. What he hears is nothing more than the sound of Layla's lute plucking out a sad Turkish ballad, but Wenceslas plays it so wonderfully that Sigismund rises, slightly drunk, tears in his eyes, and bends over the harpsichord. "Never have I heard...I feel all...."

"You are feeling the power of music, my lord," says Wenceslas, "for music, it is wisely said, softens the heart of man."

"It's true," says Sigismund, almost blubbering, "I feel I am becoming a better man. Goodness, justice, the ideal, no more chains.... Because of you.... Come with me."

He takes the musician to the table and loads him with crystal, silver, and gold. Wenceslas barely keeps the precious goods from slipping out of his hands and arms. "Prince," says he, delighted, "I accept your magnificent gifts in the name of Art, which flourishes only when the mighty sustain it."

Zamoyski is once again discreetly furious. He watches Poland, hardly rich to begin with, divesting itself in favor of a low-born entertainer. The others in the Hall oscillate between surprise, jealousy, and amusement. In the meantime, Wenceslas has knelt before Sigismund and kissed the fingers the prince has extended to him. Pleased, Sigismund walks around the kneeling musician, patting his skull in amiable fashion. "I like this," he says. "I like this. Now rise, Artist, go home, and make the world gentler with thy music."

No need to say it twice. Wenceslas withdraws, stepping

backward, dropping a few valuable objects, picking them up, losing others, catching them again, until he manages to leave the Hall, not without undergoing a few unfriendly pokes at the hands of the guards in the antechamber.

Sigismund takes a benevolent survey of the little group in the Hall. "You too, my friends, kneel to me a little, I like it. Do it, do it!"

Whereupon Gedko, the courtiers, the servants, and the guards make a circle around him, kneel, and cry, "Long live Prince Sigismund!"

"God bless you," responds the prince.

The only man who has remained standing is Florian Zamoyski, a highly visible exception.

"Now you, my good man," says Sigismund to him.

The chancellor grows pale. "I am not called 'my good man' by anyone."

"Well then, chancellor, bend your knee all the same, like the others." Sigismund is still smiling.

"Prince," says the chancellor, "for centuries the Zamoyski have enjoyed the privilege of kneeling only to the archbishop of Gniezno and the pope. To all others, an inclination of twenty degrees from the waist is—"

"I don't understand," interrupts Sigismund, no longer smiling. "Is not the heir to the throne superior to a chancellor?"

"Perhaps so; nevertheless, tradition as well as the law—"

"Take your hat off when you speak to me."

"The peers of this country keep their heads covered even before the king."

More and more afraid, the kneelers have timidly risen to their feet. They gather in a cluster as far away as possible and make themselves small. Sigismund stares menacingly at the chancellor. His gaze happens on a footstool. He knocks it over with one foot in front of Florian. And orders him with thunder in his voice: "Jump over that footstool!"

"Never!" says the chancellor without a quaver.

"Then jump from the balcony!"

"This mockery is intolerable. I am—"

"You are nothing! *They* knelt to me. So will you!"

And he draws his sword. But so does the chancellor. The colossus has strength; Florian has experience. Both throw their hats to the floor. The swords meet. The metallic clinks ring throughout the Hall. The witnesses dare not move. Suddenly the voice of a valet flies over the space. "His Most Christian Majesty!" and Casimir appears, wearing his crown, followed by Estrella, Astolof, Klotalski, and a dozen soldiers.

"What do I see?" exclaims the king. "Put up your swords! How dare you, Zamoyski, how dare you fight with my son?"

"Never, your Majesty," replies Zamoyski. "Do not be concerned. I was only showing the prince a secret thrust I learned from Carranza."

"Thank God," says the king.

The witnesses to this spectacle take good care not to contradict the chancellor. As for Sigismund, he has instinctively obeyed the king. And now father and son stare at each other. Neither closes the gap of several feet between them, which is also, as it were, the invisible but tragic void made by the twenty-one years of Sigismund's exile.

A heavy silence weighs on the Hall. Only the feeble clicks of the soldiers' weapons are heard. Finally the king speaks— speaks as firmly as he can. "My son, my beloved son, you have long known that the stars foretold the worst misfortunes at your birth. In spite of their threats, my love for you and my love for Poland have persuaded me to call you back. You will ride at the head of our armies and save our country from its foes. I beg you to defy the stars and to spread disaster not upon us but only upon those who hate us. I freed you from your chains, but beware! It may be that you are dreaming. The father who stands before you, this palace, the persons you see here, all this may vanish, and all this *will* vanish if you show yourself cruel and tyrannical, and then you shall wake once more chained to your cave, and nevermore shall you dream this dream. Be virtuous, be great, be sublime. Here is your cousin, the Princess Estrella, who gives up the throne in your favor. Here is Astolof, son of the tsar of holy Russia, who will marry her and be your valiant ally. And now, my son, my child, come, come to me, come to my arms."

Sigismund steps slowly up to his father, who is almost as tall as he. He stops all but nose to nose with him. There he lifts his arms and sets his two thick hands on the royal shoulders and, still slowly, forces the king to bend his legs and collapse onto his knees. Cries of horror ring out on all sides. Sigismund pays no attention to them. He lifts the crown from his father's head and places it on his own. "No more chains!" he shouts. Whereupon he turns on his heels and, looking neither to the right nor to the left, returns to his apartments.

Estrella, Astolof, Zamoyski, and Klotalski, rushing to the king, help the old man rise from the ground. Tears in his eyes, Casimir stammers, "I deserve no better." He stands up and stumbles away, leaning on Estrella and followed by Astolof and Klotalski.

Zamoyski remains behind and turns to the witnesses. He almost bellows. "You have seen nothing, you have heard nothing!"—sure (the fool) that this will silence them for all eternity.

Having returned to the Blue Bedchamber, Sigismund sees a little door he had not noticed before. He opens it and discovers the cabinet that will be his workplace. On a large table lie topographical maps, town plans, documents of the realm—everything he will need to take Poland in hand. It will be hard work: Sweden, Prussia, Russia, the Cossacks, the Tatars, the Turks, the Empire—a huge, dangerous world awaits him. Filled with joy, he feels ready to begin when, breathless and frightened, Klotalski appears.

"Sigismund, my boy," he groans, "what have you done, how have you dared? Your father..."

He doesn't know how to finish his sentence, but Sigismund looks at him quite calmly. Calmly he removes the crown from his head and places it in his tutor's hands. "Go," he says, "return it to him. He has understood."

eated in his study (which he has visited only twice), Astolof is writing a letter to his father. "Master of All Russia and dear papa, I don't know whether I can bear much longer my visit here. The most horrible things are happening ever since the arrival of that damnable Prince Sigismund, who has snatched from us (momentarily, I hope) our hope of seizing Poland, a wretched country (between you and me), but the possession of which would have allowed us to turn the table on the Swedes and their attempts to rob us of our lands. Can you believe, my dear father, that this Sigismund tore the crown from *his* father's head with a violence that defies belief, to place it on his own? True, I compelled the prince to return it to the wretched old man, but I can hardly change his choleric character. He is seen nosing about the servants' quarters of the castle, making friends with the basest slatterns. He is observed in town, shaking hands with street sweepers. He mouths opinions so shocking that I forbear to repeat them to you. The king is barely polite with me, while my betrothed keeps caressing the image of that scoundrel who is my rival, Bogdan Opalinski—a miniature portrait hangs on her bosom—even when she speaks to me, which is but seldom, not however that I care. Concerning this Bogdan, all the talk is about him, and I am told that his portrait and his pamphlets are broadcast by the thousands from printing shops (yes, there are printing shops in this country; do not for God's sake permit them *chez nous*, dear papa!). One of these days he is going to fling himself on Cracow, and I do believe that Sigismund will encourage him. In a word, I am in hell here, and would be happier to see the Tatars rather than those Poles. In the meantime, be so dear as to have five new flasks of Tabriz perfume sent to me, as mine are almost empty. Five will suffice, for once they are finished I shall return to Moscow, where I ask you to kiss my beloved mother. Your most devoted and humble son, the tsarevich Astolof."

Having sealed his letter, Astolof rings for his valet. Fancy his surprise when, instead of the valet, Agafya stands before him. He jumps out of his chair as if a mad dog were pouncing on him. "Go away!" he yells. "Go back to Pochinok to milk your cows!"

Second surprise: Agafya does not yell back at him. She puts a finger to her lips to signify that both should be still, she comes very near him and whispers, "Now that I'm comfortable in the castle and that the princess likes me, I hear things, and I've come to tell you what I hear."

Agafya's air of mystery troubles the tsarevich, who is used to clamors from her.

"Tell me and then go back to your work."

"Blood will flow," says Agafya.

Astolof grows pale.

Agafya continues: "Now that Sigismund has come, we the oppressed, we the poor, we the nobodies is going to get revenge. It's our turn. And there's a man in the forest not far from here what's going to fling himself on Cracow."

The very words he has used in his letter! But he manages to look cool-headed. "I know all about that. Why are you telling me?"

"Why? It's simple. You marry me, and I protect you."

Astolof's laugh is a cackle. "You're out of your mind, my beauty. I am telling you for the twentieth time that Dmitri, my Master of the Wardrobe, is ready to marry you, with a dowry, a gift of mine, of five hundred ducats. He is tall, handsome, muscles all over his body, a tangle of golden hair on his chest—"

"How do you know?" Agafya snaps at him. Astolof's cheeks turn crimson.

"Get out of here! And come back when you're ready to accept my offer."

"And the boyar?" For Agafya is willing to negotiate.

"You're dreaming, peasant-girl. Leave the room before I call one of my officers."

Agafya gives him a look both scornful and menacing. "You are going to die," she states calmly, turns about, and leaves.

But she hasn't lied. Sigismund is everywhere in Cracow. He meets with notables high and not so high; he is not afraid to encourage beggars; he drinks in taverns with anyone and everyone; he has paid a visit to the jail; and all this is well known at the royal palace. Fearsome rumors spread from Warsaw to Cracow and back again. Three times already, Casimir has summoned the Great Council, where he has heard so many contrary opinions and suggestions that, in the end, he has decided to listen to nobody, or almost nobody; for he sees much of Klotalski, the man who knows his son best.

"I am desperate, Klotalski," says the king. "True, he returned my crown, but no tenderness, few words, sinister looks, secret actions. His tongue wags only in company with the vilest rabble. What do our spies report?"

Klotalski hesitates. "The populace is arming."

"And our troops?"

"The officers are afraid of them."

"Because they know that Opalinski moves about in the forest of Sandomierz, a mere two hours' gallop from Cracow. I have one idea left, Klotalski, that of arousing a rivalry between Sigismund and Bogdan, one that will weaken them both, puzzle the people, make them doubtful, and enable me to restore order."

"Your Majesty..." says Klotalski, biting his lower lip.

"What? Don't be afraid to speak."

"Your son is urging the rebel to come; he intends to open Cracow's gates to him. Zamoyski heard the news less than an hour ago but wanted courage to bring it to you. The news is trustworthy, for it comes from his son, Colonel Janusz Zamoyski."

The king's head sinks, and then he speaks almost in a whisper. "The dream is over."

"My lord?"

"Blood will flow. It nearly flowed between Sigismund and Zamoyski. Gedko told me what really happened. Of course I had a sense of it to begin with. I made believe that I didn't. Now I must act. Swiftly. The stars didn't lie. I am a father, but I am also king. We will put him to sleep again and chain him again to his cave. And then we shall see. I am not so old that I can't ride a horse at the head of my army. I also count on that same Janusz, who is made of steel. And in the meantime...."

Out of a deep pocket he takes a small, purselike leather bag which he places slowly and meaningfully into Klotalski's hand. "This very evening. Into his wine. Gedko will help you. No delay."

Klotalski wants nothing better than to obey, but how? Sigismund is gone. Where is one to find him and how is one to hold him still? No one in the palace is aware that tonight he is supping in a squalid tavern in the capital's slum, surrounded by thugs, gypsies, beggars, dismissed officers, deserters—a spot that Casimir and his courtiers know but vaguely by way of police reports. Sigismund, instead, is already familiar with all the places of ill repute in Cracow. He tells left and right the tale of the cave, the chain, the clamp around his ankle, and shows the crowds both bare bruised ankles. They love him wherever he appears. They love him especially for his promises and his threats. Instead of returning to the royal palace, he sleeps in a brothel, and, remarkably, no matter how much wine he has swilled, his reasons stays cold; he knows what he has to do; he has his plan; Destiny hammers at the gate and he will open it.

Next day, seated in the royal study, the king and Klotalski are listening to the report of the chief of police. He can tell them where Sigismund has spent the night. But where is he now? It is almost noon. Suddenly a lieutenant of the royal guard appears, out of breath, and crying: "The prince is marching up the hill toward Wawel Castle at the head of a gang of convicts!"

"Why hasn't the royal guard arrested them?" shouts the king.

"We dared not act against the prince without your command, your Majesty," answers the lieutenant.

"He has come to murder me," says the king, rushing away from his study.

The chief of police slips away, exits Wawel Castle by a back door, softly returns home, doffs his uniform, dresses in a plain citizen's suit, and double-locks his door.

Casimir, having in part mastered his emotions, enters the Hall of Victories, accompanied by Klotalski. The king orders Gedko to be summoned. He takes the faithful maître d'hôtel aside and whispers into his ears a very few words—words obviously agreed upon beforehand. Gedko knows what to do. He produces, from a cabinet, a beautiful silver drinking cup known as the "cup of the fallen Icarus" because of the fine image carved upon it. Designed with a wide foot, it will not easily fall over and spill its content in the event of a scuffle. Into this vessel Gedko discreetly pours the powder Klotalski gave him the day before. Ten soldiers, commanded by an ensign, are posted in the Hall. Gedko places the cup on the large table, the one at which Sigismund has so recently feasted. He whispers to the lord of Zakopane that everything is ready. Klotalski passes on the message into the king's ear—the king who is just now giving contradictory messages to the poor ensign, a youth who is at a loss as to what is expected of him. Anyway, what can these soldiers do?

For a huge clamor rises in the castle's courtyard. Sigismund has arrived at the head of some twenty convicts he has freed from the jail cells in which they were rotting away. Already they are climbing the grand staircase. The king turns to Gedko. "Bring food and drink for all these rogues!" A strange command! But Gedko promptly obeys, and soon after the entrance of the jailbirds, the table is buried under bottles and victuals. Klotalski, fearing a bloodbath, orders the ten soldiers to keep away.

The hideously boisterous convicts, dragging and rattling fragments of their chains, enter the Hall by slamming through its beautiful gothic double door. They wield clubs, knives, pitchforks, axes, and iron bars torn from their cells.

"Greetings my father," cries Sigismund, "greetings old tutor, greetings Hecataeus, greetings dream of freedom, greetings my friends in chains, but in chains no longer! No more chains!"

"Long live our liberator!" yell the convicts.

"This is your home," Sigismund announces. "This palace is yours. Father, kiss me. I have been hard at work and I am thirsty."

The word "thirsty" makes the convicts merry. "So are we, so are we!"

The king knows how to row with the stream. He hugs his son and contrives to look elated. "Welcome my lads, and welcome my son! Yes, you are all at home here. Indeed, we were waiting for you; that is why the table is already set. Come, drink, there's enough for each one of you. As for you, my son, allow your father and king to serve you in person. Here is a bowl of Hungary's best."

And he thrusts the Icarus cup into Sigismund's hand.

The ruffians are eating and drinking and shouting "Long live the king! Long live Poland! Long live Bacchus!" while the king's soldiers tremble in their corner.

Sigismund raises the beautiful vessel to his lips. "I drink to the new Jerusalem!" But his eyes settling again on Klotalski, he sets it down on a low table next to him. "Klotalski, old friend, I haven't forgotten your lessons. Listen, all of you!"

One of the convicts, brawnier than his fellows, chimes in: "Peace, you pigs, our holy savior wants to speak!"

They all hush, mouths full or empty. Sigismund speaks. "Saint Luke tells you: He hath cast the mighty from their thrones and he hath elevated the humble. He hath fed the hungry and sent the rich away with empty bellies."

"Who said that again?" asks one of the gang.

"The apostle Luke, that is to say God himself."

The convicts are delighted and full of comments.

"And me that they holed up in a dungeon for stealing a loaf of bread for my children!"

"I never heard the like of it in church!"

"Wait! There's another saying in the Bible: 'He hath brought up a mighty savior.' Yes, and that savior is our Prince Sigismund!"

"Count on me!" cries out the prince. "As Jesus says: 'I have come to set fire to the earth.' Eat, drink!"

And to himself he adds the rest of that sacred text: "The father against the son and the son against the father. And so too spoke the stars."

The convicts are feasting, but Klotalski comes up to Sigismund, the fatal cup in one hand and an innocent tumbler of wine in the other. "Bravo, my lad, your memory is astonishing; I wish I had the fifth of it. And I can't help applauding your generosity, your success, your glory. To your health! Here is your silver cup of wine."

"To yours, old tyrant. No more flogging for your pupil, eh? No more Master of the Discipline of Peasants; wait till I catch him!"

The doctored Icarus cup is touching his lips when a man runs up to him, sprung as it were out of nowhere, and whispers something into Sigismund's ear. The prince sets down the cup at once. He leaps on a chair and proclaims: "Friends, I am about to show you something better than Abyssinian dancers!" He calls a lackey. "You, go find Prince Astolof, Princess Estrella, and all the nobles and gentlemen who wander about the palace. Tell them all that I want them here immediately. Yes my father, you are staring, words fail you, but the blind shall see, the lame shall stride, the lepers shall be cured, the deaf shall hear, for the good news is come to the poor. No more chains!"

The convicts echo his cry: "No more chains!" It must be said that a few of the domestics and soldiers mutter the same words, a fact well observed by the shrewd lord of Zakopane.

On his side, the king speaks to Sigismund, who has stepped down from the chair: "Poland needs you, my beloved son," and hands him the cup. "Drink, be merry, we all applaud you."

Sigismund grasps the cup, he is about to quaff the wine, but a great cry uttered by the king interrupts him. "God! It's Bogdan!"

Terrified, more dead than alive, the king retreats to the spot where Klotalski is standing; the latter takes his arm as if trying to protect him from the devil. At the same moment, Sigismund puts down the cup and turns to welcome the great rebel. In spite of their hunger and thirst (both seem unappeasable), the convicts cannot help but admire the newcomer.

For Bogdan is indeed a splendid figure of a man, with his huge hat, his pistols, his well-trimmed little beard, his doublet made of boar's leather, his boots that open wide at the level of his knees. Behind him, two of his well-armed men are holding a struggling, gagged, and bound officer. Bogdan kneels briefly to Casimir, then rises saying, "Your Majesty, I have not forgotten your kindnesses to me when I was a child. Nevertheless, I have allowed myself to request your royal guard to surrender to the small company which has accompanied me on my visit to our capital. We have also detained their commander, whom you no doubt recognize, Colonel Janusz Zamoyski, who will guarantee our safe departure from Cracow and return to the forest."

The king's lips tremble. He is unable to speak. Bogdan turns to Sigismund and kneels to him too. "Prince, I need no introduction to recognize you, you whom men already call the holy savior of the disinherited. I came at your invitation, which is an order for me, and I place myself and my army under your command."

"Rise, noble Opalinski," replies Sigismund, deeply moved, "and come with me to my cabinet, where I shall have a few private remarks to impart to you."

Before leaving the Hall, Sigismund addresses the king's

hapless soldiers. "Soldiers, do you wish to join me, to join us, to join the uprising that will change Poland forever? I am giving you this chance, but I shall not give it to you twice. Let those who decide to follow us take their places next to these men."

And he points his thumb at Bogdan's two soldiers who are holding their captive. The king's men hesitate. Eight of them, not daring to look at Casimir, walk slowly over with lowered heads. The ensign and the two others do not move. Big tears of gratitude roll down the monarch's eyes. Sigismund is in a merry mood and does not seem to bear them a grudge. He has a statement for the new recruits. "Henceforth you are the Prince's Guard, and you will earn thirty additional monthly zlotys. Your first assignment is to keep watch over all the doors and prevent everyone from leaving the Hall."

The three men who have remained loyal to the king look unhappy at the loss of those zlotys. One of their comrades calls out to them from the other side of the Hall: "Come on over, there's still time!" The three men waver, but remain where they are. "Dunderheads!" yells the convict who, a while ago, made his friends hush up. This man seems to have become something of a captain of the convicts, a fact that Sigismund has noticed.

"What's your name, you?" the prince asks him.

"I've got more than one, chief," is the reply, "but you can call me Jan the Knuckle."

"All right, Jan, keep order here until we return."

Whereupon, arm in arm, Sigismund and Bogdan leave the Hall and make for the prince's cabinet, where Sigismund hands the count a list which he has taken from under a heap of documents and maps. "Bogdan, take the unfortunate men I have set free from jail and attach them to your army. Go find, by means of this list, the landlords who have not fled from Cracow. Demand of each that he manumit his serfs and return the land to those who have farmed it since Adam and Eve. He who refuses to sign—deal with him at once."

"I understand, prince."

Back in the Hall of Victories, the two leaders turn to the convicts, to whom Sigismund addresses the following words: "Comrades, Fortune is smiling upon you a second time today. Lord Opalinski has accepted to enlist you alongside the brave soldiers who have just submitted to us. So take the oath and follow him in your own holy war."

"Not so fast," says the Knuckle.

"Why? What's the matter?" asks Bogdan.

"We want to know, Bogdan Opalinski, what you will do for us if we agree to fight under your command."

Bogdan smiles. "You are right to ask me this question. Well then, all of you, brave lads, what do you wish to obtain from me?"

The answers pour out at once from every mouth.

"Land!"

"Honest paid work!"

"No more flogging!"

"Loot for the soldiers!"

"Turkish slaves!"

"Kill the Jews!"

"Schools! Hospitals!"

"No more aristocrats!"

"No tax on beer!"

"Death to the Jesuits!"

"Bread for my children!"

Bogdan laughs. "Aren't they splendid?"

"Well spoken, lads," says the prince. "And now, swear allegiance to your new commander."

They all swear, as do the eight authentic soldiers, and all embrace and reduce to atoms the remaining food and liquor under the watchful eye of the ever faithful Gedko.

After the swearing, Bogdan steps to the side of the Hall where the king and Klotalski, feebly protected by the three remaining loyal soldiers, have been witnessing the spectacle like two men frozen stiff.

"Let me assure you, sire," says Bogdan, "that I will free your royal guard, as well as Colonel Zamoyski, as soon as I and my men are safely on our way. Remember that I whose ancestors are named in the chronicles of Gallus Anonimus have emancipated my serfs, and turned them into a people of happy farmers who love me, and who work at last without complaining. I beg you to follow my example on the royal lands of Poland and the Grand Duchy of Lithuania. Such an act will inscribe your name in the alas too meager register of men who were at the same time powerful and good; and it may inspire the noblemen of our country to imitate us in order to transform the hell in which we live into a paradise on Earth."

"Amen," shouts Sigismund, while the convicts joyfully roar.

The king finds in himself the strength and the wit to hug Bogdan. "Who can withstand you? Yes, I shall follow your example. You have opened my eyes. Those of the baron Klotalski, standing here, yes, his as well. Can you not see my tears?"

"And look at mine!" retorts the naïve Bogdan.

"Come," says the king, "let us drink to our reconciliation. Klotalski, hand a goblet to Bogdan, and pour one for yourself. Drink, Sigismund, drink!"

And he thrusts the Icarus cup into the prince's hand.

"Thank you, father; the truth is that I'm dying of thirst. I drink to the happiness of Poland!"

But at the instant he is going to drink, a lackey opens the grand double door of the Hall and announces: "Prince Astolof and the Princess Estrella!" Sigimund puts the vessel back on the table in order to open his arms to the betrothed couple. Several knights of noble mien who were escorting the couple at once note the danger and disappear. Sigismund has not seen them, nor has he noticed that Agafya has managed to slide into the Hall while they retreated and has discreetly taken cover behind a tapestry.

Seeing Bogdan, the lovely princess utters a cry, runs toward him, and throws herself into his arms. Gone is her so recent promise to "do her duty." "Bogdan! My Bogdan!"

"Faithful to me, my beloved?"

"Always and to the death, my Bogdan!"

"Look here!" bellows Astolof. He had already felt the crown of Poland slipping from his hands, and now his wife is going too! If the wretch knew what yet awaits him! He turns to Casimir as if for help, but undersands at once that the king can do nothing for him.

"Estrella, my wife!" says Bogdan, and then, to Sigismund: "Prince, now I can confess to you that if I responded so eagerly to your summons, I entertained a second reason, and here, in all its beauty, is that reason!"

Sigismund's heart is full. "Take her, my friend, take her with my blessings. And all of you: look at them. Do they not spell a romantic tale? What is life without love? If all that is happening to me here is no dream, as some here insinuate that it is, I shall have my Layla brought to Wawel Castle and have us married as well. But now, my friend: to work! Do not become a second Mark Antony, allowing the senses to distract you from your duty. That duty is already known to you. Give these men the order to follow you. Rejoin your troops. And do God's will for our Poland."

Bogdan names Jan the Knuckle chief of the crew. Jan aligns the men two by two, makes them lift the bits of fetters that remain attached to their ankles, and tells them to march like soldiers and not like cripples. "Go," Bogdan tells the Knuckle, "to the Saint Florian Gate, and wait for me there. The colonel is *my* affair."

The men leave the Hall in a rattling noise of chains and oaths, leaving behind the Prince's Guard.

"Well now, princess," asks Bogdan of Estrella, "will you be the partner of my dangerous life?"

"Yes, my hero, yes!"

"Look here!" Astolof shouts again, taking with a gesture the king, Klotalski, and even Gedko and the three hapless loyal soldiers as witnesses.

Not even looking at him, Estrella embraces the king.

"I love you, uncle, but I obey Destiny, which no one can

resist. I shall pray to God every day to protect you, and beg you to be so kind as to have my women send to the forest some clothing of the utmost simplicity."

"I will, my child, but be careful not to catch one of your frequent colds."

"Prince Sigismund," says Estrella next, "may you reign a thousand years over a happy Poland."

"And I," replies the prince, "I salute your courage, your sacrifice, your devotion to our fatherland; you will inspire a thousand Polish maidens to imitate you."

But Estrella has not forgotten the tsarevich. "A safe return to Moscow, Prince Astolof, and kindly convey to the tsar your father my deepest respect."

Stunned but furious, Astolof lets fly a vulgar word. The lovers pay no attention to it. They make an elegant exit, followed, less elegantly, by the two men who are holding the young Zamoyski, still struggling vainly in his ropes.

"Astolof," says Sigismund, "calm yourself and drink with me. Here is my lovely silver cup."

"No no no!" cries Klotalski, while the king and Gedko turn pale, "that cup is yours; look at the design!"

Whereupon he grabs an empty goblet, fills it with wine, and hands it to the unwilling Astolof. It is the last glass the unhappy youth will empty on this earth.

"To all of us," says Sigismund, lifting his cup. Astolof drinks, and as he swallows the last drop, Agafya jumps out from behind the tapestry, crying "Prince Sigismund, don't forget me!"

"Ha! Pretty Agafya!" responds the prince, setting down his cup. "Welcome! I am your man. You can count on me."

This is when the tsarevich flings himself into the abyss.

"Thundering God," he yells, "the women here have all gone mad! And you, King Casimir, what are you doing, open-mouthed, to protect me? Where is the royal guard? How are you going to arrest your scoundrel of a son? I and mine are returning to Moscow."

"Not before marrying Agafya," says Sigismund. "By

order of the scoundrel."

"You too have gone mad. Go on, marry her yourself and go live with her in a stable or, better, in the cavern to which you were bolted and in which both of you belong. Adieu!"

"Don't let him talk dirty words and run away!" cries Agafya.

To be sure, Astolof is near the door by which he came. But the new Prince's Guard, obeying orders, are barring all the exits from the Hall.

"Come back, Russian, and take Agafya's hand," says Sigismund.

"How dare you, rascal? I demand a *laissez-passer* for myself and my people. I predict eternal war between Russia and Poland, and for each Polish soldier of yours we shall be sending you three Russians and ten of our most bloodthirsty Cossacks. Enough! Open that door!"

"That perfumed ninny is trying to defy me!" Sigismund exclaims.

The king tries feebly to prevent disaster. "My son, my son, gently, let him go for the love of God, he is here under my protection, we have too many enemies, you are killing your father...."

Sigismund has not heard a word.

"For the last time, take Agafya's hand and swear to marry her!"

"Scoundrel," the tsarevich repeats, and he draws his sword.

So does Sigismund. The king and Klotalski try in vain to stop him, Agafya stands open-mouthed without a word, the soldiers—loyal and disloyal—look forward to the amazing story they will be telling their friends and wives, and Gedko watches Sigismund's silver cup for fear that it will be knocked over after all. The fight begins. Needless to say, Astolof hasn't a chance. With a single blow, Sigismund knocks the sword out of the tsarevich's hand. He shouts a command to one of his soldiers: "Open the balcony door!"

And to another: "You, run to the cathedral and summon

a priest."

Next, he seizes Astolof, whom terror and stupefaction have paralyzed, and carries him in his two powerful arms to the balcony, while the king, uttering a scream, attempts again to stop him. That scream is a small noise compared to Astolof's when Sigismund flings him over the balcony's railing onto the pavement below. *That* scream is heard as far as Warsaw. Those who stand in the Hall hear the horrid thud of the body striking the stones.

But now another cry is heard. It comes from Agafya, who rushes to the great double door, pushes away a startled soldier—she has twice his strength!—and vanishes. The king has collapsed on a chair. Klotalski, kneeling at his side, holds him in his arms.

Sigismund, leaning over the balcony, announces calmly: "A shapeless mass of flesh and ribbons. But yonder comes a priest. He will do what's needed to prevent Astolof from flying straight to Hell." And he returns to the Hall.

The king wrings his joined hands. "The Muscovites in the east, the Swedes in the north, the Turks in the south, Bogdan in the middle, the stars told the truth."

"He must imperatively be made to drink," whispers Klotalski.

"Have no fear, father," says Sigismund. "I am a giant. The tyrants fall and shall fall by my hand. Thousands of freed serfs will rise at the sound of my voice to protect the country, the land of Poland which is theirs at last. Be of good cheer, father, and let us raise our bowls together."

"Yes, yes, by all means," quavers the king. "Gedko, give me a glass."

"I drink to an invincible Poland!" thunders Sigismund.

The cup is touching his lips when Agafya appears in the doorway, respectfully followed by a priest. Clearly the girl is transfigured. Startled—as are of course the others—Sigismund puts down the beaker. She steps majestically into the middle of the Hall. Then majestically she speaks. Her words are solemn, her face shows a majestic grief, her Polish is faultless. "After laying his royal curse on Poland, Prince Astolof espoused me and expired. Father Radim was kind enough to perform both sacraments *in extremis*, and to place the royal ring on my finger."

"*Confirmatus est*," says Father Radim.

"The brief wedding ceremony was witnessed by Dmitri, the prince's Master of the Wardrobe, and Ivan, his coiffeur, who appeared when they heard their master's cry of distress. I am now Princess Agafya of Muscovy, and as such I shall give orders to my people to prepare for departure the moment I have changed into something suitably black. My beloved husband's cadaver will, of course, travel with us. As for the consequences of the treacherous act of regicide committed today in this palace, I shall only say that they will be violent. I have already despatched Captain Vladimir Alexandrovich to our capital with instructions to give an unbiased report of the crime. Our next message will come to you from the mouth of a cannon. Adieu. Father Radim, I shall want your prayerful support in my bereavement during our journey home."

Impressed, two soldiers from the Prince's Guard open the door for her, and she nobly leaves the Hall, followed by Radim.

"Look here!" cries Sigismund, who stands as if nailed to the floor.

In the meantime Klotalski repeats to the king: "Poland is dead if he doesn't drink up soon, your Majesty." And he hands Sigismund the silver cup: "Drink, my boy, and let us ponder–"

"Ponder fire and blood!" bawls the prince. "Did you hear that witch talking to me? A muddy farmgirl! I'm speechless! Your books didn't prepare me for this scene, Klotalski! The little upstart! Shouldn't I stop her?"

Gedko tells him he knows that Vladimir Alexandrovich, a demon on horseback, is surely halfway to Smolensk by now.

"Be strong my lad," cries Klotalski, "and let us raise–"

"Magic word!" cries Sigismund, thrusting his cup into

Gedko's hand. "Yes, let us raise three million serfs who will leap—what is this noise? If it's Agafya again, I'll throttle her!" However, it is not Agafya—she is far from Cracow by now—but the musician Wenceslas of Szamotuly who rushes to the clavecin and begins to play frenetically while crying, "Long live the new Poland!" This time, emerging from the instrument is that of ten trumpets playing together. At the same time, all the bells of Cracow's churches are set a-tolling madly; they toll, they toll, they toll.

Suddenly, amid this uproar, Bogdan reappears. He doffs his hat in a grand salute. "Prince, I have executed your command; I have dealt with the aristocrats who refused to sign."

At a signal, the convicts enter the Hall. The noise had kept those present from hearing them climb the palace steps. Each couple of the crew carries a litter in which lies a bloodied corpse. The blood drips and runs all along the floor. The convicts and their loads parade, as it were, in a semicircle before Sigismund and Bogdan. The latter names his victims: "The magnate Tarnowski, the magnate Pultusk, the magnate Poniatowski, the magnate Jablonowski, the serf Ladislaw Popnik, the magnate Potocki," and so forth. Some of the dead show only a little hole, or a tear; their faces are tranquil, they died quickly. Others are mutilated, drenched in blood, mouths contorted, horrified eyes wide open. Here an arm trails on the pavement, there a leg. A few lie on their bellies, blood stains their hair....

"Why the serf Popnik?" asks Sigismund.

"For trying to defend his lord the count Poniatowski."

The king, groaning, hugs and claws at himself; Klotalski, minor yet unquestionable nobleman, feels as if a knife were nearing his throat. As the parade of the dead men comes to an end, Jan the Knuckle arrives—late, because he is carrying on his shoulders unaided a corpse, whose name he happily proclaims: "Chancellor Florian Zamoyski!" and drops the blood-soaked body to the floor. The king cries out in horror and stumbles across the Hall to kneel over the corpse: "My friend, my too loyal friend...."

"Father," says Sigismund, "for ten men killed, there will be ten thousand, a hundred thousand freed and happy serfs. This sacrifice was painful but needed. Rise, rise."

Klotalski takes the king into his arms and tries to support him. Suddenly a new noise is heard, a noise that comes from the courtyard, one that mixes hideousy with the infernal bell-ringing of the churches and the trumpeting clavecin, a noise of clamors, curses, sobbing. Sigismund rushes to the balcony.

"The dead men's relations and friends," he anounces.

He is right, for the words that can be discerned are "Father! Husband! Brother! Cousin! Comrade!"

Sigismund turns to the Prince's Guard. "Run downstairs at once! Keep that crowd from entering the palace! Hit if you must!" He is obeyed at once. The soldiers arrive just in time to prevent the furious mourners from forcing the gate. They bang at doors and walls and pipes, but can do no more.

And then another kind of noise reaches the Hall, this one coming from the grand staircase. Jan goes out to look and returns, saying: "The menials are pouring buckets of water on the stairs to wash away the blood before your men come back."

"All that blood, all that water," Sigismund proclaims, "will moisten the earth, from which a new harvest shall spring, nourishing our land for all time to come. But enough. Father, Klotalski, are you for or against the future?"

"How can one oppose the future?" quavers the king, whose cheeks are wet with tears. "Let us drink to the future, my son, let us drink, let us joint wine to that blood and that water. Drink, drink."

And he gives him the Icarus cup. Sigismund raises it.

"Brother Opalinski, good work! I now pronounce you Grand Master of the Discipline of Nobles. You shall distribute to our peasants the lands of those whom you have executed so far and those you will execute in the future, except the holdings you choose to keep for yourself."

"Long live Sigismund!" cries Bogdan.

"Long live Sigismund!" cries the crowd, and even, though very softly, so cry the three who have remained loyal to the king, seeing that their lord is leading the way.

"Play on, musician, and let all the arts glorify us!" says Sigismund with his magnificently strong voice.

Szamotuly plays, the bells toll, the families of the victims weep, the king and Klotalski groan, the convicts laugh, the loyal soldiers keep their lips pressed down, the dead begin to rot, and Sigismund, throwing back his head, empties the cup of Icarus in three mighty gulps.

eated, this autumn afternoon, at the end of the great wooden table, Layla is peeling, cutting, slicing, and throwing into a saucepan a heap of vegetables that are familiar enough, but into which she mingles leaves, stems, roots, and flowers she has culled, as always, from the forest and the mountain. Usually she works at her own table, but now she wants to keep an eye on Sigismund, because he has not been quite himself since Klotalski's men brought him back asleep to the cave. Right now, for instance, at the other end of the table, he is leaning over one of the books Father Radim brought him the day before yesterday, when he came to report that the lord of Zakopane was detained in Cracow. The book is open, but she can see that Sigismund's mind is elsewhere. She can also see—and it makes her smile—that he is watching her without seeming to. Naturally, after a while, he becomes aware that she realizes that he is keeping an eye on her. "I am looking at you," he tells her, "because God only knows what you're tossing into that saucepan. I'm not denying that I enjoy what you feed me, and I know that you're pretty fond of me, otherwise I'd be afraid that you're a kind of Medea, you who wander about the forest to find herbs that Nature hides from us ordinary Poles. Delicious, yes, but often of a taste, how shall I put it?—a sort of exploratory taste. Could it be it was one of those suppers that plunged me into my dream? My enormous, rich, bloody, exciting, ravaging dream...?"

Layla has been hearing about that dream a good twenty times. As far as she is concerned, the affair is not very complicated. They took Sigismund away. He stayed away quite a while. He does not seem to have been mistreated. They brought him back. He had a worrisome dream. Well?

Everybody has worrisome dreams. Enough! She grunts and signs with her knife for the prince to go back to his book.

"You're right," says Sigismund, you're right...but I don't concentrate as well as I used to...I examine...I inspect...I try to understand why this dream...why it...but let it go. Besides, the poets are right. Listen.

The book he holds open in his hands is a pretty gathering of Polish verse. Sigismund reads with a gentle voice.

> *Farewell ye gilded follies, pleasing troubles,*
> *Farewell ye honored rags, ye glorious bubbles;*
> *Fame's but a hollow echo, gold mere clay,*
> *Glory the darling but of one short day.*
> *Welcome pure thoughts, welcome you silent groves,*
> *These leafy shades my soul most dearly loves.*
> *A prayer book now shall be my looking glass—*

Here he pauses. "My looking glass...I'd forgotten! Give me your mirror, Layla."

Layla obeys with a show of petulance. Sigismund gazes at himself in the humble little fissured object. "Imagine, Layla, a mirror taller than myself, and Sigismund in it, wonderful and regal.... And now, rags in a broken glass.... Take it back. The poets know best." And he picks up the book again.

> *A prayer book now shall be my looking glass,*
> *Wherein I will adore sweet Virtue's face.*
> *Here dwell no hateful looks, no palace cares,*
> *No lurking crimes beget pale fears.*
> *Here will I shun ambition's folly,*
> *And learn to prize a holy melancholy.*
> *And if contentment prove a stranger still,*
> *I'll seek it nowhere but in Heaven's will.*

"There speaks a wise Pole.... Did I tell you that I threw a man out of a window? No, it was a door...no, a balcony... yes, I did tell you. Ten times, I guess! What a scream he let out! I am a killer. And Opalinski too. Splendid lad! And what a fine couple. And Jan...Jan the Something...and then came the Russian girl who'd fallen from her horse...but that's natural enough...the little viper...."

"Farewell, ye gilded follies...."

Layla has finished her work. Sigismund's mutterings and ramblings do not interest her in the least. She carries the saucepan away and begins to light the torches, for day's end is at hand, although its warmth lingers. The tranquility of the huge trees, the humming of various insects, the pretty singsong of the nearby brook, the twitter of birds, and, in the distance, an animal calling to another, all this penetrates the souls of the man and the woman without their knowing it. However, Sigismund, turning the pages, has lit on a poem that makes him laugh.

"They tell us that the poets are the true sages of the world. But if they're so wise, these poets, why do they give opposite advice? Come back to the table and listen to this one." And now, rising from his bench despite the heavy chain that holds his ankle, he reads with the tough voice of a general:

> *Tis time to leave the books in dust*
> *And oil the unused armor's rust*
> *And like the falcon high*
> *Dive furious from the sky.*
>
> *So restless Caesar would not cease*
> *In the inglorious arts of peace,*
> *But through adventurous war*
> *Urged his active star....*

And now, as if in a fever: "Hail Prince Sigismund! Savior of Poland! You—down on your knees! I shatter your sword! Oh, it felt glorious, glorious! There's nothing like glory, my Layla, to whip up a man's blood."

He sits down again. "Blood, yes, there were floods of it. To be sure, it was the blood of dead rascals. On the other hand, who'd be left, Layla—Layla!"

He has noticed that the Turkish slave is drowsing off,

encouraged by the growing darkness. "Are you listening to me?"

"Hmmmm," says Layla, squeezing her eyes open.

"The question I'm asking you is, who deserves to live, if life is only for those who are good? You, of course. But who else? Certainly not I. Oh no, not I...I think too much, damn it. Opalinski didn't look left nor right before he...I gave the order, though...I think I did....

"Welcome pure thoughts....

"I was cruel to the king of Poland, my dreamfather, Layla...and to Klotalski. In that riotous nightmare of mine I made the omens come true. I was a superb beast! That silly Astolof.... How is one to interpret my dream? How would the young Moses have explained it to the Pharaoh? Either: 'Know, Sigismund, once and for all why thou art fettered to thy cave!' Or: 'Sigismund, thou art not a peasant's son, thou art the son of a king; grasp thy sword; save thy country!' What do you think, Layla?"

But Layla is carving pictures into the table with the point of her knife, though she is now rather enjoying falling asleep to the noise of Sigismund's orations.

"Have I told you," continues Sigismund, "that there was also music in my dream? And Abyssinian dancers? Wake up, play for me and sing; music will tell me what to think."

No need to ask her twice. She finds her old lute while he, on his side, pretends to ply a clavecin. She hums a song, he sings, and then he dances, dances as lightly as his chain permits, clattering out a music all its own, and at the very instant when he intones "No more slaves! No more chains!" he sees, in the half darkness of the forest before him, the figure of Bogdan Opalinski emerge, followed by that of Jan the Knuckle and three more former convicts. Sigismund, struck dumb, looks at them like a man frozen into stone. Quite otherwise, Bogdan rushes toward him, crying, "At last I've found you, prince, but shackled once more like the vilest galley-slave! Horrid spectacle!" While Layla wonders in deep astonishment who these strange men may be. "You are amazed to see me here, my prince, but God be thanked, I looked for you, and I found you."

Sigismund remains frozen in disbelief. All he can bring out is Bogdan's name. Opalinski thinks that the prince finds it difficult to recognize him, for the truth is that his costume has lost much of its elegance; it is almost rustic now, and here and there shows badly mended holes.

"Bogdan, Bogdan," mumbles Sigismund.

"Yes, I am your Bogdan. Not so finely trimmed as I was in Wawel Castle. Dame Fortune plays such tricks on men."

Sigismund can speak at last. "But it was a dream!"

Needless to say, Bogdan misunderstands. "Yes, it was a dream, but the dream remains alive, and we who are the soldiers of this dream shall make it a reality. The more so because we have found you again, gloriously alive. Look at these men. Do they look discouraged? Far from it, even though many of their comrades have fallen."

"Present!" shouts Jan the Knuckle, "and ready to fight."

Another adds: "Happy to see you again, chief. And greetings from them that isn't yet sleeping under the flowers."

And another: "And thanks again for bringing us out of jail."

And the fourth: "That's a favor a man repays in blood!"

Layla is listening. She, who works for the nobility, doesn't like pushy lowlifes, she enjoys a high tone. Didn't she cook twelve years for an Ottoman lord? In the meantime, Sigismund continues to look puzzled. "But—what happened to me? How did I return here?"

"You don't know? The scoundrels told you nothing?"

"No. Tell me, my friend, tell me."

"The savages! I'll make it brief, my prince. After your bold defenestration of the tyrant Astolof, and after they banished you again, the Muscovites came roaring into Poland, slaughtering your father's men and mine without distinction. We were obliged to regroup in the hills. Now I stand back while the two oppressors of the people massacre each other. When the historic hour strikes, I shall take to the field again and fight on—fight till doomsday if need be."

"And...Estrella?"

"A ministering angel founding hospitals and orphanages wherever we go."

"And how...how did you find me? How did you know where I was?"

"We captured one of Klotalski's men, and after an hour of friendly torture he decided to tell us where they were hiding you."

"Where is Klotalski?"

"The devil knows where the old fox is hiding. All I know is that the man is alive and that he and the young Zamoyski are looking for us. Zamoyski! Whom I nobly freed!"

And then, "my father?" This in a whisper.

"Alive."

"And I?"

"What do you mean, my liege?"

"I was banished?"

"Drugged, paralyzed, bound, and brought back here. Now I understand that the dark sleep they pressed on you has caused you to forget everything."

"True, but thanks to you I am myself again. And so must I be and must I accomplish after all what I had been almost glad that I dreamed?"

Bogdan grows impatient. "Oh my prince, our sudden appearance has shaken you. But *that* will not last once you are free again. Soldiers! Hack off our commander's chain! We'll preserve it as our holy relic!"

This is when Sigismund notices that the men have brought an anvil, hammers, chisels, metal saws, files—a workshop of tools. By the light of the torches Layla has lit, three of them attack the clamp that imprisons one of Sigismund's ankles. The prince joyfully encourages them, but Layla is angry. That Klotalski and his men took away her Sigismund for a few days was an event she deemed within the rules. Besides, the lord of Zakopane slipped a few good zlotys into her hand, along with advice concerning discretion. Instead, here is a gang of ragged beggars sprung out of nowhere. Surely, if they make away with Sigismund, it is her head that will fall. So she frantically tries all her signs and all her sounds on Sigismund to make him repel these so-called liberators. As he pays no attention to her, she grabs a frying pan and sets about hitting the convicts. Jan the Knuckle takes hold of her and pushes her to one side. "You interfere with us and we'll split your heathen skull!" he yells.

But Sigismund snaps at him: "Don't hurt her, or I'll kill you the moment I'm free!" And to Layla: "Calm yourself, woman, let them do their work, you'll be coming with me."

Bogdan is helpful: "Obey the prince, Jan, that woman belongs to us."

Layla grumbles but gives way. Is it her fate to become an outlaw alongside her fine colossus? Well, so be it. In the meantime, Sigismund's excitement keeps growing. "Hammer! Cut! Hack! Don't be afraid to hurt me!" All the same, a misplaced blow causes him to bellow with pain.

Bogdan clutches his hand. "Hold on to me, master, friend, majesty! A few more minutes, and then—"

And then he drops stark dead.

Death has struck them all except the prince; struck them amid the trees out there from which has burst a violent salvo of musket shots. Sigismund saw the sparks even as Bogdan fell. The latter's hand still holds the prince's, though the body lies on the ground. The rebel's head is shattered, his blood soaks Sigismund's legs and feet and the clamp as yet locked to the ankle. The three men who were working on it sprawl lifeless as well, but Jan the Knuckle is still twitching. Out of the dark runs the Master of Peasant Discipline who finishes him off with two shots from his pistol. Layla is dead, a bullet having traversed her throat. She has fallen on her ample bosom, her locks spread out on the soil. The executioners all emerge from the forest.

Sigismund is standing still, unharmed. The king's sharp-shooters can congratulate themselves, their fire has been unerring. Two cries, very different from each other, pierce the night. That of Colonel Zamoyski: "Beloved father, you are avenged!" He tears Opalinski's hand out of Sigismund's, kicks the cadaver away from the prince, and sends a bullet through his heart, as if to kill the killer a second time.

But Sigismund has neither seen nor heard any of this, unless it be in an obscure point in his spirit, for he sees only Layla. He flings himself, chained as he is, on the body, shouting, "They murdered Layla! Murderers! Murderers!" He tries to bring the poor slave back to life. He sobs, groans, curses the killers. Nevertheless, crouched over Layla, he cannot help becoming aware that King Casimir himself is now standing over him. Two knights light the monarch with their torches. Casimir is dressed in his garb of high ceremony, and wears on his head the golden crown of the Piast dynasty, adorned with a hundred precious stones, which is removed from the Royal Treasury only on the most solemn occasions. His aspect is dignified, imposing, magical. He addresses Sigismund in a voice so grave, the soldiers feel that one of his ancestors is speaking through his mouth.

"The murderer," says the king, "is you yourself, you Sigismund. Oh my son, my beloved son, my lost son."

But Sigismund is deaf to the words. "You killed her, you killed her," he moans. The king attempts several times to make himself heard, but in vain. Instead, Sigismund takes Layla's body in his arms, rises with it (he has the strength) and turns his back on Casimir. He wants to carry her to the grotto which had been her simple home.

Irritated, the king thunders: "Turn around and pay heed to your father and your king!" Nothing. However, several soldiers bar Sigismund's way and aim their muskets at him. So at last he turns slowly around and listens, holding Layla in his arms. His father's words seem to float sadly among and over the torches into the forest beyond.

"When I tried to make you believe, on waking up here, that you had dreamed your evil time in my palace, I wanted to protect you from too heavy a grief. But Opalinski broke in, and you learned that your crimes and your punishment were all too real. It was perhaps I, my son, who begot these crimes at the moment of your birth, for I responded sinfully to the menace of the stars. I should have defied these menaces with fatherly love and made of you a beloved loving child. Nevertheless, freedom of the will abides in you as it does in me. My sins do not efface yours, and yours are dreadful. God be praised: we have struck down the leader of the rebels, your friend, your ally, your vassal. The sons of your victims will repossess their lands. A new generation will rise to fight our enemies: the Turks, the Tatars, the Cossacks, the Swedes, the Prussians, and from now on, because of you, the Muscovites. But you, Sigismund, must spend the rest of your life shackled to your cave. You are too dangerous to be free. This sentence breaks your father's heart, but that of the king remains steady. My son, listen. We shall meet again standing naked before the Supreme Judge, who will pronounce his final and inalterable verdict. May He have mercy on us. Sigismund, let me hold you in my arms...."

Sigismund stares into space. Angered, Zamoyski and the Master of Peasant Discipline advance on him but are stopped by a sharp gesture of the king.

"Allow this good soldier at your side to take her for one moment," says old Casimir.

Nothing. Sigismund holds on more tightly to the body.

So then the king turns his back on Sigismund, as Sigismund had turned his on him, and slowly leaves, followed by the other men. The torch flames dance in the low wind that has risen. Layla's blood fills one of Sigismund's hands, and drips drop by drop onto a hammer and then to the earth around it.

The tsarevich Astolof and his retinue made their entrance into Cracow two or three days after the arrival of the baron Klotalski in the capital. I need hardly tell you that he was received with all the considerations that were his due—indeed, more than all, for it was necessary to make him understand that a genuine heir to the throne was now, as they say, "in the picture," a youth who had not only the right but also the duty to stand ahead of the Muscovite, albeit without in the least diminishing the latter's honor, nor that of his fatherland, and without setting any obstacle, quite on the contrary! to the marriage of the young princely couple, a marriage that might well lead, in the course of time, to a union between the two lands under benevolent Russian dominion. Sentences as long as this last one, only more tortuous, to which the chancellor Zamoyski helped Astolof after some sumptuous dinners and many a bottle of wine, kept the tsarevich from feeling aggrieved. Besides, he was granted the mission to fight Opalinski at the side of Sigismund, and to take the reward in substantial stretches of land. This mission pleased Astolof, for he loved making war as much as he adored women; he had just celebrated his thirtieth year by battling the Tatars in the Crimea.

Quite a man, this Astolof! And how easily we err about our neighbor when we come to conclusions about him by relying on one or two hints! Was Astolof *coquet*? Yes he was. Overly fond of perfumes? Yes or no, depending on one's taste. Does perfume prevent a man from running an enemy through the paunch? Who dares say so? Astolof feared neither the Mongols, nor the Tatars, nor the Cossacks, nor the Swedes, nor those who might want to replace him as heir to the throne of the tsars. On the other hand, he could not boast of a colossal stature like that of Sigismund. To begin with, he was a head shorter than the Princess Estrella. He was a thickset short fellow with a mighty beard. He gave one the impression of a bearded bull, but a happy one.

When he set eyes on the princess, with her thick nose, lips thin as strings, absence of chin, and elongated bony, breastless body, he decided she was good enough at any rate to bear children. She, on her side, dreamed of Bogdan (the wags at court intimated that the man had turned rebel in the forest in order to be rid of her), but she had been inculcated with the notion of self-sacrifice since childhood. Had not long ago the saintly Jadwiga been forced to renounce her Habsburg prince in order to marry a pagan Lithuanian? Be that as it may, the princess looked forward to a mission of her own, that of converting the Muscovite schismatics to the pope's true religion.

The betrothal was celebrated before the bishop of Cracow two days after Astolof's arrival. The notaries presented a multitude of documents in tiny letters and bad Latin, setting out everybody's rights, duties, privileges, possessions, donations, heritages, penalties, recompenses, and so forth. The Russian bound himself to convert to the Catholic faith before the wedding and spelled out the right of Sigismund and his heirs to the throne of Poland, should that be the wish of Poland's noblemen.

After the betrothal, the king held a secret meeting to which he invited Astolof, the chancellor Zamoyski, his son Colonel Janusz (commander of the royal guard), and the lord of Zakopane, count of Transylvania. The first decision arrived at was that no proclamation would be made to the senate before Sigismund was brought home from the grotto. Sigismund would be presented to the kingdom's magnates in a *coup de théâtre*—"cleaned up," said the colonel, that is to say in all his glory. The king counted on surprise and joy, and on some delicate hints of threats, to incite the senate (accustomed to electing kings) to acclaim Sigismund *vivente rege*—during the king's life—as his legitimate heir. What

Casimir concealed was his intention to abdicate the next day in favor of his son. To begin with, he was weary of having reigned so long. But more than that, he was thinking of the prediction of the stars—yes, he still believed in their word—that he would be made to crawl at the feet of his son. Men often speak in metaphors, so why not the stars? By the act of abdication, Casimir hoped that he might satisfy Fate without harm to himself and with happiness all around.

It was also decided at the meeting that the journey to the mountain would not be undertaken by a mob. Aside from a small armed escort, the present company would suffice. Splendidly arrayed, they would solemnly announce to Sigismund that a crown and a sacred mission awaited him. Yes, said Casimir, solemnity was the word, for the event was an immense one, both personally for himself and his son, and for the future of Poland.

Casimir staged the scene in his imagination—saw himself embracing his son and heard the latter speak a beautiful pardon. The night before the pilgrimage he could not sleep, he trembled, he prayed, he wept....

But I anticipate. Let me run the clock backward a bit and talk about Agafya.

Astolof had been duly informed that a Russian peasant-girl had pursued him all the way to Wawel Castle. The king's secretary took him aside to mention the affair the very day of his arrival. Because the girl had been put to work in parts of the castle barely known to the princess, Estrella was not even aware that a new girl was serving her. Needless to say, the news astonished the tsarevich. It was hard to believe that a farmgirl had undertaken this long, hard journey alone on horseback for the sole purpose of berating him. But when, after jostling his memory, he succeeded in separating Agafya from the other farmgirls and artisans' daughters (and wives) who had bestowed their ultimate favors on him, he recognized that this expedition of hers was altogether in character. Presently, it occurred to him that an uncommon amusement lay perhaps in store for him.

At nightfall, Agafya told her fellow servants that, as a Russian, she was curious to see her prince almost face to face. They suggested that she carry him a jug of fresh water and return with a harvest of spicy details.

The tsarevich was waiting for her. It was almost midnight. Seated, in his nightgown and robe, in a well-padded curule chair, he was reading Hasan Osman's *Treatise of Fortifications* (in a Russian translation) by candlelight, his feet resting on a Persian cushion. Nearby, in the shade, stood the softly inviting canopied bed. He was reading absentmindedly, for he was sure that Agafya would be coming.

Astolof's valet slipped into the room a few minutes after midnight to apprise him, with his customary discretion, that a Russian-speaking girl was at the door pretending to deliver a jug of water. The valet was a wag. Was he, he inquired, to send her back where she came from, seeing that jugs of water were anything but scarce in the prince's chambers? Astolof replied that he wished to see the girl out of curiosity. So the valet admitted Agafya, then withdrew to observe the sequel through a keyhole.

The prince put on a masterful show of stupefaction. He slammed the *Treatise* on a low table by his chair. "Agafya Matveyevna! What a surprise! You've traveled this far just to see me again! I'm immensely flattered. This is a true fairy tale. And prettier than ever! Come here, siren, let me kiss you."

"How dare you," hissed Agafya, "how dare you mock me! You who stole my honor from me!"

"Love was the thief, Agasha, Agashenka, love was the thief! A tsar and a humble lass, what can be more beautiful? I'm so happy to see you again!"

"You who called me a slut in Pochinok."

"And I was right. I gave you an ebony box, lined in velvet, full of ducats, and not a word from you, not the tiniest thank you!"

"You know perfectly well that my dad snatched the box

away from me and used the money to purchase the patch of land next to ours. For me, not even a flower."

"God confound him! Is it my fault that your scoundrel of a father robbed you? I should have had him flogged to teach him manners."

"And now you're getting married! You will live in Cracow."

"Of course not. I remain in Moscow. It is my duty to marry, but what of it? Do you believe that I'll renounce you just for that? Have you seen the Princess Estrella? Do you think I'm going to prefer that broom to a girl like you? Come here, I'm hungry for you."

"You don't find her attractive?"

"A woman without a chin!"

"It's true...I didn't want to say it...and she has nothing *there*."

"I have noticed, believe me. Next time—"

"You promised to marry me to a boyar."

"Well, I unpromise, I break my vow! I want to keep you to myself. The heir to a tsar is obliged to marry and furnish legitimate children to the country; but a lass like you is free; and I want you to be faithful to me. What I was about to say is this: Next time, believe me, your papa won't see so much as the hinge of a box. You shall have a new one, better filled than the first, and you shall live near me, that is to say not far from the palace, in Moscow, like a lady, with your own carriage and lackeys."

"You're lying," said Agafya, but now her voice had become so mild that the tsarevich was able to draw her toward him. "Come, my Agashenka. Say, do you remember?..."

And thus it came about that Agafya set the jug down next to the *Treatise*; she forgot her anger and grief, and he forgot Poland.

In all those days, Agafya had performed what Klotalski expected of her: she told the servants with abundant details the story of the enchanted grotto. She said she was sure that the young man in chains was a great prince. As a result, fed by ancient rumors, the notion that a son of the king would soon be saving Poland spread throughout the city. Casimir heard of this excitement. The people were looking for a miracle. They were averse to a Muscovite ruler—too much blood had flown in the wars between Poland and Muscovy. Hence it came about that on the morning of his journey to the Tatras, the king was able to rejoice in the certainty that noblemen and burghers alike would greet with rapture the crowning of his son.

ayla left her cave one fine morning to attend to her usual household chores. But first she stepped into Sigismund's cave to take another look at the sleeper. He was still unconscious, but he was fidgeting more than the day before, and she concluded happily that he would soon be waking up. Sheets were hanging between two trees. She pulled them down and returned to her cave in order to fold and place them on their shelves. After that, she sat down near the entrance to her little home and began to sew and mend some of her and some of the prince's garments. While she worked, still thinking of Sigismund, whose long and agitated sleep couldn't but worry her after all, Sigismund did at last wake up. Layla had taken good care of him during his sickness—for that sleep of his was surely a sick one. He was clean, shaved, neatly dressed. But he arose wretched to the depth of his soul. He staggered up from his cot; left the cave; the sun almost blinded him. He heard the brook and the birds, and felt a mild breeze across his cheeks. But he was alone. Murderers, he thought, had bereft him of all he had, and even they were gone.

He took a few uncertain steps outside the grotto. His gaze fell upon the great crucifix Father Radim had nailed to a tree ages ago. Nearby stood a pile of logs. Sigismund seized one of the thickest in his two hands. He was about to strike the crucifix, already he was shouting, "So it was you who made the world, satanic Christ!" and he would have smashed the image of the Lamb of God into twenty pieces had not the sharp sound of a nearby trumpet stopped him. Startled, he allowed the log to slip from his hands. He failed to see Layla, because, drawn as well by the sound, she was looking in the same direction as he. She, however, saw him, and in her delight to see him up and well, she called out to him, but her voice was covered by a magnificent drumroll. From the very same spot where Opalinski had appeared in Sigismund's terrible dream, Klotalski emerged between two soldiers, preceded by a third who held in his hands an iron casket all too familiar to Sigismund. Klotalski was garbed in the luxurious red velvet robe that he piously kept for the grandest occasions—the crowning of a king, for instance. Behind these four men other shapes were appearing, but Sigismund's attention was concentrated on the soldier with the casket. This man knelt before him, took out the great key by which, for so many years, the clamp that imprisoned the prince's ankle had been locked, and set Sigismund free. While Klotalski intoned in a solemn voice, "Long live the future Sigismund IX, king of Poland and Grand Duke of Lithuania!" the soldier threw off the chain, which went crashing onto the table behind Sigismund with an infernal noise.

A great cry arose: "Long live Sigismund!" and Casimir V came into the light. A step behind to his left walked Astolof in silver armor, and to his right the chancellor Zamoyski. Close upon them came Janusz Zamoyski. Only he was armed (one never knew), albeit discreetly. Casimir wore the traditional regal robe of crimson velvet sprinkled with little stars. On his white hairs he wore the crown of the Piast dynasty. God! How he resembled the portrait Sigismond had been looking at for years!

Eyes and mouth wide open, Sigismund gaped, unable to speak. Images clashed with images in his whirling spirit. The king moved toward him, but stopped within fifteen steps of his son. He trembled and was afraid to come closer. He wanted to speak with dignity, but his emotion made him stammer. Suddenly it seemed to Sigismund that he was meeting again the father who had crumbled...whose crown he had...to whom he had raised—

"My son, my son," said the king, "look at me...Sigismund...I am your father....your mother died giving you birth...

her name was Ludmila...God gave her time to love you...I have come to take you back with me...I care for you, my child...I committed grave errors...But the stars...You have often been told...You know why...We were afraid...afraid of you...the predictions were terrible...But now you are utterly free...Forgive us...forgive me...I want to place you on the throne...Poland calls you...the nobles wish to acclaim you... Here is the tsarevich Astolof, who will be your cousin...How tall you are! How handsome! Blood of my blood!"

The word "blood" made Sigismund shiver. But here is what happened as a result. Layla, a happy witness to this scene, thought that the prince, perhaps still feverish, felt cold in spite of the mildness of the day. She went on tiptoes into Sigismund's cave and brought out a leather cape which she tenderly draped over his shoulders.

Then, finally, the darkness was rent for Sigismund as if by a knife-slash of lightning, and he understood everything. I weight my words: he understood everything.

"Layla, Layla, you're alive!" he said laughing, holding the woman in his arms.

Embarrassed in front of all these aristocratic persons, Layla tried to free herself, but Sigismund powerfully held her.

"Let her go," Klotalski shouted, "let her go, Sigismund, and pay heed to your father, for the love of God!"

The father now spoke with the indignation and authority of a king. "Leave that woman, and leave your childhood behind you. You are my son. You are my warrior. Poland is waiting for you. Attack her enemies. Let their blood overflow our fields. Let their vile blood—"

He could say no more. Howling louder than all the country's drums: "No more blood! No more blood!" Sigismund, prince of Poland, ran into the wild mountain and pathless forest that stretched behind his cave, and vanished.

At this point, my friend Modrzewski fell silent. I thought he was pausing in order to empty his glass of beer (we were seated in the tavern—the one from which one can admire the monument of the heroic Colonel Lis-Kula)—and he did empty it, but continued to say nothing.

"And then?" I asked him, a bit taken aback.

"And then? What do you mean? And then, nothing. The story is finished."

"You're joking! Finish it, finish it!"

Modrzewski bestowed on me an unflatteringly ambiguous smile. "I find that you didn't quite understand."

"So be it. Finish anyway." I was curiously agitated.

"If you wish."

Modrzewski needed time to reflect. "Let me see, let me see," he grumbled, closing his eyes. After a couple of minutes, they reopened and he picked up the story's thread.

"Well now. Needless to say, Sigismund's unexpected flight dumbfounded the king and all the others. Presently, though, they set off in pursuit. Layla, obviously familiar with the land, guided them. Or made believe that she guided them. The party searched the difficult terrain all day. Sigismund was nowhere to be found. Night fell. The search was to resume the next morning. But during the night, Layla filled a large basket with a heap of necessaries for a long voyage and discovered the prince without much trouble. The two left together. They crossed the Carpathians and arrived in Hungary, where, as time went by, they earned their living, Layla by singing and strumming the brand-new lute they collected enough to purchase, and Sigismund by telling fantastic tales to children—he knew dozens of them thanks to his excellent education. They reached Constantinople. There,

it appeared that everybody and his dog wanted to learn
Polish, for the Turks believed they would soon be conquering
Poland, and afterward the rest of Europe. Sigismund became
a professor of our beautiful language, and thus the happy
couple was able to live in ample comfort. This, at any rate,
is what some who are familiar with the life of Sigismund
affirm."

"They are probably right. Why not?"

"Others, on the contrary, declare that Sigismund was
simply eaten by a bear."

"An idiotic ending!"

"Such is life: its endings are often idiotic. However,
still others in the know tell us that Sigismund *was* found
by Klotalski's men, some of whom were almost as well
acquainted with the region as Layla, and brought back by
force to Cracow. But there he stubbornly refused the crown.
At last he obtained permission from Casimir to enter the
friary of the Bernardines at Lwow, which is a mendicant
Order. After the noviciate, he received the tonsure, and is
known thereafter for his charitable work among the sick, the
orphans, and the poor."

"And Layla?"

"She returned—"

"No!"

"So sorry! She went to work in a thriving inn near the
marketplace of Lwow, washing and mending the linen. She
had her own little room—everybody was fond of her—and
since Brother Sigismund habitually roamed the streets doing
good works, he was often able to gratify her with pious
visits."

"That's as it should be. And Agafya, and Astolof?"

"You're insatiable! Well, it was just as the tsarevich had
promised. He settled Agafya not far from the Kremlin, and
they enjoyed the bliss of love for a long time. Eventually the
bliss faded gently on both sides. Agafya sold her mansion
and returned to Pochinok, where, though she strutted about
as the *grande dame* of the district, she consented to marry

the customs inspector, a man by the name of Omelko (if you really want to know), but don't ask me for his Christian name, for I never knew it."

"Now Astolof."

"Good. For him, I advise you to consult the historians. Like most Occidentals, you know next to nothing about our marvelous history. Know, at any rate, that our nobles refused to elect a Russian king of Poland. Astolof returned to his father feeling ill-used and leaving Estrella in Cracow. By the way, you display no interest in our homely princess, and yet she was to become queen of Bohemia! I won't talk about Astolof's murderous raids on Poland (or ours on Muscovy), except to say that they bore one good result: he killed Opalinski (not, of course, as a favor to us) and so squashed that particular danger."

"Did Casimir live long?"

"Casimir the Survivor, as he became known after his death?" Read the chronicles, my friend, I am bone tired."

"Poor king.... What else?"

"Oh! I suddenly remember a kind of speech made by Astolof after he became tsar. One day, when some courtiers reminded him of our Sigismund's great refusal, he said to them: "If this Sigismund had become king of Poland, would his country, would mine, would the world, have differed greatly? Perhaps. Perhaps not. History is capricious. Sometimes it is twisted this way or that by a man, or even a woman. Other times nothing that a man, or a woman, does can compel it to change the course it is bent on taking. What is to be concluded? I say one thing remains: Let each of us take care of the soul he has."

The End

AFTERWORD

The notion of "doing something" with Pedro Calderón de la Barca's *La Vida es sueño* is one I entertained for many years before writing the present tale. It seems that I wanted more, somehow, than what the poet himself had produced out of his haunting central images of the terrible omen, the prince chained to the wall of a cave and the noble stratagem of the dream (a pseudodream in the Spanish text) with its grim consequences. In truth, I longed for more of the Segismundo matter, less of the Clotaldo-Violante-Rosaura-Astolfo-Estrella romances, and much less of the *gracioso* Clarin—less tinsel, as I would call these portions of the Spanish play if I dared. When at last an overarching theme suggested itself to me, a master idea which was, to be sure, completely alien to Calderón's, I was able, step by step, to extract a new story from the Spanish classic. Nevertheless, everyone who has read *La Vida es sueño* will recognize not only my underlying indebtedness to it, but also a few playful near-quotations from it.

My retelling began as a play, titled *Sigismund, Prince of Poland: a Baroque Entertainment*. It was published in 1988 by the University Press of America (a house I would not recommend to a friend) and is technically still in print at this writing. An improved version of the play can be read in my *Reinventions: Four Plays after Homer, Cervantes, Calderón and Marivaux* (2002). Sometime in the following years, I turned the play into a narrative in French, giving it the title *Du rêve que fit Sigismond, Prince de Pologne*. The prose tale, while it sticks to the philosophical center of the play, differs from the latter in numberless details. The present version is my English translation (fairly free) of the French original.

A trifle more mindful of Polish history than Calderón, I made free and fanciful use, in play and tale, of Norman Davies's excellent *God's Playground: a History of Poland*.

The name of Bogdan Opalinksi combines those of Bogdan Chmielnicki, the ferocious warlord, Cossack leader and scourge of Poland, with Krzysztof Opalinski, the liberal and enlightened author of certain admired *Satires and Warnings*, which I have not read.

For Hecataeus, whose works are conveniently lost, I went to Herodotus, Book Two.

In the tenth chapter, Sigismund quotes an anonymous seventeenth-century English lyric, followed by a modified section of Andrew Marvell's Horatian Ode on Cromwell. The reader is asked to suppose that Sigismund is reciting some fine Polish verse which I have translated into English.

OSCAR MANDEL
A CHRONOLOGICAL BIBLIOGRAPHY

1961 *A Definition of Tragedy.*

1963 *The Theatre of Don Juan: a Collection of Plays and Views 1630–1963.*

1964 *Chi Po and the Sorcerer: a Chinese Tale for Children and Philosophers.*

1967 *The Fatal French Dentist* [comedy].

1967 *Gobble-Up Stories* [fables].

1968 *Seven Comedies by Marivaux* [translations, essay].

1970 *Five Comedies of Medieval France* [translations, essay].

1970–72 *The Collected Plays* (2 volumes).

1971 *Three Classic Don Juan Plays.*

1974 *Simplicities* [poems].

1976 *Amphitryon* [comedy after Molière].

1976 *The Patriots of Nantucket: a Romantic Comedy of the American Revolution.*

1978 *The Land of Upside Down by Ludwig Tieck* [translation, essay].

1981 *Annotations to "Vanity Fair."*

1981 *Collected Lyrics and Epigrams.*

1981 *Philoctetes and the Fall of Troy: Plays, Documents, Iconography, Interpretations.*

1982 *"Ariadne" by Thomas Corneille, with essay: Ariadne and Neo-Classical French Tragedy.*

1985 *The Book of Elaborations* [personal essays].

1987 *The Kukkurrik Fables: 43 Mini-Plays for All Media.*

1988 *Annotations to "Vanity Fair,"* second edition, in collaboration with John Sutherland.

1988 *Sigismund, Prince of Poland: a Baroque Entertainment* [drama].

1990 *August von Kotzebue: the Comedy, the Man.*

1993 *The Virgin and the Unicorn: Four Plays.*

1994 *The Art of Alessandro Magnasco: an Essay in the Recovery of Meaning* [art history].

1996 *The Cheerfulness of Dutch Art: a Rescue Operation* [art history].

1996 *Two Romantic Comedies: The Spaniards in Denmark (by Prosper Mérimée) and The Rebels of Nantucket.*

1997 *Fundamentals of the Art of Poetry.*

2002 *Reinventions: Four Plays after Homer, Cervantes, Calderón and Marivaux.*

2002 *L'Arc de Philoctète* [drama].

2003 *Amphitryon, ou le Cocu béni* [comedy after Molière].

2003 *Prosper Mérimée: Plays on Hispanic Themes* [translations, essay].

2003 *Le Triomphe d'Agamemnon* [drama].

2004 *Chi Po et le Sorcier* [fiction].

2006 *Where Is the Light? Poems 1955–2005.*

2007 *La Reine de Patagonie et son caniche* [fables].

2010 *Cette guêpe me regarde de travers* [poems in French and English].

2012 *Comment faut-il jouer "Le Misanthrope"? Six études sur le théâtre, de Sophocle à Brecht.*

2013 Être ou ne pas être juif [essay].

2013 *Théâtre dans un fauteuil: huit comédies et drames.*

For more details, go to oscarmandel.com.